DONUT SUMMER

DONUT SUMMER

ANITA KELLY

Quill Tree Books
An Imprint of HarperCollinsPublishers

HarperCollins Children's Books,
a division of HarperCollins Publishers,
195 Broadway, New York, NY 10007

HarperCollins Publishers, Macken House,
39/40 Mayor Street Upper, Dublin 1, D01 C9W8, Ireland

Quill Tree Books is an imprint of HarperCollins Publishers.

Donut Summer
Copyright © 2025 by Anita Kelly
All rights reserved. Manufactured in Harrisonburg, VA,
United States of America.
No part of this book may be used or reproduced in any manner whatsoever without written permission except in the case of brief quotations embodied in critical articles and reviews. Without limiting the exclusive rights of any author, contributor, or the publisher of this publication, any unauthorized use of this publication to train generative artificial intelligence (AI) technologies is expressly prohibited. HarperCollins also exercises their rights under Article 4(3) of the Digital Single Market Directive 2019/790 and expressly reserves this publication from the text and data mining exception.
harpercollins.com

ISBN 978-1-335-01289-0

Typography by Catherine Lee
25 26 27 28 29 LBC 5 4 3 2 1

First Edition

For Manda,
from the middle of nowhere to everywhere

DONUT SUMMER

ONE

College Fund: $20 (from Grandma Jean's Latest Birthday Card)

I'm contemplating the imperfect perfection of the apple fritter when Mateo della Penna walks into Delicious Donuts and ruins my life.

Again.

For a moment, I'm merely irritated at the universe. Of course Mateo would show up on the first day of my first-ever summer job. Of course! It's like when my uncle Dave tells the same joke over and over, even when it's long ceased being funny.

Mateo della Penna appearing in Delicious Donuts at 5:40 *freaking* a.m. is the worst Uncle Dave joke ever told.

God, I hope Mrs. Arshakyan doesn't force me to serve them as my first Delicious Donuts customer. Or that if she does, we can get it over with quickly and painlessly. I can focus on learning the intricacies of the POS system instead of their face and thereafter return to my regularly scheduled Mateo-less summer.

Clearly, Mateo feels the same. They freeze the moment they see me, eyes widening and then closing, as if they're preparing to pray. They mutter something under their breath that sounds a lot like "You have *got* to be kidding me."

Which seems a *tad* much for having to survive ordering a donut from me, but whatever. Mateo being annoyed at my existence is nothing new; I experienced it for the entirety of last school year. Said annoyance just . . . wasn't how I'd pictured kicking off my summer employment.

But then Mrs. Arshakyan—or Elen, as she'd asked me to call her when I walked in this morning—smiles and says, "Mateo! Good to see you. Let me show you where you can put your things, and then I'll grab your apron."

I blink.

Those were the first words she said to me too, ten minutes ago. When she'd grabbed *my* apron.

I watch in horror as Elen and Mateo walk into the kitchen.

Elen had mentioned there'd be another new employee coming in, that she'd be training us both this morning, but there is no way—*no* way—

Mateo emerges from the kitchen and walks behind the counter. Ties on their very own maroon apron. Tries, and fails, to keep the scowl off their face.

You have *got* to be kidding me.

"Penny, this is Mateo! Mateo, Penny."

"Yeah, we . . ." Mateo clears their throat. "We already know each other. From school."

"Perfect!" Elen claps her hands once. Elen is tall with shiny black hair and the most flawless eyebrows I have ever seen. Not to mention her cheekbones. And perfect posture. She's friendly while maintaining an aura of unquestionable bad-assery. She is everything I want to be, and I cannot believe she's doing this to me. "I thought that might be the case. Now, Mateo, before we get started, I was just asking Penny the most important question of all. What"—she holds out an arm to the racks of fresh donuts behind us—"is your favorite donut? Penny has already chosen the apple fritter."

"Oh, uh . . ." Mateo glances at the donuts in their metal trays. "Boston cream, probably."

"Oh my *God*," I burst out before I can stop myself. "Boston cream is the *worst*."

Both Elen and Mateo turn to stare at me. And I know, I *know*, disrespecting one of Elen's products is not a particularly intelligent way to begin the morning, but my short-circuiting brain needs to fight back somehow against Mateo wrecking my summer before it's even started.

"The whole point of donuts is that they're easy to eat, but a Boston cream is *not* easy to eat, because the moment you bite into it, that awful custard goes everywhere. And then it's a race to make it *stop* going everywhere, and the frosting on top is so rich and gets stuck to the roof of your mouth. It's all too much."

It is possible I have been gesturing with my hands too emphatically for 5:45 a.m.

Mateo's right eye twitches. They stare at me hard before pointing at my selection.

"And an *apple fritter*—the most extra donut of all the donuts—*isn't* too much?"

"No," I rebut immediately, clamping my hands on my hips in an effort to make them control themselves. "An apple fritter has the most satisfying texture of anything here. While a Boston cream is a gloopy mess, the fritter has substance. It has a slight crunch, *and*"—my right hand escapes, darn it—"softness inside. The glaze is sweet, but the cinnamon makes it not *too* sweet. It's easy to hold. It's perfect."

"It's a *pastry*," Mateo bites out. "It's not even a *donut*, really. It doesn't count."

My mouth opens, but Elen cuts us both off.

"Okay!" She's holding out her hands, eyebrows raised. "I am . . . glad? I think? That you are both so passionate about our products. Although maybe don't expound on your feelings to the customers."

My stomach plummets. I *really* want Elen to like me. "Sorry," I mutter to my fingernails, stopping myself from digging too harshly into the cuticle on my thumb, a nervous habit.

Even though I'm not truly sorry. A Boston cream is gloopy as hell.

Elen waves a hand. "Let's move on. Allow me to introduce you to the most important part of the shop. Even more important"—she glances at us again as she pauses, and I think she's trying to hold back a smile now, which I tell myself is good. A smile means she won't fire me. Probably—"than apple fritters or Boston creams. Say hi to Mr. Bun-Bun."

She pats the top of the ancient Bunn coffee maker with affection.

"Hi, Mr. Bun-Bun," Mateo says, and when I glance over at them—how could I not, after hearing *Mr. Bun-Bun* escape their lips—they're smiling now too. I also fully process that they have redyed their hair in the week since our sophomore year of high school ended, because of course they did. They are always redyeing their hair. They let it get long this year too; it falls past their chin now. One side is a rich purple, the other a bright, shiny pink. Perfectly symmetrical, split down the center of their scalp.

It is so ridiculous and cool I could *scream*.

Instead, I force a smile. Because we are all smiling now. Because Elen is going to like me. Because I am going to get through this.

Because, while it might just be in a donut shop, this job is important for me. Not as capital-*I Important* as, say, the Hatfield Marine Sciences Bridge Internship, which would have given me hands-on scientific experience and college credit and made me feel like I was doing something to further my future career and help our entirely screwed planet—but I am not thinking about Hatfield. I am thinking about donuts! Donuts that translate into a chance to earn money I very much need. For a future I very much want. So that I *can* do something Important someday.

"The extra bags of coffee beans are down here." Elen opens the cabinet under Mr. Bun-Bun, then shows us how to work the grinder and which buttons to avoid if we don't want to give ourselves third-degree burns.

And then the small gold bell above the glass door starts to jangle.

Soon, it doesn't matter that Mateo is here, at *my* summer job, because that little bell doesn't stop jingling, and Elen, Mateo, and I don't stop moving for the next two hours. There is a lot to learn: the donuts (regular and specialty), the bagels (and the fixings), the drinks (hot and iced), and how to unfold and fold the donut boxes (how am I so bad at unfolding boxes?).

Speaking of the boxes (which are covered in a shiny pink film I am certain is not recyclable), the amount of waste we send out the door—the plastic drink cups alone!—is a bit alarming, but I try not to let it get to me. Maybe I can convince Elen to invest in more compostable materials. You know, further down the line, when I've convinced her I'm competent and she shouldn't fire me.

Then there's learning the prices and the POS system. Where extra stock of everything is, both behind the counter and in the kitchen. Learning how to not take it personally when customers are grumpy.

That one is . . . difficult.

And while I can never exactly avoid Mateo, being that it's a small space behind the counter and their hair is incredibly bright, my brain does eventually start to focus in, like a comforting laser. It pauses in its *New things to learn! New things to learn!* happy hum only when Elen lays a hand on my arm at eight o'clock and tells me to take a break.

"But—" I stare at the steady stream of customers still walking through the door.

"But it's the law for employees to take breaks." With a gentle shove of her hip, she pushes me away from the register. "Grab a donut and go relax for fifteen minutes. You've been doing great. Hey, Sunny!"

All morning, Elen has been greeting customers like this—by name and with a smile—even if some return her salutations with only a grunt. It shouldn't have surprised me that she knows everyone; Delicious Donuts has been a staple in Verity, Oregon, for years. It's plopped right at the end of tiny Main Street, across from the library and next to the run-down park. Still, this level of familiarity has been unexpectedly fascinating to me. Take, for instance, Sunny, an old hunched-over white man who's about to pay for exactly one donut, which makes me irrationally sad. Does he come in every single day and order that same solitary donut? I bet Elen knows his deal. Does he—

"Penny." Elen lifts a perfectly sculpted brow. "Go."

I am defenseless against that brow. I would do anything Elen Arshakyan told me to do.

I go.

TWO

College Fund: $51

I walk through the doorway that leads into the kitchen, where Elen's son, Alex, started making donuts at some ungodly hour in the middle of the night. I passed him on his way out this morning, a quiet blur of golden skin and curly black hair.

Across the scuffed brown tiles of the kitchen is a tiny office, where my purse now hangs next to Mateo's messenger bag. I sit in one of the two possibly structurally unsound office chairs and attempt to relax.

Fun fact about me: I am superbad at relaxing.

I feel it almost as soon as my butt hits the seat. I was good when I was behind the counter, constantly moving, mind occupied. But now that my body's still, it descends: The slight tightening in my chest that makes it hard to take a deep breath. The sinking knowledge that the sensation might not go away for hours. The way my thoughts scatter and then simply disappear, leaving my brain blank and fuzzy. Slowly, steadily, I become adrift.

Except not in a fun way. Not in the way I imagine bros who live by the ocean feel adrift: bobbing over waves on surfboards, drinking fresh smoothies, smoking weed.

My brain feels adrift in the sense of floating helplessly into space. Untethered and directionless, my feet grasping for purchase.

I hate it. I hate it, I hate it, I hate it. I hate that I can't control it, that it never seems to make sense, that somehow my anxiety takes me by surprise every time even though I've been living with it for almost as long as I can remember. I hate that it is happening now, on the first day of a job that is supposed to be simple and fun, before it's even reached 9 a.m.

I take a (limited) breath. Try to consider reasons my brain might be having a hard time.

There is the fact that I woke up at 4:30 a.m. today, a not-normal occurrence. And I slept horribly before my alarm went off, my stomach full of nerves about donuts. And embarrassment about being nervous about donuts. What a ridiculous summer already.

And then—*and then!*—Mateo della Penna, the one person in Verity who I know hates me, showed up unexpectedly before the sun had even risen in the sky. It's an intimate thing, being around a person that early. I've felt half naked all morning.

Looking back now, I should have predicted I would be working with someone I knew. Verity's a small town.

But why couldn't it have been someone like . . . Roman Petroski, maybe. Roman would have been perfect, actually. Or if not Roman, one of my friends from Knowledge Bowl, or band, or iTuna (International Teens Upholding Nature Association), or even the ever-fledgling Spanish club. Sure, it was rare I actually hung out with most of these friends outside of school or school-related events, because friendship was weird and hard, but this could have been the perfect opportunity to finally change that! Why didn't I convince Swapna or Julian or Lani to apply to Delicious Donuts too?

And while the actual job part seems to be going *relatively* well, people have dramatically sighed at me more than I would like. I'm terrified of the espresso machine. Honestly, even Mr. Bun-Bun makes me a little unsettled.

These are all rational reasons to be stressed, I tell myself. As opposed to the other reasons I often get stressed, like not being able to stop climate change or eliminate gun violence or fix antibiotic resistance. Or just thinking about the general existence of Facebook. My therapist, Hannah, tells me these things are outside of my control and I should focus on what I do have power over, but it's hard when my brain's in space.

I tug on one of my braids, the braids I practiced for almost an hour yesterday, that I executed far more poorly this morning at 4:45, my eyes dry with non-sleep. My exceedingly boring brown hair is thin and stick-straight and doesn't easily stay in a braid, but with enough precision, hairspray, and positive thinking, I can sometimes make it happen. And as I lack the gumption to go for a pink-purple duotone, braids are the most interesting thing I have to work with. I figured my hair should be off my face in any case, to comply with OSHA regulations.

Mama D would have done a better job.

But she and Mom were still sleeping this morning when I left, even though Mom had promised she'd wake up to see me off.

And Mama D hasn't braided my hair in over six years.

The strands are already starting to unravel in my hands.

A thought slithers into my brain, pulling the air in my lungs tighter still: If I can't even handle an espresso machine . . . I mean, I probably couldn't have handled Hatfield anyway.

I need to distract myself.

I scream inside my head as I look at the clock above Elen's desk. Somehow, only four minutes of my break have passed.

Wait. Okay. The clock.

That could work.

I remember the centering exercise Hannah taught me, and I stare at the clock—something I can see. It's a little dusty but cute, with different illustrated pastel donuts for each hour of the day. I breathe in the slightly stale but somehow comforting scent of cardboard that permeates the office—something I can smell. I listen to the distant murmur of Elen and Mateo talking to customers out on the floor, the slight buzzing of the lamp over Elen's desk—things I can hear. I run my hands over my jean shorts—something I can feel.

By the time I return to my place behind the counter, the constriction in my chest has eased the tiniest bit.

Elen has me stay on the register, and the more I get used to it, the more competent I feel, the more the tightness behind my breastbone dissipates. Whenever there's a lull in customers, Elen has more to show us. Working with Mateo continues to be capital-*F Fine*. We ignore each other when we can, are cordial to each other when we need to communicate.

The only time I get thrown is when a young kid—seven or eight, maybe—smooshes their face up against the glass barrier that separates customers from the specialty donuts on the counter. Their dad straggles in behind them and gently pulls on the kid's shoulder to remove their nose from the glass. As he does, the kid looks up at Mateo, who's waiting to take their order, and gasps.

"Whoa," they breathe. "Your hair is *so cool*."

Mateo smiles at them.

And it's this that does it.

It's a quiet moment in the shop; the kid and their father are the only customers in line. I'm waiting at the register. I have nothing to do except watch Mateo's smile.

It's an almost shy, entirely adorable thing. Different from the polite one they've been throwing Elen and other customers all morning. The last time *this* smile was actually directed at me was the first time I met Mateo, when they moved here from California in eighth grade. I was their student ambassador on their first day of school, walking them to their classes, eating lunch with them, explaining the ins and outs of Verity Middle School. I loved being a student ambassador, but sometimes it was awkward, depending on whether the new kid actually wanted my help.

Mateo, though, looked at me that day like they are looking

at this kid now. Open, kind. Like they were entertained. Like they wanted to be your friend.

Eighth grade feels like a century ago.

"Maybe you can ask your dad if you can dye yours when you're older," they say.

The dad ruffles the kid's hair. "Maybe."

When Mateo turns toward me to hand off their donuts, the smile fades away.

Just as I knew it would.

I take my lunch in my car, whom I call Dolly, while listening to my "Be Better, Brain" playlist, which is mostly full of up-tempo pop music I always hope will make me happier. I'd say it works 36 percent of the time.

I got Dolly this spring from Uncle Dave after I passed my driver's test; he insisted that he was ready for a new car anyway. He wasn't necessarily lying; Dolly is twenty years old. She's not the prettiest girl on the road. But she's perfect for me. I almost always feel okay in Dolly.

I watch customers stroll in and out of the shop as I eat my Uncrustable. Watch cars drive away from the downtown strip along Main Street, toward Route 72 beyond.

Route 72 is where most residents of Verity actually spend the majority of their time, shopping at the Walmart and stopping for fast food or, on special occasions, eating at the Olive Garden.

I used to be on Main Street a lot when I was a kid, though, back when Mom still had her stationery store, Rosemary &

Time, at the opposite end of the block. I still remember the smell of it—the vanilla and cinnamon of the candles Nancy Jo Cummings made that Mom sold by the front counter, the slightly earthy smell of fresh cardstock, the tangy mineral of ink. Before opening the store on Saturday mornings, Mom would give me a five-dollar bill and send me down here to get a donut for each of us.

But ever since Rosemary & Time shut down six years ago, it's rare for us to come downtown. (Calling it *downtown* always feels a little hilarious, since it's so tiny and, you know, Verity-ish. The tallest building is three stories high.) It's something of a miracle that I was here a few weeks ago, when Mom got a hankering for takeout from Golden Sun Chinese Food Palace, and I saw the Help Wanted sign in Elen's window. I'd applied to lots of places this spring—after my dream of applying to Hatfield died—places where I thought I could still make a difference while also collecting a paycheck: Treehuggers, the tree-planting nonprofit where I already volunteer. The Nature Conservancy. The Audubon Society of Corvallis. The Oregon Department of Fish and Wildlife.

Sure, it was possible I wasn't *completely* qualified for a lot of these positions, being as I was a sixteen-year-old with no employment experience, but—yeah, no one had gotten back to me. (Well, James from Treehuggers had said, "Penny, you realize hardly any of *us* are paid, right?" and then handed me ten Douglas fir saplings to plant.)

Donuts it was.

Most of the time, when it comes to Verity, I'm dying to

get out of this place. But as I'm staring down Main Street through Dolly's passenger-side window, this funny wave of nostalgia washes over me, sudden and vivid. Even though I haven't been down here much lately, I still know it all so well: Antiques 'n' Stuff, the library, Golden Sun. The corner store, Goldie's Flowers, Olivia's Books & Tea. The empty storefront at the end of it all that used to be my mom's. The bank and the real estate office.

It's like one of those moments where you blink and all the things that normally blend into the background come into focus.

Anytime we drive up to Portland or even over to Salem, all the neighborhoods I thought I knew are shifting like salamanders—growing new skin, shedding the old. It's kind of nice that so many of the businesses on Main Street that have been here since I was a kid are still here. Like they've watched me grow up.

And for just a second, sitting there in Dolly, I feel almost . . . content. That I'm here on Main Street again instead of at the Hatfield Marine Science Center on the coast with barnacles and seaweed, datasets and strangers—real-life scientists ready to share their expertise.

Maybe it's okay that I'm surrounded only by things I know.

I try to take a deep breath. It flows through my throat a shade easier.

When I get back, the rush has continued to die down; Mateo takes their lunch next and sits in one of the seven orange booths that make up the Delicious Donuts dining area. There's a cup of black coffee from Mr. Bun-Bun in front of them, half a glazed old-fashioned. (I notice, conspicuously, that they did not choose a Boston cream.)

They hunch over one of their sketchbooks, the pencil in their hand blurring back and forth. They break only to occasionally punch something into their phone.

I try not to look at them while they draw. I really do. But it's such an odd feeling, seeing their colorful hair flopped over their ears, that familiar wrinkle of concentration on the bridge of their nose, here, where I didn't expect to see it.

I've seen some of Mateo's work. There was always at least one of their pieces rotating through the display boards in the art hallway at Verity High. They work mostly in black-and-white, sketches in pencil and charcoal. Still lifes of what I assume are various parts of their world: mangoes on a kitchen counter, a messy stack of books with a used coffee mug balancing precariously on top, a cup filled with paintbrushes in Ms. Fuentes's art room. Occasionally, a scene I recognize: a bike leaning against the corner store, underneath the board full of flyers and business cards.

Despite myself, I'm always curious what they're working on. They have their sketchbook out constantly during the school year, except for when a teacher makes them put it away. I want to protest whenever it happens. It just feels . . . mean. Like it should be as obvious to teachers as it is to me that the sketchbook is simply an extension of their body. That they need it.

It is very irritating, this strange protectiveness I have for Mateo's sketchbook.

"Hey, Alfredo!"

I jump as Elen greets a new customer. She throws a rag over her shoulder and walks around the counter to hug him. "How's Shelly doing?"

I study the buttons on the POS screen I haven't used yet.

"Oh, fine, fine." Alfredo shuffles toward me, Elen's arm still wrapped around his shoulder. "The treatments are hard. But she's having a pretty good appetite day. Thought she might like a treat."

"This treat'll be on me, okay?" she says as she joins me again behind the counter.

I step back, watch Elen do her thing. There's half of a lump caught in my throat, even though I only know Alfredo vaguely, the way I vaguely know everyone in this town. I have no idea what's happening with Shelly. But if she's sick . . . Mama D works at the local hospital. She actually knows everyone and everything. I bet she would understand this interaction.

Elen gives Alfredo another hug before he goes. Whispers something that makes him squeeze her hands for an extra-long moment.

I avert my eyes. Until I realize I'm back to staring at *another* set of hands—Mateo's, again. Their skin is light, but has *just* enough clicks more melanin than mine that I bet they tan well in the summer. As opposed to turning into a supercool lobster at the barest hint of sunshine.

I have seen the tips of their ears turn pink, though, sometimes. When they've been particularly upset with me.

I turn all the way around and focus on memorizing the

flavors of syrups behind the espresso machine.

By the time Mateo and I reach the end of our shift two hours later, I'm exhausted. My feet hurt, my left arm is sticky for reasons I can't remember, and despite Elen's warnings, I did burn my pinkie on Mr. Bun-Bun.

But when I take a deep breath, I can feel it claw its beautiful way up from the bottom of my lungs.

Okay, I think gratefully. *Okay*.

We head to the parking lot together, me to Dolly, Mateo to their bike, chained to the rack. It's full daylight now, so I try to tell myself it isn't so weird, being side by side with them outside of school. I fiddle with the strap of my bag, turning toward them before I open Dolly's door.

"Hey."

I don't know exactly what I'm going to say next, but I'm trying to remember that nice feeling that washed over me out here during my break. *Let's decide not to hate each other, at least for the purpose of our employment? Elen seems like a good boss, right? Is this your first job too?*

Whatever was in my head disappears when Mateo turns to me, stuffing their bike lock in their bag.

"An apple fritter is messy as fuck. And it's *not* a donut."

With that, they hop on their bike and pedal away.

I watch them, stomach churning, as they swing right and disappear down Hoodview Road, their pink-purple hair waving in the breeze.

THREE

College Fund: $103

Bruno throws open the front door before I've even made it up the driveway.

"Penny! Did you sell a billion donuts?"

Billion is Bruno's current favorite word. He cycles through a few a month. Whenever he latches onto a new one, he uses it as often as possible, usually in ways that make no sense. This was actually a decent use of *billion*. I am semi-impressed with his kindergarten education.

"Hey, Bruno." I pat his head as we walk through the door. "Probably not a billion. But a lot."

He shoves his face into my shirt. "You smell like donuts." He nods his approval at this new development. "Awesome."

"Penny!" Mom sweeps into the foyer as I'm slipping off my shoes, Nikki on her heels; Bruno has already sprinted away toward the kitchen. "Oh, honey, I'm so sorry I didn't wake up in time to send you off. I must have slept right through my alarm." Mom pulls me into a hug while Nikki wraps herself around my leg. Entering the Dexter-Laroche household is a full-body experience sometimes. "How was your big first day?"

A tiny chamber of my stomach twists, the part of me that wants to be mad at her. Mad that I wasn't surprised she slept through her alarm. That it was one of only a *billion* promises that she or Mama D had broken since the triplets were born six years ago.

But the truth is, I've never been very good at staying mad at either of them. I welcome the hugs, the press of Mom's soft belly into my side and her rosy cheeks against my hair, Nikki's crayon-stained fingers around my calves.

"It was good," I answer, the easiest answer, even if everything feels more complicated than that. "Elen's really nice."

"Elen is the best." Mom steps back, puts her hands on her hips. "I knew you two would make a knockout pair." A wistful look enters her eyes, a bittersweetness that makes any selfish chambers of my stomach clear completely. "You think it'll be nice?" she asks. "Spending your summer on Main Street again?"

I swallow, my throat suddenly thick. I think of that moment earlier in Dolly.

I think of how our summers used to be.

It's not just the smell of Mom's store I remember. It's everything. The way life was before, when it was just Mom and me.

Mom started dating Mama D when I was in fourth grade. Their wedding seemed to follow in a blink, and I welcomed it all, the fact that Mom had less time to spend with me, the shift of becoming a household of three. Mom was so happy, and I loved Mama D immediately right along with her. I hadn't ever had a second parent—my dad was never in the picture—and suddenly having one felt so exciting.

And then when I was in fifth grade, we found out the triplets were coming. That felt exciting too.

At least, it felt exciting before it felt terrifying.

Mom was thirty-eight when she got pregnant with the triplets. She and Mama D had both wanted another child, even though they knew getting pregnant later in life came with more risks. But when we learned there were three little bodies growing in Mom's uterus, the risks multiplied.

I probably wouldn't have felt nearly as scared about everything if there weren't a vent in my bedroom situated right above our living room that lets me hear Mom and Mama D's late-night conversations when they think I've already gone to sleep.

I've learned way too many things from that vent.

I heard all the tears of Mom's pregnancy, tears of joyful anticipation and gratitude but also of constant, ever-increasing stress. Medical phrases I didn't fully understand came in whispers through the floor of my room every night, culminating in a message I did understand: They were worried about complications not just for the triplets but for Mom.

There is truly nothing worse in the world than hearing your moms cry and knowing there is nothing you can do to help.

By the time they rushed to the hospital for delivery, I wasn't thinking about my new siblings so much as I was really, really worried about something happening to my mom.

Bruno, Emma, and Nikki arrived early, as was expected with triplets, and they came out mostly breathing and screaming—at least, so Mama D says; I wasn't there for that, because gross—but Nikki was even smaller than Bruno and Emma. And so much more blue.

Most hearts need two strong ventricles to pump blood and oxygen to our bodies, but only one of Nikki's was functioning. The other was barely formed.

Uncle Dave and all my grandparents came to help take care of me while the triplets and my moms stayed in the NICU. Bruno and Emma came home much sooner than Nikki. But eventually, after surgery, Nikki came home too.

Rosemary & Time closed its doors for good a few weeks after that.

The store—my mom's dream—had been struggling for a while, I learned through the vent. But even if it hadn't been, she didn't have the time or the mental capacity to run a small business with a medically fragile infant at home and two other infants on top of it all. Her old employees helped sell the last of the stock.

Nikki has needed more surgeries since then; she's still smaller than Bruno and Emma. She might eventually need a heart transplant. But for now, she's strong enough to give the best leg hugs.

I love my family in all its loud, imperfect chaos. But the year the triplets were born changed all of us, I think. Made me grow up faster than I'd thought I could.

Mostly, it made me more aware. Of all the things in the world that could go wrong.

My stomach started hurting a lot that year. It became harder to breathe sometimes.

Anyway, it's simply different now, is all. Mom doesn't have time to hear about Mateo or my fear of the espresso machine or Alfredo and what's possibly happening with Shelly.

"I'm so proud of you, honey." She pinches my cheek, even though she knows I hate it. I roll my eyes, batting her hand away. "Are you hungry for lunch? There's a pot of mac 'n' cheese on the stove."

"Sure."

"Oh, and Penny," Mom says over her shoulder as I follow her to the kitchen, "you're still good to watch your siblings later so I can run to the store?"

"Sure," I say again. I babysit a lot since Mama D works at the hospital so much. And while Mom hasn't had time to look for another traditional job since the store closed, she still sells custom calendars and planners online, the products that had always been her favorite to design for Rosemary & Time. Even when orders are slow, she needs help getting things done around the house, so I do what I can.

Although, as the triplets have gotten older, *babysitting* is more accurately described as *keeping the triplets from gravely injuring themselves and/or one another and barely succeeding.*

"Hi, Penny," Emma says from the kitchen table. She doesn't look up; she is deep in concentration over her pile of Legos.

"Hey, Ems." I ruffle her curls before I head to the stove.

Whoever Mom and Mama D's sperm donor was, they contributed some curly-hair genes to both Emma and Bruno that I am deeply jealous of. Nikki's, at least, is straight like mine, wispy around her pale, sugar-sweet face. Bruno has some of my freckles too. Although no one has as many freckles as me.

I hate my freckles almost (*almost*) as much as I hate my anxiety. In books, there are always descriptions of characters having a "sprinkling" of freckles, a "dusting" across their nose or cheeks. Charming! Cute!

My face, on the other hand, is more like a hailstorm of freckles. During summers, especially, it becomes hard to tell what's face and what's freckle.

There's even a huge, *weird* freckle on my upper lip. I catch people staring at it sometimes.

I grab a bowl from the cabinet next to the stove and peek inside the pot. My spirits lift when I discover it's the fancy mac 'n' cheese, made with a packet of sauce instead of powder, and Mom's even added peas to it. Gourmet, by our standards.

I join Emma at the table, which is next to the bay window that looks out over the backyard. The sill is covered in plants Mama D fusses over—when Mama D's actually home.

"What are you making?" I ask around a mouthful of processed cheese and nominally nutritious vegetables.

"Rocket launcher." Emma picks up a red brick, brow furrowed. "Well, a rocket launcher and a rocket, but the nose cone isn't working."

I nod like I know what she's talking about. "Hmm," I say. "Nose cones are tough."

"They are!" she shouts, finally looking at me. She sniffs. "You smell like donuts."

"Right." I swallow another bite. "That'll probably keep happening. As I'll be selling donuts all summer."

"Oh, yeah!" Her eyes brighten, as if she's just remembering. Emma tends to hyperfocus when she's working on something—most often, it's Legos—but whenever she returns to the world, she's the most thoughtful of the triplets, the most oddly grown up. "How was your first day?"

"Harrrrrrruuhhhhhh!" Bruno barrels into the room before I can answer, clad now in white pants and a new T-shirt. His swinging arms knock a pile of mail onto the floor. "Oh." Mom glances at me from where she's unloading the dishwasher. "And can you possibly take Bruno to his tae kwon do class in a half hour? I was going to drop him off, but I'm not sure I'll be able to get all the shopping done before I have to pick him up again."

I shovel in the last of my mac 'n' cheese before dropping the bowl in the sink.

"Sure. I'm just going to hop in the shower first."

Nikki and Emma and I can walk over to the pond that's behind the strip mall where Bruno has tae kwon do. Count the ducks until he's done. I have Verity pretty much mapped out in terms of Places Where I Can Keep the Triplets Semi-Entertained.

I'm up the stairs and throwing my bag in my room when my phone chimes.

A small hit of dopamine swings into my veins when I see

it's a text from Swapna. Someone who definitely likes me, and not just because I'm related to them and can help with their errands.

Swapna: plans for KBGB are AFOOT!!
Swapna: are you free mid-July-ish?

Knowledge Bowl Goes Bowling was pretty much the biggest social event of my summer last year. I have no reason to believe it won't be the highlight of this one too.

Penny: you know my literal only plans this summer are slinging donuts
Penny: so yes, i'm around
Penny: can't wait!!

And even though I actually want to keep talking to Swapna, triplet duty beckons.

I wait until the temperature of the water in the shower is almost scalding—just right—before stepping inside.

Okay. All right. Okay.

I've figured out with Hannah that manageable goals and hopeful intentions work for me.

Time to strategize.

I force my exhaustion from the day down the drain along with the water. Urge the steam to clear my head.

I need this summer job—working at Delicious Donuts—to go well.

Because the curse of my bedroom vent actually came in kind of clutch this year. Most of the things I've overheard since the triplets' birth have been boring or embarrassing. I've pretty much tuned the conversations out by now.

Until one day several months ago, when my moms' tone from the floor below dropped into those Hushed Decibels of Concern I hadn't heard in so long.

It was like muscle memory. I couldn't stop myself—I scrambled over the carpet, ear to the floor, straining to hear. I picked up bits and pieces of their serious-sounding sentences.

Bills from Nikki's surgeries they were still struggling to pay off.

A change of health insurance. Unsure if it would still cover Nikki's pediatric heart specialist. Something about property tax rates.

And then, from Mama D: "But Penny's college fund—"

Mom's gentle voice: "I know, baby. I know."

I'd backed away from the vent then.

I've never asked them about it outright, because I can't think of anything more awkward to discuss with my parents than their finances, but I could read—well, hear—between the lines. I want college more than I want almost anything else in my life. A chance to get out of Verity. A chance to learn how to fix something in our dying world. To save some of its beauty while we can.

A chance to do something important.

Maybe I'll find this chance in the oceans, or maybe on land; truthfully, I haven't decided exactly which field of environmental science I want to pursue yet. Hatfield was simply the closest and most prestigious internship that was open to sixteen-year-olds.

But no matter which college program I pursue, I'll have to pay for it on my own.

Which is fine. Honestly, it is. If it's Nikki's heart or my college fund, I would choose Nikki's heart too, every time.

It just meant no Hatfield. Like most internships for high schoolers, the Hatfield Marine Sciences bridge internship isn't paid. And although there were cost-benefit analyses I tried to work out—mostly concerning the two free college credits that came with the program—in the end, I knew cold hard cash was what I really needed to start accruing. I never even bothered to apply.

In other words: I need this job.

And while it was a hard pill to swallow at first, turning my back on Hatfield, I'd looked forward to one aspect of employment, outside of the cash: Having something to fill my summer days, even if it wasn't the thing I'd originally envisioned. Something that wasn't ennui and low-key depression. Something that wasn't babysitting. Something new.

Because other than Knowledge Bowl Goes Bowling . . . ever since Rosemary & Time shut down, ever since the triplets were born, ever since my elementary school friendships twisted away inside the weird atmosphere of middle school, it's just . . . I can't figure it out. How to find those carefree Julys and Augusts I've seen portrayed in books and movies, starring teenagers who always seem very different from me.

I don't know if other kids swim in the pool of summer loneliness too or if I'm just . . . more of a freak with way fewer friends.

Anyway, what I'm saying is, maybe working at Delicious Donuts will help. Not just with the college fund but with . . . a different kind of Penny summer.

That is, if I can figure out a way to work alongside Mateo, a person who made their distaste for me clear over the past ten months of my life. But if I survived sophomore year, I can survive this summer too.

I talk myself through my new intentions as I towel off my hair.

I will let myself enjoy a simple summer of donuts.

I will save every penny so I can cover application fees, eventual enrollment deposits, the first year of textbooks (hopefully). Everything will be worth it for these small steps forward.

I will conquer the espresso machine.

I will smile.

I will ask Mateo questions about their life.

I will thank them every time they help me with a task.

I will shower Mateo della Penna with good vibes and good vibes only.

And they are going to like it, damn it.

FOUR

College Fund: $464
College Application Fees: $400 ✅

A week later, my first attempt at steaming milk does not go well.

In fact, it's slightly painful. Like, physically.

I hiss, yanking my hand away, and stick my pointer finger in my mouth like a child, all while scalding-hot white liquid bubbles over the metal pitcher onto the counter.

"Whoa." Mateo reaches over me, turns off the heat, and extracts the pitcher full of burned milk from underneath the steaming wand. "You okay?"

I scowl at them. And remember my Good Vibes Only plan a few seconds too late. I pull my finger out of my mouth and struggle to form a half smile.

"I'm fine."

Except I'm not. I hate that I'm not good at this a full week into the job, while Mateo has been able to handle the espresso machine so easily. Plus my finger hurts, and it's been a bad brain morning. Ever since I woke up, I haven't been able to stop thinking about things such as *What if today is the day Nikki's heart stops working? What if someone runs a red light and hits me when I'm on my way home from work? What if the Yellowstone super-volcano finally lets loose and we all die in horrifying ways?*

So the distraction of being totally incompetent at this very basic task is . . . good, probably.

"Thank you," I add belatedly.

"Sure." Mateo glances at me, and I suddenly realize that we are much too close to each other. That I am still standing uselessly in front of my failed frothing while they have swooped to my side to clean up my mess. I can see the light brown of their irises, the small mole on their right cheek, the iridescence of their hair entirely too well. "You should probably run that under cold water."

They point at my finger, which I'm holding strangely in the air like I'm about to cast a spell. Their fingertip almost touches mine.

"Right." I turn my back on their finger—their nails are painted with sparkly black polish that I could never pull off—and the half-sympathetic, half-amused look on their face as they remake the drink and hand it over to the patiently waiting customer.

Mateo's right, of course; the cool water makes my finger feel better immediately. I try to move on in my head. *We should refill the chocolate crullers, maybe the rainbow-sprinkles too.* I dump spent coffee grounds from Mr. Bun-Bun and wipe off my hands.

"Think we should brew another pot of decaf?" I say. There's only a tiny bit left, but it's eleven o'clock, so maybe not worth it. Coffee orders, along with business in general, tend to trickle off from around now until the midafternoon rush.

"Penny." Mateo's still standing by the espresso machine. They scratch at the back of their head, shifting their shoulders awkwardly. "We can . . . we should practice *this* while no one's here."

I shove a fresh filter into the metal basket a little too aggressively.

They are being, like, weirdly nice to me. It's possible my Good Vibes Only plan is simply working as intended—other than this current upsetting moment of Attack by Espresso Machine, I have been friendly as hell since our first day—but it also feels . . . odd. "I'll have Candace give me some more tips tomorrow."

Candace is the other full-time summer employee of Delicious Donuts. She graduated from Verity High a year ago, has worked at Delicious Donuts for three years, is studying computer science at Benton County Community College, and, like Mateo, is infinitely cooler than me. She's been super-nice so far, though. She has a nose ring and a small neck tattoo. I'm a little obsessed with her.

"You don't have to—" I start to say to Mateo, but I'm not sure how to finish my sentence. *Baby me? Be nice to me? Teach me something I clearly should have grasped already since we were both trained at the same freaking time?*

I let the sentence hang instead. Mateo doesn't have to do anything. The end.

I walk to the racks of backup donuts in the kitchen and pull out a tray of chocolate crullers. There's only an hour left in our shifts before Candace and Elen come in to finish the afternoon. I'll go back to Good Vibes Only Penny tomorrow.

Except as I refill the trays behind the counter, the store remains annoyingly free of customers. And Mateo annoyingly persistent. They cross their arms over their apron, leaning their hip against the counter next to me.

"You just have to practice," they say. "You'll feel better the more you try."

I keep placing donuts in trays. They keep staring at me.

Eventually, I sigh. "Fine."

They smile at me. And—oh. They're smiling at me, that charming, adorable smile they smiled at that small child on our first day. The smile I haven't been the intended audience for in so long. I swallow as they turn and head back toward the espresso machine, my cheeks heating for no discernible reason.

This is good, I tell myself. *My plan is working.*

Or maybe they've just come to the same conclusion I did—that this summer will be much more enjoyable if we treat each other like . . . oh, I don't know. Like the other isn't the *worst*.

The memory comes to me unbidden, as it often does; such an embarrassing fleeting moment to obsess over. Mateo at their locker a few minutes after the last bell, the first day of sophomore year. Their best friend, Talanoa, leaning next to them.

For what it's worth, I also hadn't quite been able to believe it as that day progressed—the fact that Mateo and I somehow had every single class together.

Every. Single. Class.

It was like the counselors had gotten lazy when they'd arrived at the *D*s and stuck our class schedules together.

There were other kids in our grade I'd had plenty of classes with over the years—in a small town, schedule overlap was natural—but since middle school, I couldn't remember having *every* class with a particular person. It didn't help that *Dexter* and *della* often landed next to each other on class rosters, so in the classes with old-school teachers who set up their rooms in alphabetical rows, we were often *literally* next to each other.

Which was super-annoying, because I actually prefer the old-school rows (the social anxiety of sitting in a random *group* is a nightmare), but I couldn't even enjoy the soothing organizational logic of an alphabetical row last year since it meant Mateo was always in front of me, with their sketchpad and their very cool hair. I had, against my will, memorized every single inch of their neck.

So, yeah, it had been an odd first day of school. But by the time sixth period was over—Algebra 2 with Mrs. Nguyen—it also felt kind of funny. Mateo and my relationship, if one could even call it that, had turned strange after that day I was their student ambassador in eighth grade, but I'd planned on joking about our schedule at our lockers. Because Verity High still used ancient lockers. Which were *also* assigned to students in alphabetical order. Maybe Mateo would think it was all funny too.

Except when I got there that day, a bit delayed because I'd had to stay after to ask Mrs. Nguyen about my access code to our online textbook, Talanoa was blocking my own locker and saying this, loudly, to Mateo:

"She's really in every single one of your classes?" His voice had been tinged with laughter.

"Yes." Mateo faced their open locker, their back to me. "It's the *worst*."

And then they'd clanged their forehead against the top of the locker for emphasis. Talanoa had burst into actual laughter, and I'd turned on my heel and raced down the hall. Even though I needed my flute, which I'd shoved in my locker at lunch. My face had felt like it was literally on fire as I collapsed into my bus seat.

I've thought about it a million times since, why this one small snippet of overheard conversation hurt so much. It just felt like... someone taking every irrational worry I'd ever had about myself and shouting, *Guess what! Hannah's been lying to you—it's all true!*

Because maybe I *am* the worst.

But I didn't want Mateo to think that too.

Anyway, the rational part of my brain knows I should accept it, this newfound Mateo friendliness inside of Delicious Donuts. So I follow them to the dumb machine, where they're already pouring fresh milk into a clean pitcher. They place the milk back in the industrial fridge that's underneath the counter, kick it shut with their shoe.

"You want to make sure the tip of the wand is near the bottom of the pitcher when you start. If it's too close to the surface of the milk, it'll make huge bubbles."

I cross my arms over my chest and bite the inside of my cheek. *Friendly Penny*, I remind myself. Instead of shouting *Elen already told me that ten times!*

"You want to move the pitcher down slowly as it heats up and be really careful to make the foam without actually breaking the surface. You just kind of . . ." Mateo shrugs as they move the pitcher around. I can tell they're producing perfect foam from the noise, a pleasant, consistent steaming sound instead of the angry hisses the machine makes at me. "Feel it."

I bite my cheek harder.

"But I *do* all that," I can't stop myself from saying. Because I *do*. Mateo must simply possess some espresso-machine sorcery I was not granted at birth. One that Elen and Candace also possess. Magically.

"Then let's try it." They click off the heat and wipe the wand again before taking a step back. "Show me."

I pick up a clean pitcher from the counter and pour in some milk. Stand in front of the machine, spine straight, shoulders back. I do not care that Mateo is a mere foot away, watching me. I do not care that this machine is evil. I am competent. I can do this.

"Good," Mateo says after I've turned on the heat and kept the wand in the milk without killing us for approximately point five seconds. I barely manage to hold in an eye roll. "Okay, start lowering the pitcher just a little," they say, *right* before I am about to do exactly that, and I can feel my temper rising along with the temperature of the milk. "Keep an eye on the gauge as you're working on the foam; it tends to get really hot really fast when you're—"

I release a yelp as the tip of the wand accidentally lifts above the surface, spurting angry bubbles.

"It's okay!" Mateo reaches their hands toward mine.

"I got it!" I shout, submerging the wand again before Mateo can hold my hand, literally, through the simple correction. "I got it," I repeat at a slightly lower volume.

"Okay." Mateo retreats, shoving their hands into their hair and fisting their fingers in the bright strands as if to prevent themself from reaching out again.

Tentatively, I move the wand around, attempting to get some decent foamage going on, even though I already know it won't be as good as Mateo's. I'm feeling pretty good about it, actually; there's less hissing, fewer ominous bubbles than before. Maybe Mateo was right. I just needed a little more practice. I bet eventually, I could—

"Penny," Mateo says. "Watch the temperature. It's—"

Too late, I shift my gaze from the semi-decent foam I'm creating to the temperature gauge. Which is—which is way past the red, holy crap, and the milk is somehow expanding in volume every second and—

Mateo stabs their finger against the Off button a breath before I do, our fingers jamming into each other. I leap back from the pitcher as scalding milk pours over the side.

I take a shaky breath as I wrap the finger that just jammed into Mateo's inside my fist and hold it to my chest.

I do not look at Mateo.

An awkward second drags by.

"That was better," Mateo says.

I can't help myself. I glare at them.

"It was!" They hold up their hands, imploring. "Way less explosive. You just have to make sure you turn off the heat before the gauge gets into the red."

"Yeah." I sniff the air. Despite the horror of the past five minutes, I think it does smell slightly less . . . scorched this time. "I know."

"Want to try again?"

I bite the inside of my cheek once more. I absolutely do not.

"Yeah," I say.

And when I look at Mateo, they're smiling again. It's so alarming, being so close to their smile, that for a moment I can't move.

The bell above the door jangles.

"Yoo-hoo, kids!" It's Bao, who works at the pharmacy halfway down Main Street. She waves her hand high above her head, as she does every time she walks in. "It's Friday-afternoon treat time!"

Bao, I've learned, also celebrates Monday-afternoon treat time. And Wednesday-afternoon treat time.

I practically leap away from the espresso machine to reach

the end of the counter where Bao is standing, a fierce look of concentration on her face. It feels at least ten degrees cooler over here.

I'll practice more tomorrow.

"What today, what today..." Bao sings under her breath, standing on her tippy-toes to look over the counter. I move to the side to make sure she can see the array of trays behind me. Bao mixes it up; I never know what she's going to order.

I'm surprised, actually, at how many customers' orders I do know, even after only a week of shifts. I'm not at Elen level or anything, but it's weirdly satisfying, knowing what kind of donut Mr. Davies from the lumber shop likes and how Keena, a physician assistant who works at the doctor's office in the next town over, likes her coffee. And that Adrian, a postal carrier, orders a blueberry bagel with extra cream cheese at the beginning of each week.

Bao claps her hands once, loud, like she does every time she reaches a decision.

"Oreo," she announces.

I am delighted for her.

"Good choice," I say as I place the cookies-and-cream-filled donut into a small paper bag.

"Donuts are always a good choice," she says. I smile, finding it hard to disagree, my frustration with the espresso machine fading into the sugary air.

I know I might feel different by the end of the summer, but

I'm not sick of the sweet, doughy smell of the shop yet. Still smiling at Bao, I move to ring her up at the register—

And bump into Mateo, who's already standing there, Bao's Oreo-frosted donut already rung up on the POS system.

"Oh." I push Bao's bag across the counter and step away. God. Mateo and I worked together all morning totally normally, and now I can't seem to find personal space.

Bao glances back and forth between us a few times.

"Thanks so much, have a delicious day," I say in a rush and twirl to disappear into the kitchen.

It is possible I spend an unnecessary amount of time organizing the remaining racks of donuts.

When I return to the floor, Mateo does not ask me to practice steaming milk again.

A string of lunchtime customers occupy most of the next hour. A group of parents with strollers come in for a donut playdate, taking over most of the orange booths. Their children crawl over the chipped laminate tabletops, along the scuffed floors. Which is totally gross—I know what those floors look like under those booths now—but their parents don't seem to care, and the kids are having a great time. They remind me of the triplets when they were younger. I cross my eyes and stick out my tongue at them over the counter while Mateo restocks milk from the big fridge in the kitchen.

Each time I risk a glance at Mateo, something like shame starts to build in my gut over the way I handled their foaming lesson, the way I'm treating their kindness with suspicion instead of gratitude.

I know, even without Hannah explaining it to me, that my brain tends to get in its own way a lot of the time. And when I look back at our shift today, Mateo has been nothing but nice, plain and simple. I should at least thank them for trying to help me.

I turn toward them after they close the fridge.

"Mateo," I start.

But I'm interrupted by the jingling bell and, half a second later, Roman Petroski gliding through the door.

FIVE

College Fund: $483

"Penster!" Roman croons with his signature toothy grin. "I didn't know you were working here this summer."

I feel more than see Mateo step beside me.

"And Mateo della Penna!" Roman's smile shines even brighter, his voice lingering over the syllables of Mateo's name. Roman's golden curls have platinum streaks from the sun; his skin is a shade darker than the last time I saw him, like he's been summering *hard*. He's wearing a loose tank top, the kind with the weirdly long arm holes that guys wear, showing off his defined biceps and an indecent amount of side stomach.

Roman Petroski is . . . a lot of things. He's a year ahead of us, one of those teenage unicorns who is both a star soccer player *and* a lead in every spring musical. Both beautiful and kind. Academically successful and effortlessly cool.

He's also a member of iTuna, the environmental-justice club I was vice president of last year and hope to be president of next year.

Roman and I are not *friends*, per se, but I've been angling to get more on his radar for the entirety of my high-school career for a few reasons. First, Roman's support for my iTuna presidency would basically seal the deal for me. It's hard to disagree with Roman Petroski.

Roman talking more about iTuna at all would give us a boost, really. It's a struggling club; the membership is almost as nerdy and weird as Knowledge Bowl's but not nearly as driven. Roman himself shows up only half the time, which is probably the only thing about him that frustrates me—but honestly, the fact that he shows up to any of our meetings is something of a miracle.

I think if I held the reins, though, I could get us motivated to run more effective campaigns. Things I could write about in my college essays. Things Roman—and his dad—could be proud of.

Because, second, his dad is sort of my hero. A professor at Oregon State, he visited our science class in eighth grade to talk about his research into the effects of rising sea temperatures on coastal wildlife. He helped get congressional approval for a marine sanctuary off the southern coast. He repeatedly advises the Oregon Department of Environmental Quality on how to reach their carbon-reduction goals. He is, like, a mega-expert on sea sponges, of which there are more than eight thousand known species. Eight thousand!

It's possible I have been lightly stalking his work ever since that eighth-grade presentation.

Because the thing is, no matter what else I've tried, no matter how many anxiety-soothing methods Hannah has taught me, the only thing that ever *actually* helps my brain relax is reading about people who are trying to make the world better.

Hearing about people who are doing important things.

Knowing that change, however small, is possible.

"Hey, Roman," Mateo says. "What kind of donut do you want?"

"No donut for me today." Roman rubs his stomach. Which means I am now staring at Roman's far-too-visible stomach. It's a little obscene. I bet he's been kayaking a lot in the past week and a half. Or rock climbing. Or wakeboarding. His family's into all that stuff; he talks about it all the time in iTuna on the days he shows up. It's why, in addition to his dad's work, he cares so much about the environment.

Which is definitely the most attractive thing about him. Caring about the environment. Not . . . other stuff.

"But I would kill for an iced latte," he says. "We're heading down to the coast today with Eli, and I didn't get to sleep until, like, two a.m."

"I got it!" I squeak. Like, my voice actually squeaks. Like I'm twelve and adjusting to new levels of hormones.

"Dash of caramel in there?" Roman adds, and I spin on my heel with a nod and head for the espresso machine. Gather ice in Roman's cup while the espresso shots pour. Iced drinks I can handle. Kind of.

Mateo and Roman chat about their summers so far, about theater people they both know and what everyone's been up to.

Think of something cool to say! I shout inside my head.

But instead of conjuring up anything intelligent, *Penster*, said in Roman's charismatic voice, is the only thing that echoes idly around my skull.

"Thanks, Penny," Roman says with a wink when I hand him his drink. It would be ridiculous if that wink made my skin heat. Roman probably winks at the scary old guy who works the deli counter at the IGA.

With a friendly wave, he heads toward the door, then stops at the last second.

"Hey!" he says as he turns. He points at me and Mateo. "Both of you. Make sure you're at my party in August, all right?"

Roman waves once more and shoves out the door before we can respond. I watch it swing shut after him while my brain fills with a surprised fuzz.

On top of his other accomplishments, Roman Petroski is also known for the epic parties he throws at the end of the summer every year. I've known about them since seventh grade, when he hosted the first one. I'm sure Mateo attends, because all the theater kids do.

I am not, generally, a party person.

But I have also never been directly invited before.

And . . . well. *A different kind of Penny summer.*

Right? Maybe I could try a Roman party. Maybe it would be fun.

Maybe I could get to see Dr. Petroski's office.

When I realize I've been spacing out too long and blink my

way back to reality, I discover two things: I'm smiling a weird smile, and Mateo is staring at me.

"What?" I snap, embarrassed, forcing my lips down.

Mateo only shakes their head and turns away.

I take a deep breath, trying to remember what I'd been about to do before Roman walked in. Eventually, since the shop remains quiet, I wander into Elen's office to restock our paper supplies.

I'm grabbing a stack of sixteen-ounce cups when I see it.

SIX

College Fund: $487

For the record, I wasn't *trying* to snoop around Elen's office. We have to go in here all the time; it's where a bunch of supplies are kept. And the document was just . . . there, sticking out from under her draft of next week's schedule.

It's impossible to miss the logo of Northwest Donuts: a fir tree inside a big pink-icing-with-sprinkles circle.

And when I tug at the paper, just a little, the words in all caps underneath that recognizable logo are also impossible to miss:

OFFER OF PURCHASE

I yank the whole thing out and scan it, heart thudding in my ears.

A minute later, I stuff it back where I found it and march out to the floor.

Where the hell is Mateo? Oh, there they are, sitting at their favorite booth with their sketchbook. Vaguely, I remember them saying they were going to take their last ten just before I went to look for the cups. Which I totally forgot back in Elen's office. But who cares about cups now!

"Mateo."

They jump as I slide in across from them, smacking their elbow into the hard plastic booth. "Fuck," they say. "Ow." They glance toward me, scowling, then down at their sketchbook. Their eyes go wide, and they slam it closed, scowl deepening.

I would roll my eyes—as if I would try to pry into their art at a time like this—but I'm too stressed for annoyance.

"Did you know Elen is selling Delicious Donuts?"

Their scowl shifts into a frown, the bridge of their nose bunching. "She is?"

"To Northwest Donuts!" I practically shout. I look around to make sure we're still the only ones in the shop. "I saw the paperwork in her office," I hiss across the table at a slightly lower decibel, just in case a customer opens the door.

Mateo frowns a bit deeper and rubs their forehead. "Well, that sucks."

"Um. *Yes*." Oops, I got loud again. "What should we do?"

"I mean . . . nothing?" Mateo lifts their shoulders for a long second, then drops them. "If she's selling to Northwest . . . at least it'll still be a donut shop? We probably won't lose our jobs."

"Who cares about our jobs!" I'm back to hissing, and okay, I'm being weird. I will my body to regulate itself. "I mean," I say, backpedaling, "I care about our jobs. It's just . . . Elen can't sell Delicious Donuts. It's been here forever. It's a staple of downtown Verity!"

"Look, I don't like it either," Mateo concedes. "But I'm sure if Elen is thinking about this, she has a good reason."

"I feel like the shop does good business, right?" I bite my lip. I've worked here barely a week and a half, and yeah, it's almost lunchtime and the shop is dead, but mornings are always busy; I imagine the ebb and flow is the same at any donut shop. I think of Bao, Mr. Davies, Keena, Sunny with his single donut, Jack the librarian, who always travels across the street for an iced coffee. The way Elen squeezed Alfredo's hands.

Elen has loyal customers. This place might be only a small stop in people's days, a tiny store on the edge of a quiet, possibly dying Main Street. Just like Rosemary & Time was. But . . . it matters. I just can't fully form the words to explain why.

"I think it does," Mateo answers. "But maybe she wants to retire. I'm sure Northwest Donuts would give her decent bank for this place."

"But what about Alex!" I think of Elen's son, dutifully here so early every day. The more this sinks into my head, the more it doesn't feel right. "He's always here making the donuts. It's a family business. Why isn't she passing it on to him if she wants to retire?"

"Maybe Alex doesn't want to make donuts for the rest of his life." Mateo shrugs again. "Or maybe he wants to make donuts but not take over the actual business part."

"But—" Ugh, Mateo is being so *irritating* with their calm logic. Why aren't they more upset? They should be more upset. "But if Northwest Donuts buys this place, it'll be a corporate chain taking up space on Main Street. It'll be like Route 72's taking over the whole town, you know? First it's Northwest Donuts eating up this place, next it'll be . . . Panda Express buying Golden Sun!"

"Okay, but Panda Express is *delicious*." Mateo is smiling now! Smiling! They're slumped against the back of the booth, shoulders relaxed. I want to reach across the table and shake them. "Sometimes Talanoa's mom drives us to a Panda in Salem when—"

"Mateo!" I smack the table. Mateo jumps. "Fine! Panda is delicious! But it doesn't belong *here*." I ball my hands into fists. "We have to do something."

"This is absolutely none of our business, Penny. It's Elen's business, literally; we're just two kids who definitely weren't supposed to see that paperwork. On another note, Elen will be here soon, and if we *do* want to keep our jobs, she probably shouldn't see us both just hanging out in a booth."

They move to leave. I reach out and grab their wrist. "Wait."

God, I hate what they just said. *We're just two kids.*

I know, I *know*—even in my adrenaline-fueled brain—that saving a local donut shop isn't the same as fighting climate change. It's not the same as saving the rainforests or coral reefs or polar bears or honeybees. I know I'm not Greta Thunberg. But it's *something*. Stopping larger corporations from gaining more power *is* connected to everything. And Delicious Donuts . . . it's a small business and a longtime part of Verity, but it's also *good*. And saving one thing in this world that doesn't suck? It feels worth it.

Maybe I *was* destined for donuts this summer. Maybe saving this place is something important I can do.

It won't boost my college applications or change our carbon footprint. But it would still be something.

And maybe I can work with Elen on the carbon-footprint thing.

I realize, too late probably, that Mateo is frozen halfway out of the booth and that I'm still holding on to their wrist. The warmth of their skin under my fingers hits my brain all at once. I yank my hand away, face flushing.

"Wait," I say again as they unfreeze and rush away from me, back toward the counter. "Listen, Mateo, I know we're new here. But . . ." I huff out an aggravated breath as they tie their apron back on. "Delicious Donuts hasn't changed since I was a kid. It's part of the community. Getting to know the regulars . . ." I flail my hands around. "It's like—people are awful to each other most of the time, you know? But people aren't awful to each other here. That's important to keep."

Mateo glances at me as they fiddle with the espresso machine.

"All right," they finally say. "But I don't see how having a different logo on the door will change that."

I look away, absently picking at a cuticle. I'm starting to feel a little silly for being so upset while Mateo is still so unaffected.

"There has to be something we can do," I say, pressing on anyway. "Give the shop a fresh shine or something. To at least remind Elen that Verity cares about this place. That we don't want to see it go."

And even though we're not supposed to have our phones with us on the floor, I dig mine out of my pocket and google *Delicious Donuts Verity, Oregon.*

"I'm going to refill the cups," Mateo says.

I let them breeze past me. It appears Elen doesn't even have a website? All I can find is a Facebook page. Which—ugh. But I guess it makes sense. Even though I applied online for every other job I'd tried to get this summer, I applied for *this* one in person on a paper application, like it was the 1990s or something.

"Mateo," I say when they return. "Elen has, like, zero social media presence." The Facebook page doesn't count. It looks like it was last updated three years ago anyway.

Mateo raises an eyebrow at me while they rip the plastic off a sleeve of cups. "Does Delicious Donuts really need a social media presence?"

"Uh, yes? What kind of business these days doesn't even have an Instagram account?" I may not know how to magically boost Delicious Donuts' sales or convince Elen not to sell, but I can make an Instagram account. I can grow our followers.

"I don't know." Mateo leans against the counter, crushing the ball of plastic in their hands. "I kind of like that this place doesn't have an Instagram. It doesn't need it, you know? It's old-school. It doesn't need, like . . ." They wave a hand toward the empty store. "Monstera plants and fancy lighting for hip shots that are constantly trying to sell you something."

Wow, I would not have taken Mateo to be such an Instagram hater. Also, I want to strangle them.

"You know you're totally making my point for me, right?" My temper flares again. "That's exactly why we need to save this place! Because it's old-school!" I huff at my phone, clicking through a few more searches to make sure I'm not missing Elen's accounts. "The Instagram doesn't need to be hip. It could just be like . . . funny stuff. Donut puns, I don't know. Or basic things like highlighting the weekly donut specials. Reminding people that the store exists, that they should visit downtown more."

Because maybe if people visited Main Street more, they'd remember Verity used to be an actual town, a unique place with history, before the chain restaurants and box stores on Route 72 took over.

Maybe if people visited Main Street more, that empty storefront at the end of the street could be filled with my mom's designs again.

Maybe money wouldn't be so tight.

Maybe life could be more like it used to be.

"Mateo." My gaze snaps back to them. "Your art! You could design a new logo!"

Mateo gives a bit of a snort. They shove twenty-ounce cups into their holder.

"Penny, if Delicious Donuts doesn't need an Instagram, it doesn't need a new logo either. And anyway—" They toss their trash away, still not looking at me. "I don't know how to do that kind of stuff. I just draw shit; I don't know graphic design."

I scoff. I am 100 percent positive Mateo could produce an amazing logo. But fine. "Okay, so you could draw, like, cute donut cartoons and stuff. For the Instagram. People would love it."

They roll their eyes and go to Elen's office. I hustle after them.

"I don't do cute donut cartoons either."

"But you *could*," I press, hovering over their shoulder as they lean down to reach the plastic cups for iced drinks on the bottom shelf.

"I don't even know what *cute donut cartoons* entails," they say, voice muffled.

"You know." I wave my hands behind their back. "Donuts. Sprinkles. Maybe little cups of coffee. Being cute."

They stand before I'm ready for it, their shoulder brushing against my arm on the way, their chest entirely too close to mine once they're fully upright.

I take a step back, crossing my arms.

"Or—" I clear my throat. "We could get one of those stand-up chalkboard things to put out on the sidewalk? And you could do cute drawings on there! Or at least some nice lettering advertising different things. It could catch people's attention."

Once I say it, I'm a little shocked that Elen doesn't have one already. Not having a website, fine, but not having one of those cute sidewalk signs when we have a very ample sidewalk? Unacceptable.

"Maybe," Mateo says, noncommittal. They shoulder past me, literally, their arm hitting mine again. "But I still don't think that would save Delicious Donuts from being sold," they call over their shoulder as they walk away.

"But you have to start small!" I shout, running after them back to the floor. I am aware, distantly, that I'm buzzing around them like a sweat bee, but it's not my fault they won't stop working to listen to me. "Any real change *has* to start small. Because otherwise you get overwhelmed. But if you do one small thing, it can lead to other small things, until it turns out you've done a lot."

If I didn't remind myself of this start-small system, how doing even one small thing to help solve a problem is worthwhile, then frankly, I'd freak out. Like, all the time.

I lean my back against the counter, mind still whirring. "Maybe Candace could start a TikTok," I say.

Mateo smirks as they dump out some used coffee grounds. "Candace's TikToks *are* pretty hilarious."

And just like that, a little bump of hurt cuffs me on the chin. I only said it because clearly Mateo isn't interested in helping, so maybe I can rope in Candace. But Mateo certainly doesn't follow *me* on TikTok. Not that, like, they should. I don't post anything anyway. I'm mostly just on there to follow scientists.

I turn away, eyeing the donut trays. Seeing if there's anything

I can restock before Elen and Candace come in and I go home to babysit.

Mateo's right.

Elen's probably made her decision already.

We're just kids at a donut shop.

And if that fact weirdly makes me feel like crying, well, that's for me to discuss with Hannah or the inside of my own head.

Thankfully, a customer finally comes in, and for a few minutes, we're distracted. I'm already mentally locking the past embarrassing half hour away when Mateo speaks.

"Why do you want my help, anyway?"

I turn, surprised out of my thoughts at the tone of their voice. Their frustration is echoed in the furrow of their forehead, their dark eyebrows scrunched toward each other, their long lashes hitting their cheeks. They're at the espresso machine again, running hot water into the shot glasses.

"What do you mean?" Except even as the words leave my mouth, I realize that the past fifteen minutes of me trying to convince Mateo to help save Delicious Donuts was the longest real conversation we've had in . . . a long time.

When they don't say anything, only give me a *look*, I swallow and pull my gaze away from their face.

"I'm not as creative as you," I force out. "I think whatever we could do . . . it would be a lot better. With you."

I cringe internally. Why didn't I say *with your design skills* or *your art*? *With you*. It sounded so . . . familiar. Like—

"I don't—" Mateo lets out a huff, running a hand through

their hair. My eyes can't help but be drawn to them again. "But we're not friends, Penny. Remember?" Their brown eyes meet mine, and for a second, I can't breathe. "You made that super-clear last year."

The door jingles, and Candace walks in.

"Hey there, kids!"

She pops gum between her teeth. Her hair is bright orange, like a radioactive pumpkin, stuck into two short pigtails underneath her ears, bangs hanging over her eyebrows. She gives us a salute as she heads into the kitchen.

My face feels hot.

Mateo wears this leather bracelet around their wrist, a plain brown strap tied together by string, the dangling ends of which are adorned with four small beads. They worry the beads between their fingers now, gaze dropped.

"Mateo," I say, but somehow Candace is already back, clocking in at the register.

"Dead as shit, huh?" She pops her gum again, then spits it into the trash. "How was the morning shift?"

"Fine." Suddenly, Mateo's brushing past me. "I gotta go."

I feel Candace's eyes on the side of my face as I watch Mateo barrel into the kitchen.

"Huh. Weird vibes in here," she remarks.

My words remain stuck in my throat as Mateo returns, messenger bag slung across their chest, and walks swiftly out the door.

SEVEN

College Fund: $504

Once more, for the record: I have always wanted to be Mateo's friend.

Ever since that first day as their student ambassador. They hadn't started dyeing their hair yet, but it was long, close to what it is now. Before they shaved it all off freshman year.

I remember the way they tucked the brown strands behind their ears as we ate lunch together in the Verity Middle School cafeteria. How they quietly said, "My, uh. My pronouns are they/them, by the way."

"Oh," I'd said. "Cool. Mine are she/her." And then, because if there was one thing my brain was good at, it was questioning absolutely everything: "At least, I'm pretty sure they're she/her."

They smiled back and echoed, "Cool."

And then I led them to their fourth period, and they proceeded to disappear into a black hole for the rest of eighth grade.

We didn't share many classes then, but even when I happened to see Mateo in the halls, they would avoid eye contact, act like I didn't exist. I wondered all year what I had done wrong. If I'd had broccoli stuck in my teeth that first day or something and that was the only reason they'd smiled at me—because they had been secretly laughing at me.

I am pretty much always worried people are secretly laughing at me.

And high school—well, freshman year was... a year of truly unfortunate events. Like the time I spilled an almost-full Baja Blast down their back, which they *had* to have known was an accident. Or the time they walked in on me during a bad anxiety day when I was simply trying to peacefully hyperventilate by myself in my favorite solo practice room in the band wing, the one in the very far corner that smells kind of weird. The one I escape to when I need a minute alone. I... hadn't reacted super-well. It's possible I screamed at them, a little. Embarrassment makes you do embarrassing things.

The optimistic part of me, the part Hannah always tries to encourage me to listen to more, wondered if I was just making it up, this awkward, tense vibe that had developed between us. Overblowing it with my overthinking, as I tend to do with... everything.

Until the first day of sophomore year.

And what had I actually done to them, really, that made sharing classes with me "the *worst*"? Other than—okay, there had also been that one time we were doing an egg-drop challenge in STEM and they happened to walk onto the stairs *right* when I dropped my contraption and . . . yeah, fine, my egg cracked on their head. Right on their hair, which was dyed blue at the time. And I had maybe yelled at them then too, but my contraption had been *good*, and they had walked right past the sign that said we were dropping them!

It was also possible I spilled nacho cheese sauce on their shoes in the cafeteria once.

Also an accident.

But other than that! It felt unwarranted.

Just one more thing I couldn't stop thinking about, a thing that I wanted to fix, that felt completely, frustratingly out of my control.

So after that first day of school last year I decided to harden myself. I would no longer care what Mateo della Penna thought of me. They were fully in with the theater kids by sophomore year anyway; they certainly didn't *need* me to be nice to them. They had a bunch of friends, and I had a 4.0 to maintain and an internship to work toward. And three younger siblings to take care of. And a disintegrating world and fragile hearts to worry about. It was fine.

And that's what this past year had been: fine.

I had laid it out for Mateo that next morning, the second day of school, when I met them at our lockers.

"Look, we don't have to be friends, okay?"

This was a sentence I'd never said to anyone before. I am, in general, a person who wishes the entire world could be friends so as to prevent the stockpiling of nuclear weapons and the tragedy of borders and the irrational need to argue with strangers on the internet.

But I had felt proud of myself for setting boundaries. Regaining a tiny bit of control.

I'd keep out of Mateo's way as much as possible, and they'd keep out of mine.

They had seemed confused at first, which made me even angrier somehow, but they'd agreed. And so we had a very fine year of glaring at each other every single day.

There had been only one real *incident* this year, when I accidentally lit their favorite shirt on fire during a chem lab, which I suppose did violate our staying-out-of-the-other's-way rule. But in my defense, Ms. Kellogg had made us work together, and I hadn't *known* it was their favorite shirt. And while it had been legitimately scary for a half a second, it turned out all right in the end. Ms. Kellogg, who's a bit . . . eccentric, seemed thrilled about getting to use the fire extinguisher. Which she used with, like, surprising speed. Mateo's shirt was barely singed, their skin totally safe.

Although I think the chemicals from the extinguisher did end up ruining the shirt, in the end.

There was also, of course, all the times we had to participate in discussions in our US History class, and Mateo always seemed strangely antagonistic toward my opinions in particular. I can barely think about American history now without, like, vibrating with rage.

I just didn't realize until Mateo said that thing at the end of our shift yesterday—*But we're not friends, Penny. Remember?*

How much I had already unhardened myself around them

inside of Delicious Donuts.

It's not just because of some Good Vibes Only plan. It's also because, unconsciously, I probably *want* to.

Because it's easier, sometimes, being soft.

I can't stop thinking about the fact that they remembered me saying it to them, my line about not being friends. I have to assume that's what they were referring to; it felt so . . . pointed. Like they might still think about it. Like how I think about them saying "It's the *worst*."

Some weird part of me hopes they do remember. That they weren't just stating a general fact. Because if they were affected by me saying we weren't friends . . . that must mean they *care*, right? In some twisted way.

I stay up most of the night thinking myself in circles about it.

I almost text Swapna: *Was I too much of a bitch to Mateo last year?* But even though I'd consider Swapna one of my closest friends, we mostly excel at discussing Knowledge Bowl drama and hypothesizing about our teachers' personal lives. We're not . . . text-each-other-in-the-middle-of-the-night friends.

I don't think I really have any of those.

Anyway. To distract myself, I spend some solid time obsessing over that paperwork too, for funsies. My brain flips between Mateo's smile and *OFFER OF PURCHASE* all night long.

Even though I'm exhausted, I show up early for my afternoon shift the next day. Instead of going into the store, I leave

Dolly in the parking lot and stroll down Main Street. Maybe a short walk before facing Elen will clear my head.

Because I know I have to say something to her. Another not-fun-at-all fact about me: I am bad at keeping my mouth shut. No matter what I told myself yesterday about Mateo being right, about accepting that I can't do anything about Delicious Donuts possibly being bought out, I can't make myself *not* care. It's just . . . who I am.

Annoying. Tiring. But who I am.

It's a cloudless, late-June blue-sky day, yet I am the only one strolling past Bao's pharmacy and Golden Sun Chinese Food Palace, past the real estate office and Antiques 'n' Stuff. A second later, I stop outside my old haunt Olivia's Books & Tea. I spent a lot of time here when I was a kid; my mom always considered a bookshop a soul sister to a stationery store. Olivia's sold some of my mom's cards, and my mom sold their tea sachets at Rosemary & Time. They had each other's business cards on their front counters.

But it was middle school when I really made Olivia's my own, after Rosemary & Time was gone, when I needed to be *alone*, away from three screaming toddlers at home and confusing social dynamics at school. I made one of my moms drop me off here at least once a week so I could get some homework done. I step inside now and it smells exactly the same as it did then, when I'd sit in a back corner and pretend I was worldly and sophisticated, like old books and Earl Grey.

I run my fingers along the edge of a display table of new releases. But the moment I'm tempted to pick one up, I snatch my hand back. My checking account/college fund is higher than it's ever been, but it's still paltry in terms of what I need. What am I doing here? I can't afford new books.

I attempt to amble casually and not at all awkwardly back out the door, like I've totally been here for more than four seconds. I let out a breath when I return to Main Street and, on muscle memory, turn left.

Where, just as abruptly, I stop.

Two more storefronts before the corner where Rosemary & Time used to live. I know it's still sitting empty. A thrift store opened there after Mom closed her doors, but it petered out after a year. And even though Mom seems to have moved on, I suddenly don't want to face that empty space.

I jaywalk across the street instead, hustling to the opposite sidewalk to complete my loop back to Delicious Donuts. I make it a good five steps before my sneakers halt once more, this time in front of Goldie's Flowers.

The painted gold lettering on the window is still there, but beyond it, the sun shines into . . . another completely empty storefront.

Okay, now. When did Goldie's close? Do Mom and Mama D know?

I frown.

Not that we ever had the time or money or need for flowers, but Goldie's storefront had always been so pretty. Full of color, changing for the seasons. And next to the displays of picture-perfect bouquets, there had been this sign tucked in the corner of the window with rotating dad jokes that were so bad but always made Mom belly-laugh whenever we walked by.

By the time I shove open the door of Delicious Donuts and grab my maroon apron from its hook in the kitchen, I'm breathing heavily. I close my eyes, press my palm to my diaphragm, try to recenter. People, I've found, are more amenable to your requests if you approach them with positivity and a few simple ideas instead of, say, blurting out, *Do not sell your donut shop or you will be contributing to the destruction of Verity's downtown core.*

"Hey, Penny." Elen smiles at me when I step into her office, but her eyes quickly drift back to her computer screen. She squints through purple-framed glasses that sit at the tip of her nose. "How's it going?"

"Good!" I chirp. "I actually had sort of a proposition for you. You're free to say no to any of it, of course."

Elen clicks around on the screen, adjusts a number.

"I've really enjoyed working here so far," I continue, "and I was thinking of some ways we could maybe help boost the visibility of Delicious Donuts in the community? I have a lot of experience running advertising campaigns for different groups I work with at school, so I have some ideas. Just simple things we could do, you know? To maybe bring in some new customers or remind old ones what a great place this is."

Elen's pointer finger freezes on the mouse.

"I hope that doesn't sound"—I clear my throat, nerves re-revving their engines—"like I'm overstepping. I just think there's a lot of cool things we could do. For instance, we could increase our social media presence, which is free!"

When Elen doesn't say anything, I panic. "Plus, I'm not sure if you know, but Mateo is really great at art. I was thinking we could get one of those A-frame boards to put out on the sidewalk? And Mateo could draw on it, advertising specials or just writing fun things on it to make people smile."

I could probably still convince Mateo to help me if I take a different angle with them. Probably.

Elen finally turns away from the screen; she removes her glasses to stare at me.

"Huh," she says. Totally deadpan. I have no idea how to interpret this *huh* at all. My nerves do a little extended jig.

I bluster onward. "And maybe," I say, "we could create a new logo that we could use for merch? Stickers, T-shirts, hats, stuff like that. There's a lot we could do with merch."

"You think," Elen says slowly, "people would want Delicious Donuts merch?"

"Oh my God, *absolutely*."

She stares at me some more.

"You know we're just selling donuts here, Penny." A corner of her mouth twitches, and I realize, with a mixture of relief and embarrassment, that Elen is holding back a smile. "I do appreciate your initiative, but I can't exactly afford to hire a social media or merchandising manager."

"Oh, no!" I once more gesture perhaps a bit too wildly with my hands. "You wouldn't have to pay us anything extra. I want to do it. I think it would all be fun. I bet even people who have moved away from Verity would follow us online and want to buy merch to remember their hometown, you know? Delicious Donuts is such an important part of this place."

I reel myself in. The arch of Elen's eyebrow and my Spidey sense tell me I'm waxing *too* poetic about Delicious Donuts.

After a pregnant pause, Elen neatly collapses her glasses in her palm, a single hand move that is, like, oddly sexy. I swallow.

"Are you looking for community-service hours or class credit? If so, I'd need the paperwork from your teachers to make sure we're on the up-and-up."

"No." I shake my head, trying to keep my hands from flailing again. "It's not anything like that. I just want to do it. I think working on stuff like this is fun."

This—also for the record—is true.

But when Elen stares at me a moment more, I break.

"I saw the paperwork on your desk yesterday," I say, voice small, casting my gaze to the floor. "From Northwest Donuts."

I hear her sigh, a slow exhalation followed by a quiet hum.

"Penny," she eventually says, her voice now equally quiet. "Sit."

She kicks the second chair from the side of her desk toward me with the toe of her shoe. I sit.

"You know," she says, "I remember when you used to come here when you were small. Running down the street from your mom's store."

I'm fidgeting with my hands, totally messing up my cuticles, but I snap my head up at this. "Really?" She hadn't said anything during my interview or my training.

"Of course." She smiles, eyes crinkling, and my body fills with relief at the warmth of it. "It's hard to forget those freckles. And your hair always attracted so much static electricity—I remember handing you your donuts over the counter and those little brown strands would just be—" She explodes her fingers into a halo around her head. I'm glad she's smiling now but I hold back my own sigh. So my hair *has* always sucked. Great.

Her smile fades as she examines me. I see the calculation in her eyes, how she's contemplating exactly what she wants to say.

"The offer from Northwest was a surprise," she says eventually. I sit up straighter. "And I haven't made any decisions yet. But . . . there are many reasons why it's an attractive offer to me, Penny. And I don't know if merch is going to change that."

"But we could try," I blurt out. "It never hurts to try." And for some reason, I belabor this point. "The A-frame sign would be a great way for Mateo to display their work too. They're really talented."

Another eyebrow arch. Another long, searching look.

These eyebrow arches are really killing me.

"You're right," she says slowly, at length. "That could be cute."

I squeeze my hands together. "So cute."

"What do you want to do after you graduate, Penny?"

The question throws me off, but I try not to show it. This whole conversation has gone both better and worse than I'd hoped; it feels more important than my interview for this job was.

"I want to study environmental science," I answer. "I want to try to . . . save things."

She nods. And then: "I'm not promising you anything, Penny. But you can make the social media accounts if you really want to. Run stuff by me first, though. And if you start getting any weird trolls, you tell me right away."

I exhale all the way from the bottom of my lungs for the first time since I entered this office. It gives me enough strength to grin.

This is good. Better than good. Anything that's not an outright no is always a start to enacting change. I know I'll get her to see the light on merch. And once I do, I'll bring up the other ideas I ruminated on when I couldn't sleep last night.

"Thank you so much, Elen."

I bounce back out to the front before she can change her mind.

My grin fades when Candace and Mateo turn to look at me.

"Hey, Pen!" Candace waves a plastic-gloved hand at me before returning to restocking a tray of jelly-filled. Mateo looks away.

Right. I'd forgotten for a second about the other conversation I have to have today.

Except then the door jingles, and I don't have time to think about the myriad of awkward ways I could approach Mateo, because we have a flood of customers. I step to the register; on my left, Candace grabs food, and on my right, Mateo prepares drinks. For the first few minutes of the abrupt rush, standing between Candace's neck tattoo and Mateo's neon hair, I feel like the dullest girl in Dulltown. Like if Holly Black wrote books about girls with boring hair and anxiety instead of fae.

The insecurity fades, though, the busier the rush gets, the more efficient we become. Without speaking about it, the three of us are a well-oiled machine.

I've never done drugs, so I suppose I don't *really* know, but it's kind of a high.

And then the rush fizzles to a trickle, and Candace clocks out. Elen leaves soon after, and then it's just me and Mateo. Closing shift.

It's possible my heart's beating too fast.

I turn to where they're still stationed behind the espresso machine before I lose my nerve. Good Vibes Only Penny. *Honest* Penny. I want them to work with me on the espresso machine again. I want them to work with me to save Delicious Donuts. I want to be their friend. Even if we run in different circles. Even if we have weird history. Even if I'm not, never was, and never will be as cool as them.

"Hey," I say. "Mateo."

They glance up. A lock of purple hair escapes from behind their ear, brushes the side of their cheek.

"I'm . . ." Except the word gets stuck in my throat. All the question marks of last night, of the past *year*, poke their way into my brain once again. I know the animosity between us hasn't been one-sided. I need them to apologize too.

I force the word out anyway:

"Sorry."

They lift an eyebrow. And say nothing. Which is infuriating.

"For . . ." I gesture with my hands. They have to get what I'm saying. "You know. The thing you said about not being friends? I would love to . . . change that."

Their face shifts. The eyebrow drops. A look passes behind their eyes I can't read, quick and then gone.

"Yeah?"

"Yeah." I clear my throat, gesture again, back toward the kitchen this time. "I talked to Elen before I clocked in, and she sounds open to some of my ideas. I think she's going to buy your chalkboard sign for the sidewalk!"

I smile at them, projecting hope. A corner of their mouth twitches. I might also be projecting that I think they're trying to hold back a grin.

"Pretty sure it's your sign, Penny."

I shake my head. "Nah. Start practicing your cute-donut drawing skills, della Penna."

This time I'm sure. They shift their eyes away from me when it happens, but that is *definitely* a real Mateo smile.

Even if it falters a second later.

"So." They stretch out the syllable a beat too long, staring at the espresso machine. "You want to be friends . . . so that I'll help you save Delicious Donuts?"

My mouth opens and closes. That . . . sounds bad. It's not exactly what I meant, even if it's also not exactly untrue.

"No. I mean. Maybe. But—" I blow out a breath. "I mean,

we work together now. I just think we should be friends!"

Their eyebrow goes up again. Because, fine, maybe that came out sounding angrier than I intended. God, why does being around Mateo dial my temper up to an eleven every time?

I backtrack, scrambling for an olive branch. "But, like, if there's anything I could ever do for you, I would love—"

"Hey." A new voice enters the conversation. I literally jump. "Penny. You know how to drive a stick shift?"

EIGHT

College Fund: $518

"What?"

"Stick shift," Talanoa repeats. Because Talanoa has apparently been here, on the other side of the counter behind the espresso machine, the whole time.

Awesome.

"Noa," Mateo says, annoyance threaded in their voice. I'm momentarily brought right back to US History. Mr. Humphries is about to sigh at us any minute.

Still, it's a strange relief to know I'm not the only person Mateo talks to with this specific tone.

Talanoa ignores it.

"So?" he prompts, piercing me with a questioning stare. Talanoa's hair is freshly buzzed, dark and fuzzy on his light brown scalp, showcasing the wide wooden plugs in his ears.

I shift on my feet. "Yeah. I do."

Talanoa reaches over the divider and slugs Mateo in the shoulder. "See? Just like you said."

Mateo stares daggers at him.

"What?" I repeat. I could really use more sleep.

"And you have your license, yeah?" Talanoa pushes on. "Not just your permit?"

"Yeah," I say, more slowly this time. "I do."

I got my permit and then tested for my license as soon as I could last winter. You spend six years of your life living with triplets, you take the opportunity to be able to leave the house on your own when you can.

Plus, as soon as I sat behind the wheel for the first time, I knew I would love driving. It was terrifying at first, but once I got a handle on it, it granted me all my favorite feelings: Feeling in control. Competent. Free.

When I'm able to not think about the statistical likelihood of crashes, driving might be the only thing in the world outside of science that truly eases my anxiety.

Which is awful. Because driving is absolutely horrible for the environment. Dolly isn't even very fuel-efficient.

But sometimes you have to do what you have to do and not feel bad about it if it makes you happy.

At least, that's what Hannah says.

"There you go!" Talanoa claps his hands, raises them in the air. "Can you teach Mateo?"

"What?" I say. That's thrice.

"Mateo needs someone to teach them how to drive a stick shift."

"*Noa—*"

"And *you* want Mateo's help with . . . something. Saving

donuts." Talanoa claps his hands again. "Bada-bing, bada-boom."

Mateo sighs heavily and hangs their head. I stare at their hairline briefly before turning back to Talanoa.

"Why don't you teach them?"

"Please." Talanoa scoffs and takes a step back as if even the suggestion is dangerous. "You should barely trust me on these streets with an automatic."

At that, Mateo laughs. The reappearance of their smile makes my shoulders relax.

"This is true." Finally, they glance at me. "You don't have to."

"Would you *want* me to?" I try to keep the incredulousness out of my voice. They shrug, but there's a discomfort in it, like they're trying to play off being casual.

"Sure. I do . . ." They swallow, cheeks darkening, eyes already back on the espresso machine. I think Mateo is *blushing*? "I, uh, do unfortunately need to learn to drive a stick shift this summer. So I could . . . help you out with trying to save the store. In return. Like Talanoa said. If you want."

This is the most awkward Mateo I have ever witnessed. I would feel gratified by it if I weren't so thrown by this entire conversation.

They toss another glance at me, a bit longer this time.

I only start to actually consider the proposition then. It still feels . . . strange. But I can see it somehow in their eyes. They're uncomfortable, but they mean it. They want me to help them learn how to drive.

I shift on my feet again, digging my thumbnail into my

opposite thumb's cuticle. I do like teaching people things. Being helpful. It's why I signed up to be a student ambassador in middle school, why I volunteer once a week during the school year as a tutor with the Honor Society.

"But you said it wasn't any of our business," I say. "Yesterday, about the shop. That we're just kids."

They shrug again.

"I mean, if Elen's down . . ." They glance at me once more. "We could try. Right?"

Now I'm the one to look away. If they said the exact wrong thing to me yesterday, this is the exact *right* thing to say to me now.

We could try.

"Okay," I hear myself say. It comes out oddly quiet. I clear my throat. "Yeah. Sure. If you're sure."

"I love when a plan comes together," Talanoa says in triumph, walking backward away from the counter. I had somehow forgotten he was still here.

"Dude," Mateo says, head swiveling back to him. "You're not even going to buy anything?"

"Honestly?" Talanoa holds a hand over his heart. His wide shoulders almost fill the entire frame of the door. "The sweetness of this situation here is all my body needs."

"I am going to fucking—"

Mateo swallows whatever they were going to say upon seeing Talanoa open the door for Jack, the children's librarian who works at the Verity branch of the Benton County Library across the street. I see this interaction from the corner of my eye; I'm busy gaping at Mateo for dropping the F-bomb while *on the floor*. I mean, yes, Talanoa was our only customer at the time, but *still*.

They refuse to look back at me, continuing to stare at Talanoa after the door shuts behind him. He's still walking backward on the sidewalk, making ridiculous hand motions at Mateo I don't fully understand, ending with his fingers curled in a Taylor Swift heart before finally walking out of view. Mateo mutters something unintelligible underneath their breath.

"Hey, Jack," I say, stepping toward the register, trying to shake off... whatever the hell just happened. "How are things at the library?"

"Big day," Jack answers as he parks his wheelchair in front of the counter. "Snake guy's coming in this afternoon."

"Oh!" I smile, big and easy this time. "I love the snake guy."

"Everyone loves the snake guy," Jack says.

Mom doesn't love the snake guy. She always closed her eyes and squeezed my hand real hard when she took me to his program each summer when I was a kid. Before the triplets.

Now that I think of it, it's wild that we haven't taken the triplets to see the snake guy. At the same time, it doesn't completely surprise me. It's weird, but ever since the triplets arrived, it's like... we're busier than ever before, but we also somehow *do* less than ever.

Anyway, Bruno probably shouldn't be trusted around snakes.

"Can I get an iced coffee?" Jack asks. "I'm trying to curb my caffeine intake, but I need the strength today."

"Got it," Mateo says.

"Can I get some hazelnut in there too?" Jack asks with a hopeful lilt in his voice. "And a dash of oat milk?"

If there's one thing I've learned in the past couple weeks, it's how happy coffee makes people. Even though it's gross. I refuse to believe Mateo actually enjoys the black sludge they're always drinking whenever they're here. Still. I like being able to give Jack a little extra strength for his day.

I open the door for him a minute later; he gives a wave over his shoulder as he rolls back across the street, like he always does. The sidewalks are full of American flags, silvery stars strung between buildings, Main Street gearing up for the Fourth of July.

And then it's just me and Mateo again.

They move past me to clean the coffee station by the door, the one with the sugar and cream and napkins. I pick up a rag and clean the already clean back counter for a while before it bursts out of me:

"What did Talanoa mean, before?"

I turn my head in time to see Mateo freeze, their fingers pausing on the handle of the half-and-half carafe.

"What do you mean?"

I bite my lip, trying to remember the exact phrasing.

"When I said that I know how to drive a stick shift, he punched you and said something that made it sound like you'd discussed it before."

They push the half-and-half back into place and walk

behind the counter again.

"My dad will give me his truck if I learn how," they say, checking the filter in Mr. Bun-Bun. "But learning with him is . . . not working. I just reached the six-month mark of my license, though, where I can drive without an adult, so . . . Talanoa and I were trying to brainstorm who else could teach me."

They lean their palms against the counter by the sink, staring out the window at the scraggly bushes behind the building. "I bet that you probably knew how."

My brow furrows. "Why?"

A beat of silence, another shifting of their shoulders.

"Because you're good at everything."

I blink a bunch of times in a row, trying to comprehend this.

The statement itself is . . . extremely, patently false. I don't think a person who's good at everything would suffer from debilitating anxiety.

Or light their chem lab partner's shirt on fire.

But falsehood aside, Mateo's statement *sounds* like a compliment, one that's making my heart beat too fast in my chest again, since I can't remember the last time Mateo offered me a compliment. The fact that I even came up in their and Talanoa's conversation at all is—

Except the way they just said it. *You're good at everything.* I could be making it up, but . . . there was this *edge* to it. Like they're mad I'm good at everything.

A desire to fold into myself, to just disappear into the floor beneath the thick rubber mats, flushes through my body.

"I'm not good at the espresso machine" is all I manage.

Mateo's still staring out the window, but they crack a smile.

"I know," they say. "It's weird."

Despite myself, I laugh a little.

"We could start in the Walmart parking lot," I say after a moment. "That's where Mama D taught me."

They nod, their elbows unlocking, shoulders lowering. "Yeah."

And then, surreally, Mateo della Penna and I exchange numbers.

"Want to practice a little more?" they ask as they stuff their phone in their back pocket, gesturing toward the espresso machine.

"Yeah." I nod, mentally unfolding. "Let's try."

NINE

College Fund: $602
College Application Fees: $400 ☑
Enrollment Deposit: $200 ☑

My first driving lesson with Mateo does not actually start in the Walmart parking lot but at their house. Because we have to get the navy pickup truck Mateo wants to learn how to drive out of their driveway and to the Walmart parking lot first.

Which makes sense. But driving to Mateo's house still feels uncomfortably personal, like I'm wearing someone else's clothes. It's late Sunday afternoon, only a day after our last shift together at Delicious Donuts when this plan was somehow concocted. It's a perfect time to practice driving, lots of empty parking lots and quiet roads. Still, my skin tingles with nerves as I park along the curb of 510 Stonyfield Lane.

It's so . . . private, seeing someone's house. Like suddenly they are this fully formed person who exists outside of school—or work—in their own domain, where they eat and sleep and watch TV and play video games and argue with their family. And draw. I wonder how much time Mateo spends drawing at home, if the walls of their room are covered with their work or if they hide it all under their bed.

Not that I'm expecting to see Mateo's bedroom. Or anything inside their house, really. But even just knowing their address, their neighborhood, makes me blush, just like I did when I entered their number in my phone.

I barely have time to turn off my engine or fully take in the dark green siding, the clean white door, or the roses in bloom out front before Mateo is striding across the yard.

I picture them sitting at their living-room window waiting for me. I close my eyes, take a deep breath, and step out of Dolly.

"Hey." Mateo stuffs their hands in their pockets, rocking back on their heels. Nervous energy radiates off them in waves, even worse than my own. "Ready?"

"Nah, I thought we'd stand here awkwardly in the middle of the street for a while first."

I don't mean to start this interaction off with snark. But they need to chill. Because *one* of us needs to be chill.

Luckily, the corner of their mouth twitches into an almost smile.

"Sorry," they say with a small shake of their head, "to hardly give you a second to park. It's just, if we don't go soon—" They look past me and close their eyes. "Shit," they mutter under their breath.

I turn to see the white door opening again. A woman, who I assume is another della Penna, saunters across the lawn toward us. She's tall and wearing sweatpants and a tight black tank top. She's smiling, but she has this sense of authority about her, this swagger—like Elen, but with younger skin—that makes my stomach swoop.

Mateo sighs behind me. "My sister."

"Hey, bambinos," Mateo's sister sings a second later, propping an elbow on Dolly's roof. Her voice is bright and cheery, but my body tenses anyway. Her hair is so shiny. "You must be Penny." She holds out her other hand. "Lía."

"Hi!" I try to make my voice bright and cheery in return, but I'm pretty sure it only sounds squeaky. Again. I shake her hand. "Nice to meet you."

"Y tú también." Her grin deepens, and my brain catches on the language. I know *della Penna* is Italian—it's possible I'd googled it, after meeting them—but I *thought* I'd heard Mateo mumbling in Spanish under their breath sometimes. I wonder if their dad's Italian but their mom isn't, or— I'd never felt close enough to them to ask.

There's a lot I'd never felt close enough to ask.

"Mateo has told me so—"

"We really gotta get going, Lía." Mateo's voice is loud, right behind my ear. "Need to start practicing before it gets dark."

"Sí, sí." Lía's eyes flicker to Mateo before settling back on mine. "Be careful with my sibling, you hear, Penny?" Almost unconsciously, my back straightens. "And if you wreck my dad's truck . . . te matará."

"Oh," I say on a surprised puff of air. I had been so distracted thinking about Mateo's house on the drive over here that I hadn't made room in my brain for the possibility of familial interrogation.

"Ignore her, Penny," Mateo says. And to their sister: "Fuck off, Lía."

Lía's lips pull down in an exaggerated frown. "Can you also teach Mateo some manners while you're out there?"

"Come on." Mateo loops their arm through mine and pulls me toward the truck sitting in the driveway. "Can you drive to Walmart, please?" they ask, voice low against my ear, arm still curled around mine as my feet stumble to keep up. "If we start here, Lía will just stand there and stare at us. And possibly my dad will too." They glance at the house. "Which would actually be worse."

"Sure," I say, like I am feeling casual about any of this. We reach the driver-side door, which must alert them to the fact that they're still holding my arm, because they look down and drop it with a suddenness, practically leaping away from me. They take the keys from their pocket and throw them toward my hands—I reach out my palm just in time to catch them—before walking around the hood. They slam the passenger side door behind them.

I turn back to Lía.

"We'll be careful," I promise, trying to take a breath. Lía sticks her hands in the pockets of her sweats, her stance looking funnily similar to Mateo's when they'd greeted me at my car a few minutes ago. They have a lot of similar features, now that I'm looking more closely at her. Same tilt to her mouth, same brown eyes. And when she smiles at me now, it seems gentler than before. I wonder if it's because Mateo's out of earshot.

"I know you will, Penny," she says, all the tease gone from her voice. Her boobs look incredible in that tank top. I am, overall, embarrassed about the existence of my boobs, but maybe I wouldn't be if they looked like that. I can barely even comprehend what it would feel like to look like Lía della Penna. "Have fun."

She turns toward the house, pauses, turns back.

"My dad really will kill you if you wreck the truck, though."

I swallow. "Noted."

She hesitates another moment before adding, "Thanks for doing this. For Mateo."

"Oh." I sound surprised again. "It's not a big deal."

At least, I have spent the last twenty-four hours convincing myself it's not.

Lía nods and walks away for good, her long hair swinging behind her.

When I climb into the truck, Mateo is bouncing their knee, staring out the window as they worry the beads at their wrist. They say nothing.

I take a couple of minutes to orient myself, adjust the mirrors, study the dashboard. I'm pretty sure I can do this, but I've never actually driven a truck before. Dolly's a compact automatic, and when Mama D taught me manual, it was with her old Subaru. I feel so *high* in this thing, and I'm not used to the lever gear shift, but I'm sure I'll figure that out. As soon as I back out of this driveway, I'll be fine.

I know both Lía and Mateo's dad are safely inside the house, but I swear I feel their eyes on me anyway. It's almost a relief

Mateo isn't looking at me, even though you'd think they'd want to, to see what I was doing. Whatever.

I press the pedals with both feet a few times until I feel comfortable, then push down on the clutch and brake and turn the keys in the ignition. The truck roars to life, loud and rumbly, and I smile. It's sort of cool, now that I've had a second with it, being so high off the ground. Mateo's driveway is on a slight incline, but the road behind us is empty and wide. I check the mirrors and ease us down, a flare of satisfaction kindling in my chest when I brake smoothly at the end of the turn without a stall. I switch from reverse to drive and get us into first gear, then second, driving out of Mateo's neighborhood with only the slightest of hitches between gears.

My brain hums. I can *totally* do this.

We're out of Mateo's neighborhood and on Route 72 heading toward the Walmart before Mateo speaks.

"You know I don't, like, *actually* talk about you to Lía or anything." They shift in their seat. "I mean, she knows we work together, but, like—"

"Oh, I know." It's funny to me they would even be concerned. Like I really think Mateo and Lía sit around gossiping about Penny Dexter. "A girl came to pick you up she hadn't met before, and she wanted to give you a hard time." I shrug. "I get it."

Mateo's quiet again. Which is fine. I'm focused on fourth gear and maintaining the speed limit.

But when they say, "You have older siblings that give you a

hard time too?" it's been so long that I have to think back to remember what I'd said.

I shift down for a stop at a red light. "Um," I answer. "No. All my siblings are six years old. That's just . . . I don't know. How older siblings act on TV, I guess."

My face heats as the light turns green. At least I'm more confident in my shifting abilities now, accelerating back into first gear as we roll through the intersection.

"Wait," Mateo says, and while my eyes are focused on the road, I can hear the confusion in their voice, and I know that wrinkle between their eyes is probably back. "All your siblings are six?"

"Triplets," I confirm. "Emma, Bruno, Nikki. My moms had them kind of late, when I was in fifth grade, after they got married. You didn't know?"

At this point, I sort of figure everything about my family is common knowledge. Two moms, triplets. Not exactly your run-of-the-mill Verity household. Word gets around in a small town.

"No." Out of the corner of my eye I see Mateo shake their head. We're getting close to Walmart now. "I knew about your moms, but . . . yeah. That's cool, though."

I almost tell them that the triplets *are* cool. That Bruno leveled up in tae kwon do last night, and to celebrate, Mom took us all to the Dairy Twist, where Bruno ran to every picnic table, telling any stranger within hearing distance all about it. That Nikki got rainbow sprinkles in her hair, which Bruno thought looked cool, so he tried to dump his own soft serve on top of her head too but Mom caught his wrist just in time. That Emma let me finish the last crunchy bites of her cone when she got full.

But even with this shaky agreement Mateo and I now have to help each other this summer, Talanoa's interruption yesterday prevented Mateo from truly answering my request that we be friends. I don't know how much Mateo actually wants to know about my life. I keep my mouth shut.

But Mateo keeps talking.

"Lía just got back from her first year in college, and . . . I don't know." Their knee starts bouncing again. "She seems even more clingy than normal or something. Always in my face."

"She's in college?" A flutter of my heart. "Which school?"

"USC."

I hold in a gasp. "Like, University of Southern California?"

A small sigh before Mateo answers, "Yeah."

"Wow."

"Yeah."

USC would be a dream school for me—if I thought I'd be able to afford anything out of state. "What does she study?"

"Anthropology."

Oh my God. Fantastic boobs and an anthropology major at USC. It's possible I am in love with Mateo's sister.

I almost ask Mateo more—whether she likes USC, what got her into anthropology, why did Mateo sigh when they talked about it—but we've already reached the Walmart parking lot. I ease the truck into a space at the far edge over by the garden center, where it's empty. When I turn off the engine, I realize something.

I have just had an entire conversation with Mateo della Penna. Not because we were forced to by school or work but just, like . . . because. And it was . . . pleasant.

Almost like we're friends.

I hop out of the truck and switch places with Mateo before I can overthink it. I turn on teaching mode in my brain as I click in my seat belt on the passenger side.

"Okay!" I push enthusiasm into my voice. "So you said you've tried this before? With your dad?"

"Yeah." Mateo is hunched over the steering wheel, their knuckles already white as they grip at 10 and 2. "Hasn't gone well," they mutter.

"All right, soooo . . ." I start to reach out to push back their shoulders, to ease their death grip on the wheel. But me and Mateo do not, in fact, casually touch. I pretend I meant to scratch my forehead instead. "Maybe you should relax a little?"

Mateo sighs. They lean back, slightly, in the seat. They do not release their grip.

"Great!" I chirp. "So, then, you're familiar with the clutch?"

"Theoretically," they mumble.

Their confidence is inspiring.

Nonetheless, I talk them through starting the vehicle, how to slowly let go of the brake to step on the gas, balance lifting up on the clutch, and—the truck bolts forward. I might screech a little.

The truck stalls.

Mateo's forehead hits the steering wheel.

"Stalling's going to happen," I say, really wishing I hadn't made that embarrassing sound. "You just have to accept it and keep trying. So let's try again."

Mateo does not move their head. This is going great.

After an awkward minute of silence, I venture, "Is this truck your only option? Maybe you could use your savings from working at the shop this summer to buy an automatic?" Most kids I know can only drive an automatic. Mama D taught me manual because, like . . . I don't know, she's butch, and sometimes she wants to do these butch things, like teach me how to drive her Subaru, and I can tell it makes her happy. But for most intents and purposes, driving a stick shift feels sort of like a dying art, like film photography or cable TV.

I think for a moment that Mateo is never going to lift their head from the steering wheel. We might die here. I might have to go into the Walmart for provisions. It was a smart move, doing this in the Walmart parking lot.

"I can't drive unless I drive this truck," they say eventually into the steering wheel. They lean back and add, voice clear, "Real men know how to drive stick shift."

I suck in a breath. "Oh," I whisper.

I think of Lía telling me how their dad would kill me if we wrecked his truck, and it doesn't take a lot of brainpower to deduce who said this to them.

Mateo stares straight ahead through the windshield. Their mouth is set in a hard line. I look away.

I guess I don't know exactly how Mateo identifies, whether

they're nonbinary or genderqueer or agender or something else, but in any case, it has never been hard to know them that way, as belonging outside the binary in some shape or form. Like, it is literally *not hard* to see Mateo for who they are. Even just hearing Mateo say that line about *real men* makes me feel sick to my stomach.

I can only imagine how it makes them feel.

When Mama D taught me how to drive stick, it wasn't because she thought it would magically make me butch too. It wasn't attached to a weird ultimatum. I did it because I like learning new things, and I like spending time with Mama D. It didn't feel . . . like this.

This sucks.

"Okay," I say after another minute. "Let's try again."

They nod. And we do.

We keep trying and we keep stalling, over and over again. It is not fun. But eventually, finally, Mateo hits first gear. And stays there.

"Oh, shit," they say as the tires successfully roll across the asphalt of the parking lot. "Oh, shit," they say again. "What do I do?"

"Steer!" I yell. "Keep going!"

The engine starts to whine as Mateo steers around the edge of Walmart, toward the loading docks. "Try to shift to second!" I shout. "Just push in the clutch again, and—"

The truck stalls.

But Mateo, miraculously, is still smiling. "Cool," they say, almost to themself. And then: "Let's try again."

An hour later, we're driving smoothly around the Walmart parking lot and laughing each time Mateo successfully navigates a stop sign. And, holy crap, there are a lot of stop signs in this parking lot. Every time they successfully shift, I yell.

I've never been very into sports, but I imagine the adrenaline I feel as Mateo drives around Walmart is akin to what sports people feel during a good game. Which, like, I get it now, Sports. It's a rush. It's almost funny what a rush it is. Which is probably why Mateo and I keep laughing.

When I feel they have a good handle on things, I ask, "Do you want to drive home?"

"Nope." They slide into a parking spot and turn off the engine. "Not even a little bit."

"Fine," I say on a dramatic sigh. "Next time."

"Next time," they say as they click out of their seat belt.

As I navigate back out to Route 72, the sun's starting to bleed toward the horizon, and I feel . . . I don't know. Smug. Satisfied. Happy. Not just because I'd rate that as a pretty fine first lesson, but because I *knew* it. There's still a lot of stuff I'm confused about, but I knew Mateo and I could be friends. Middle-school dreams never die. Is that a saying? It should be.

"Do you mind if I put on some music?" Mateo asks. When I look over, they're already scrolling through playlists on their phone, purple hair cascading over their face.

"Sure." I shrug. They scroll a few seconds more before they plug into the aux cable and hit play on a song. They stare out their window as soon as the beat starts.

I have no idea what song this is. Of course I don't. I imagine I've never heard of half the bands Mateo likes. It's surprisingly quiet, though, just drums and acoustic guitar and this person's, like, really vulnerable voice. It's . . . pretty. Which shouldn't surprise me; I don't know why it does. Everything Mateo draws is pretty. Their hair is pretty. Their nails are pretty.

But as the first song blends into the next—this one equally as soft but sung in Spanish—and the early summer sky turns from powder blue to peach, I swallow. The air between us feels different now, with nothing but the pretty songs, and it feels . . . *too* intimate. More intimate than seeing Mateo's house. More intimate than working together before the sun's up. This is like seeing-Mateo's-bedroom intimate. This is like . . . romantic-date intimate.

And clearly, I am not built for dates—which is likely why I've never been on one—because by the time we approach Mateo's neighborhood, I am *sweating*. I can feel my pulse pounding in my fingertips, and my throat is dry, and I can't focus on anything, like how I feel before an anxiety attack. But I am simply driving while listening to objectively enjoyable music. Mateo isn't doing anything but sitting there. There is absolutely nothing wrong, and I absolutely want to die.

I pull into Mateo's driveway, and frankly it's a miracle that *I* don't stall out.

As soon as I park, I toss the keys in their general vicinity without looking at them.

"Ouch," I hear them mutter, and I hope, belatedly, that I

haven't hit their face. Because their face is, you know. Pretty. Objectively.

"See you at work," I say on my way out the door, and then I am marching toward Dolly.

I am still sweating once I'm blissfully inside.

But it's nothing Dolly hasn't seen before.

TEN

College Fund: $690

To regain a tiny bit of control, I send Mateo a spreadsheet on the Monday following our Walmart parking-lot excursion.

Spreadsheets I understand.

On Tuesday, I greet them with "Did you look at the list of username possibilities?"

"Um," they say around a yawn. "I thought we were strategizing after our shift?"

I swallow my disappointment. Sure, it's 5:50 a.m., and they are technically correct. We agreed to have our first Save Delicious Donuts! campaign meeting (the exclamation point helps give me confidence) after our opening shift today.

But also, it was a relatively short spreadsheet.

Candace pops her gum as we hustle to get the store ready for opening, and I mentally put the spreadsheet aside for now.

"Isn't chewing gum on the floor an OSHA violation?" My 5:50 a.m. mouth isn't as filtered as it should be.

Thankfully, Candace just grins at me before she spits it in the trash.

"You're cute," she says. And then she unlocks the door, flips on the neon Open sign. "Hey, Jay! How's the insurance biz going?"

This is Candace's thing, asking everyone how their *biz* is going. Jay with his insurance biz, Jack with his library biz, Mr. Davies with his lumber biz. She knows as many people in this town as Elen does.

"Have a delicious day!" I wave at Jay a few minutes later as he leaves, black coffee and plain glazed in hand.

"You know that's not a thing." Candace leans against the back counter. "No one else says 'Have a delicious day.'"

"Yeah, and it's weird," I respond, a bit testily. If Candace can ask everyone about their biz, I can tell people to have a delicious day. I can have a thing too. "It's a natural setup. Alliteration!"

Before she can laugh at me, the door jangles once more, and we're swept into the early-morning rush.

Even though the three of us are so different, my shifts with Candace and Mateo are my favorite ones. Whenever customers are mean, Candace always makes me laugh as soon as they're out the door. I feel less pressure to be perfect without Elen around. And it's obviously better than any shift I've worked with DJ, who's part-time and completely useless even though he's ten years older than me.

The morning rush is just starting to taper off when I look up and gasp.

"Mom!" I shout before I can contemplate how dorky it is to shout *Mom!* in the middle of my place of employment. But whatever, my mom is here! Along with the triplets. Bruno immediately smooshes his face against the glass.

"I want a donut with a billion sprinkles," he demands, looking at Mateo, who's standing at the register. And, when Mom gives Bruno a slight nudge on the shoulder: "Please."

"Uh." Mateo looks at the donut racks. "I'm not sure if we have—"

"What's your name?" Emma demands next.

"Mateo." Mateo looks a little overwhelmed at being shouted at in such quick succession. It's like they're not even used to living with three six-year-olds.

"Muh—tay—" Nikki starts to sound out the name quietly, across from me. This is a thing she does—sound out new words slowly to herself to make sure she's got them. Which doesn't have anything to do, I don't think, with her developmental issues; it's just another part of her signature Nikki cuteness. She mouths the syllables to herself a couple more times before she looks up, eyes bright, and pronounces, "Tomato."

"Are you nice to Penny?" Emma asks, chin in the air. Mateo glances over at me, mouth opening in an awkward non-answer.

"Yes," I fill in to save us both. "Everyone here is nice to me, Emma."

"Yeah, we are." Candace sidles up next to Mateo and holds out her hand. "Candace. And you are?"

"Nikki!" Nikki shouts with a shy grin that's hilarious in contrast to the enthusiasm of her voice, the sparkle in her eye. Emma introduces herself next, the only one to take Candace's hand in a serious shake.

"*Mateo-tomato! Mateo-tomato!*" Bruno shouts, jumping up and down.

"And that's Bruno," I note, glancing at Mateo to gauge their reaction to this nickname. But before I can fully ascertain it, Nikki's tiny hands are reaching toward me over the counter.

"Penny hug!" she demands. I slide past Mateo to get out from behind the counter and give Nikki her Penny hug while Mom slinks her arm around my waist for a side squeeze.

"Hope it's okay we stopped by, honey."

"Of course." Part of me suddenly feels a little self-conscious about being with my family in front of Mateo. But most of me is thrilled they're here, that they even had the idea to come see me.

"Bruno was in need of a billion donuts." Mom raises an eyebrow at Candace. "Hopefully that's doable?"

"Oh, yeah," Candace says. "Definitely."

"*Spring-kuuuuuuls.*" Bruno runs back over and yells into the glass. It fogs up, which makes him breathe on it even harder.

"Okay, bud." I pull him back by his T-shirt. "How about we leave the glass alone."

"Donut, donut, donut," he loud-whispers to himself, jumping up and down again in rhythm with his chant to see all the choices.

"Were your parents mad when you did that to your hair?" Emma asks next, still going full throttle with her Mateo interrogation.

"Um." Mateo scratches the top of their head. "The first time I dyed it, yeah. But now they're kind of used to it."

"Mom." Emma spins toward her. "Can I do that to my hair?"

"How old are you, Mateo?" Mom asks.

"Sixteen."

"When you're sixteen, dear." Mom pats Emma's head.

"Ugh." Emma stomps. "Being little is the *worst*."

"I know, love. Life is hard. You can each order *one* donut, okay?"

While the triplets crowd the counter and shout at Mateo and Candace, Mom pulls me to the side.

"How's work going, Penny Bear?"

"Good," I say. I haven't burned myself in the name of someone else's caffeine and no one has yelled at me about donuts. In my newly employed status, I'm counting any days where no one yells at me and I don't hurt myself as good ones.

"I was wondering if I could ask a favor of you," Mom says, brushing a stray hair off my forehead, and I already know what's coming next. "Mama D took an extra shift tonight. And I'm supposed to get dinner with the OTLB. I know it's selfish of me to ask, but Laura's daughter just had a baby, and Chandra's got a new—"

"Mom, it's fine," I say. Because it is fine, and it's not selfish of Mom to ask; she loves her get-togethers with the Out to Lunch Bunch. Mom deserves a night out with her friends.

And I know every time Mama D takes an extra shift at the hospital, she's helping save more people's lives. It feels selfish to get mad at that.

Even if I do miss her lately.

Watching the triplets for a few hours during the day is different from a full night with them, though. This means I'll have to get them all to bed, which is always an intense level of chaos. And there's a new National Geographic documentary I'd been planning to watch, and I need to keep up my Duolingo streak, and I just got to a really good part in my book last night—

"Thank you." Mom kisses my forehead. "You're the best."

I paste a smile on my face.

I keep it there until the triplets have gotten their donuts and Mom has paid. Until they've all made their way out the door to Mom's minivan.

And then I let it drop.

It really is fine that Mom wants to go out with her friends, that Mama D is making extra money for us that I know we need. I can watch the documentary after the triplets fall asleep. If they fall asleep.

It's just—for a second, I thought they had come by to see *me*. But really, Mom only needed to make sure I could babysit again.

"Your siblings are hella cute," Candace says. I nod and march into the back to restock our milk supply under the espresso machine. I make three trips of 2 percent before Mateo steps in front of me.

"Hey." They frown. "You okay?"

"Yeah." I inch around them on a mission for two more whole milks. "I'm fine."

Because Mateo has actual problems with their dad. They don't need to hear me complain about how I'm sad that my moms don't want to hang out with me. And don't most teens, like, actively avoid their parents? God, I'm a loser.

Mateo and Candace let me sulk for a while. It's unfortunate timing, because the shop has sunk into a late-morning dead zone. Which means more empty space for my brain to spiral out. Until—

"Oh!" I practically tap-dance as I remember. I rush to get my phone from Elen's office. "The spreadsheet!" I burst out when I return to the floor. Mateo laughs. My gut instinct is to be annoyed—they promised they were in this with me!—but, well. Part of me just likes hearing Mateo laugh.

"What's this, now?" Candace asks, and Mateo briefly fills her in while I bring up the list on my phone.

To my immense satisfaction, Candace is also appalled by the idea of selling to Northwest Donuts.

"Listen," she says. "I'm not working here anymore if Elen's not my boss."

"Exactly!" I shout. "Elen's an integral part of Main Street!"

"Damn straight she is," Candace agrees. I kind of want to kiss Candace right now.

"So I have to admit I didn't actually open the spreadsheet," Mateo says, and my smile turns into a scowl.

"Of course you didn't," I mutter, but there's barely any heat in it. I'm still too thrilled about Candace being on my side.

"Hit us with these usernames," she says.

I start from the top.

"Delicious.Verity."

"Sounds like you're a monster about to eat the town," Mateo says immediately. I scowl at them again but mark it off the list.

"Okay. DeliciousDonuts.Verity? Any and all iterations of just *delicious donuts* have already been taken, so I think *Verity* needs to be in there. But maybe it's better for SEO to put it first? Verity.DeliciousDonuts? So that way, anyone googling *Verity* might have it pop up."

"Do you actually understand how SEO works?" Mateo asks over the wall of cups at the end of the counter.

"Of course she does," Candace answers before I can respond. "Didn't you just tell me the other day that Penny's a super-genius?"

Mateo promptly disappears behind the wall of cups to mess with something on the espresso machine. My jaw unhinges.

"I'm not—" *You're good at everything.* "I don't—" I try again. Because, truly, what is happening here?

And the thing is, I don't even know if I *do* know what SEO means. My mouth often just says things that my brain realizes an hour later I should have fact-checked more.

"I'm, like, seventy-two percent sure I used it semi-correctly," I say when I finally have some semblance of control over my brain again. I stare desperately at my spreadsheet. "Do you have feelings about a dot versus an underscore?"

"Dot," Candace says. "No question."

"Agreed," Mateo throws in.

"Okay." I swallow, crossing a few more things off my list. "Candace, I'm going to make an Instagram account, but do you think you could make a TikTok? Could you cross-reference which names are already taken on there?"

"On it, boss." She grabs her own phone, and we work together to verify what would work best until the door starts to jingle again, and we slide our phones into our pockets.

The rest of our shift goes quickly, and when Elen comes in and relieves Mateo and me, we head outside to the parking lot. I lean against Dolly, dig out my phone, and click to the spreadsheet once more.

"You don't see many yellow cars these days," Mateo says as they give a light, affectionate kick to Dolly's front tire. I stare at the screen in my hand, pretending Mateo's approval of my car means nothing to me.

Because maybe I'm reading it all wrong again. Maybe that curve of their mouth isn't affectionate at all. Maybe they're laughing at me and my old, weird car.

"Yeah, well," I say, bringing up the doc I linked to in the second tab of the spreadsheet. "People are boring. Did you get this?"

I point my screen their way. They glance at it and join me against Dolly's side.

"Yeah. Opened it on my break. The designs are cute."

"If you're able to work on something like these, I really think we should order stickers ASAP. Printing and shipping can take a while, and we're already past the best part of summer, so if we're going to convince Elen to save Delicious Donuts"—I picture the exclamation mark in my head—"by September, then we have to move fast."

"Two questions. No, actually, three. One: I thought Elen said no merch?"

"Stickers hardly count. They're just a simple thing we can put by the register, an easy upsell, and then it's free advertising when people put them on their water bottles or anywhere, really. I'm going to talk to her about it this week."

"Okay. Two: What do you mean the best part of summer is over? It's barely July."

"Yeah," I say. "And July is pretty much just a countdown to August, and once you hit August, it's all over. The last two weeks of June are the best part of summer. Everything still feels wide open and exciting."

Even for me, summers don't hit their peak of Penny depression until July. I've been so busy these past couple of school years that I enjoy the chance to breathe at the end of June, to imagine the freedom of a few months of sunshine and laziness, the dream of summer that everyone else seems to hold in their hands so easily.

Until June ends, and I remember that being lazy actually makes me feel really sad, and endless West Coast sunshine results in drought and wildfires.

Mateo huffs out an amused breath.

"I agree about August," they say. "But I couldn't disagree more about July. July *is* summer."

They're not exactly *close* to me—I'm right by my side mirror, and Mateo's down by Dolly's gas tank—but they're still close enough that a whoosh of the breeze sends their scent my way. It's something floral, like roses. I've been able to catch it in the past when our seats were right next to each other in class. Inside the shop this summer, though, the smell of donuts and coffee is so strong that it's been mostly hidden.

But here, outside, combined with the fresh air, it smells just right. Like the color of their hair. Like an Oregon garden. Like July.

I blink back down at my phone. "What was the third question?"

Mateo sighs, runs a hand through their hair. Even if I couldn't see them out of the corner of my eye, I could *feel* their mood plummet.

"These already look good on their own. Why don't you just make the stickers from these?"

I turn to look at them head-on and shove my phone toward their face.

"These are just graphics from Canva that I made in ten minutes! Delicious Donuts deserves better than ten-minute Canva. Seriously."

Mateo shrugs. "Most people won't have any idea. They'll just be like, 'Hey, cute donut,' and pick it up."

"But yours will be *better*. They'll be original. Unique."

Mateo kicks at the asphalt with their shoe.

"But what if they're not? I told you, I'm not good with digital design. I barely know how to use any of the programs."

I shrug back at them.

"Well, maybe this is your chance to try some of them out."

"The good ones are expensive."

"Mateo." I gust out a frustrated breath; a few loose hairs blow away from my cheeks. "I know there are some free programs out there. Come on. Just try it."

They kick at the pebbles of the parking lot for another sullen moment before the corner of their mouth quirks back up.

"And when is this homework due, Professor?"

"Well." I fold my arms across my chest, squinting. I'm blushing, even though I don't fully understand why. "I was hoping you could show me some ideas tomorrow."

"Right." Their lips curve up farther. "Of course. In that case"—they shove off from Dolly's side—"I ought to get moving."

"Mateo?"

They pause in front of me. I bite my lip. I should probably just let them go. But I haven't been able to get that moment with Emma from earlier out of my head. The question bubbles out of me:

"Why *are* you being nice to me this summer?"

I can tell from the way Mateo sticks their hands in their pockets and looks down and then away, the discomfiture that once again takes over their shoulders, that they know exactly what I'm talking about. That they remember Emma's question too.

"Like you said," they finally say after a beat that veered just a few seconds too long into awkward territory. "We're working together now, so."

I guess this makes sense.

But . . . it still doesn't make *enough* sense. Not really. Not to me.

It feels like a half answer. Like there's more lurking in their brain that they're holding back from saying.

Still, I know I can't force more out of them. I don't know what it is I'm even hoping to hear. I'm just opening my mouth to tell them to have a good bike ride home when—

"Why are *you* being nice to *me*?"

I frown. I'm *nice*. Ask Bao or Jack or any of the regulars! Ask Swapna or Julian or anyone on the Knowledge Bowl team or any of the teachers at Verity High. I'm a nice person!

Except.

I shuffle my feet, staring at my shoes.

"Because I'm tired of not being nice to you," I eventually say.

Because this last school year wasn't *fine*.

It sucked.

It sucked a lot.

When I gather enough courage to look at Mateo, their mouth is curved again. It's a barely there smile, but their eyes are gentle.

"Okay," they say. When they move toward their bike, one last question jumps out of me:

"What kind of car would you want if you could get something other than the truck?"

Mateo doesn't hesitate, turning to answer.

"A dusty-pink Bug."

Despite all the uncertain feelings swirling around my gut, I can't help my grin.

"That would suit you."

"Yeah." Their answering smile is bigger this time, easy. "I don't even know if dusty-pink Bugs actually exist, but it's what I've always pictured."

"We'll find you one," I say. "By the end of the summer."

"Sure, Penny." They laugh a little, a bob of their throat I see more than hear, and throw their bike lock into their bag. "We can try."

ELEVEN

College Fund: $854

Two days later, on the Fourth of July, Instagram account @verity.deliciousdonuts has its first official post.

Mateo and Candace stand behind the counter in the photo. Mateo's shoving a chocolate donut with rainbow sprinkles into their mouth; Candace has one arm wrapped around Mateo's neck, her other hand giving a peace sign. They both have goofy looks on their faces. The caption gives our summer hours and an all-caps COME SEE US!! I've read conflicting things about whether hashtags actually affect the algorithm, but I add them anyway: #donuts #donutshops #verityoregon #oregonsmallbusiness #smallbusinesses #downtownverity #gonutsfordonuts #haveadeliciousday.

We get thirty likes. Most of which are from the friends and families of me, Mateo, and Candace, whom we made follow us. But I feel positive we can increase our interactions with each post.

Every time I look at the photo, I remember the way Mateo

dropped my arm that day we had our first driving lesson, like it had burned them.

It hurts my feelings only a little that they don't have a problem with being so casually close to Candace.

The A-frame chalkboard sign shows up on Saturday.

Mateo agrees to stay after their shift to work on it. I run to get a pack of chalk from Bao's pharmacy on my ten.

We had our second driving lesson yesterday, and Mateo grew confident enough to venture out of the Walmart parking lot onto Route 72.

Until they stalled at their first stoplight and, following some honking, pulled into the Burgerville parking lot posthaste and demanded I take over. But still.

Candace's first Delicious Donuts TikTok got a bunch of views.

I am so excited I can barely stand it.

"Stop hovering." Mateo frowns at me. "You're messing with my process."

"You haven't even started yet," I point out.

"Yeah, because you keep *hovering*." They glare and walk the sign and their chalk to the very last booth on the far side of the shop.

Fine. They're right. But now that Mateo's off the floor, I'm alone with DJ, and he smells particularly strongly of weed today.

I force myself to stay behind the counter anyway. An afternoon rush starts, and DJ is, again, useless, so I have to work double-time, which at least helps the minutes go by. Two full hours pass before I'm able to approach the booth where Mateo is still sitting, hands scrunched in their hair.

"How's it going?"

To my delight, they don't tell me to go away. At least, like, not immediately.

And even though their elbows are covering up part of it, I can see their progress on the sign. *Welcome to Delicious Donuts*, it says in bubble letters at the top, above a dancing pink donut. There's something else written in fancy cursive at the bottom, but Mateo's hunched-over torso is covering it.

Ripped-out pieces of their sketchbook sit on the table next to the sign, countless drafts of donuts and letters drawn in pencil. I bite my lip to hide my smile.

"Hey." I dare to reach over and shove their shoulder. "Let me see."

Mateo's wrists are covering their eyes. "This is the most embarrassing thing I've ever done."

"Oh my God, it is not." I roll my eyes and give them another shove. This conversation is starting almost the exact same way as the one about their sticker designs did three days ago.

Which weren't embarrassing at all, by the way. I had only the smallest bit of feedback.

"I can already tell it's perfect. Come on, let me see the whole thing."

With a sigh, Mateo drops their arms and leans back in the booth.

Their face is covered in dusty patches of chalk. A swath

of pink sits above their right eyebrow. A bit of white is splashed in the purple side of their hair. It is . . . really, really adorable.

I force my eyes away from their face and toward the board. *Come on in!* the cursive says.

"There's no good place to put a mouth on a donut, you know that?" Mateo grouses. "Or a nose."

"The mouth is perfect." Mateo's situated it off to the side, near the bottom of the donut, by its in-mid-step stick legs. "And I don't think donuts need noses, personally."

"But then they can't smell themselves," they say. "Which would be sad." They cover their face with their hands again. "I think I'm losing my mind."

"Is there something on the other side?" Carefully, so as to not whack Mateo in the face with it, I flip the sign over. *Not Just Donuts!* the bubble letters proclaim on this side. A list of our espresso drinks and a drawing of an iced coffee follows. I have absolutely zero feedback this time. "Mateo, this is amazing!"

"You know what they always say," Mateo mutters, kicking the underside of my bench with the toe of their shoe. "The best way to get into art school is through drawings of dancing donuts and coffee."

I look away from the sign and back to their chalk-dusted face.

"You want to go to art school?"

Mateo glances at me before quickly averting their eyes, fiddling with a piece of chalk.

"Um. Yeah. It probably won't happen, though. Forget I said that."

"No, that makes total sense! Clearly, you should go to art school. Is there a specific one you have in mind?"

"Penny." They sound irritated now. "I'm not going to art school. Real men drive trucks and they don't go to art school, okay?"

I flinch.

It feels just as awful and *wrong* to hear them say it as it did the first time, back in the Walmart parking lot. Like I've swallowed something rotten.

"Mateo," I can't keep myself from saying. "Stop. Don't say that."

They only stare at me, eyes hard.

My anxiety flares. It's been a few days since they've looked at me that way. But it makes sense that they're frustrated with me; I'm forcing them into doing all this extra work, work they obviously don't want to be doing when they could be hanging out with Talanoa or Roman or doing whatever they normally do during their summers, and I keep saying the wrong things to them about . . . everything.

My excitement about Save Delicious Donuts! whispers out in a blink. All I want to do is finish this shift with DJ and get back home, where I will complete approximately fifty lessons of Duolingo.

"Thank you for doing the sign," I say quietly to the drawn cup of iced coffee. I start to slip out of the booth. "It really does look great."

Mateo kicks out a leg to block my progress, their shin making a cross against mine. The contact makes me freeze.

"Penny." Mateo sighs. They gather up their messy stack of papers, the scattered pieces of chalk. "I'm sorry." Their leg is still pressed against mine; the texture of their black jeans is rough against my bare skin. I feel weirdly cocooned by it, boxed in but safe. The edges of my brain buzz, a sensation I've never quite experienced before.

They move away only when they stand. I miss that leg next to mine immediately. And wonder if maybe *I'm* losing my mind.

"I should get going," they say, sticking the pack of chalk and their bunched-up papers into their messenger bag.

I swallow, staring down at the sign. "You're okay if I put this out?"

"Sure."

"If you can send me those tweaked designs, I can order those stickers tonight too. Elen gave me a purchase order for it."

Mateo sighs again, forcing a smile before they leave. I hate myself a little.

But I really should order the stickers soon.

My break's probably over by now, and lord knows DJ can't be trusted to run the place by himself, but I sit at the booth for a moment more. I run my finger along the wooden edge of the sign. Stare at the lines and shapes Mateo's created.

Wonder which art school they'll end up at.

My phone beeps from the pocket of my apron. I dig it out,

welcoming the distraction. I'm surprised to see the text is from Elen.

> **Elen:** Can you post this on the Instagram? Maybe with a message about how hard he works? Thank you 🖤

Attached is a photo of Alex in the kitchen. His face is down; he's focused on the trays of donuts that surround him, everything neatly spaced and impeccable. I smile, post it immediately, and add a #donutstopbelieving hashtag.

I take another minute to reread the comments on the first post.

> omg i remember this place, i used to go all the time as a kid!!
> CUUUUUUUTE
> 🍩🍩🍩🍩
> yes.
> Delicious Donuts is the best! We love Elen!
> candaaaaace
> 😍😍😍

I wonder, briefly, what the Instagram account for Rosemary & Time would have looked like. Mom never had one, but looking back, I think the store was made for a cozy filter. I could have helped her with it. The entire grid would've felt like golden fall leaves drifting in the sun.

I pick up Mateo's sign and put it outside. We're open for

only two more hours, but it pops on the sidewalk, all of Main Street stretching out behind it. I bite my lip and snap a photo.

I'll post this one tomorrow.

"Penny Bear," Mom says to me on Monday morning, flying around the kitchen. "Now, where did I put that piece of paper?" she mumbles, picking up a pile of mail by the phone. I know she'll get back to what she wanted to tell me eventually. Mom is kind of a whirling dervish of a person, always on the move. I think it's entirely possible she has undiagnosed ADHD. She and Bruno together are an absolute disaster, which I say with the highest level of affection. The only person who has ever been able to slow her down is Mama D.

When I look back, I think I knew I loved Mama D when I first saw her do that. Mom had been bustling around the house, looking for something she desperately needed and could just as desperately not find, when Mama D laid a hand on her forearm and said, "Sadie. Take a breath."

And Mom . . . did.

When she told me a few months later that they were getting married, my first thought had been *Thank God*.

"Oh, darn it to heck," Mom says now. "Oh, well." She swipes her keys from the hook and turns to me, hands on her hips. "Penny Bear, you remember you'll be picking up Bruno and Emma from Chandra's today after your shift?"

I swallow my bite of cereal.

"I am?" I'm working a short midday shift today, covering

the transition between opening and closing crews. I have no memory of having any extra duties after that, which probably means Mom just never told me, but it's fine. It's not like I have any pressing social plans.

"Nikki has an appointment in Portland." Mom checks her watch. "Mama D should be home any minute to head up with us, and we're dropping Emma and Bruno off at Chandra's on the way."

"An appointment with Dr. Tran?" My spoon drops into the dregs of my milk, my brain temporarily wiped clean of thought.

"Yeah, just a check-in and an ultrasound." Mom frowns at the look on my face. "I swear I told you, honey."

"Yeah, no." I force myself to speak, to make a casual expression appear on my face, even though I know I'm failing. "Of course. I can do that."

She walks over to squeeze my wrist as I hear Mama D's Subaru crunch into the drive.

"Everything will be fine, Penny."

I nod, even though I actually *hate* these kinds of platitudes Mom always says. Because there's no possible way she can know everything will be fine. No way she can know what will show up on Nikki's scan this time, what Dr. Tran will have to say.

She releases my wrist as Mama D walks into the kitchen.

"Hey." Mama D kisses Mom's cheek and drops her own keys on the hook. "Just gonna change out of my scrubs. Hey, Penny." She walks over to give a quick ruffle of my hair. "Good to see you."

I bite back the observation that *Good to see you* feels like the kind of remark a teacher makes in September after not seeing you for a few months, not something a mom says to her kid.

But also—the truth is, it *is* good to see her. Her hand helps center me, just a little bit, just like it does Mom. Even if it's only for a second.

Even if she and everyone else in the house are gone five minutes later, and I'm still here, at the kitchen table in my pajamas, watching Mama D back out of the drive, my chest tight against my will, throat threatening to close.

I close my eyes and grip the table. Feel the light scratches in the wood along my fingertips, listen to the quiet tick of the clock above the sink. Something I can feel, something I can hear. Something I can smell—the citrus candle Mom always keeps on the kitchen counter, the same kind she used to sell in the shop, that her old friend Nancy Jo handmakes in Eugene. Something I can taste: my last bite of Honey Nut Cheerios.

I don't know what will happen today in Portland. But I can still get through this day. I can focus on the moment. I can fight for a deep breath.

And I do. I put my bowl in the dishwasher and listen to a podcast about an endangered species of burrowing owls finding refuge in a decommissioned military base. I show up to Delicious Donuts on time and relieve Elen, who steps off the floor to do some paperwork for a few hours, and I serve people donuts alongside Candace and then DJ. I focus on my breathing. Candace asks if I'm okay before she gets off shift, noting that I'm quieter than usual, and I feel so touched I almost cry, which I know is weird. But I also need to pick up Emma and Bruno and act normal, so I make myself smile and breathe and breathe and breathe.

When I park outside Chandra's house, my phone pings with texts from Mom.

> Mom: All good here. About to get a late lunch and head back home
> Mom: Let us know when you've got Emma and Bruno
> Mom: We love you very much

I know the last text is an apology for making me pick up Emma and Bruno, for not telling me earlier about the appointment. I know they do love me.

But *All good here* tells me just as much concrete information as *Everything will be fine*. I want details. Mom should know by now that I need details.

I try for another deep breath before I go inside to gather my brother and sister.

Mom and Mama D walk into the house three hours later with Nikki in tow, who looks half awake. She always falls asleep during car rides longer than fifteen minutes. I want to feel better at the sight of her wispy blond hair; I want to feel better having the whole family home at the same time for once. I *should* feel better.

But I just . . . can't. I can't get this excess energy that's been in my system all day to bleed out.

"I think I'm going to stop by Treehuggers," I say.

Mom looks up from where she's kicking off her shoes by the front door. "Right now?"

"Yeah, I should get there before they close, while there's still sunlight."

Even though it's July in Oregon, which means there will be daylight until nine.

"Can you go another day? We were thinking of ordering pizza for—"

"Go ahead, Penny." Mama D appears from the hallway and lays a hand on Mom's forearm. "You haven't been there in a while, have you?"

"I haven't. Thanks." I slip on my own shoes, grab my bag. "You don't have to wait for me for dinner. I won't be back late, though."

Mom looks like she wants to say something else, but Mama D's still holding her arm. She looks up at Mama D. Mom's a big woman, but short; she has big arms, big hips, short legs. Mama D, in contrast, is tall and lean, solid in all the places Mom's soft. They exchange a look while I hover by the door. Finally, Mom looks at me and says, "Be safe, okay?"

And I'm gone.

It's true I haven't been to Treehuggers in a while, and it would be a good place for me to go right now. I know James would prefer at least a *little* notice about when I'm going to volunteer. But he also knows planting saplings for them helps calm my anxiety. I think he knows because my moms expressly told him it does, which is kind of embarrassing, but whatever. Dirt is super-therapeutic.

But once I reach Route 72, I turn in a different direction.

I try to focus on the feeling of being in Dolly—in control, competent—instead of the fact that I have left the house on my own without a single plan, something I'm not sure I've ever done before. *A different kind of Penny summer!* I think; I sound high-pitched and frantic even in my head. I'm branching out and being brave! Not acting totally unhinged.

I drive past Walmart.

And then I drive a little more. I take a left, and another.

A few minutes later, I'm parked along the curb in front of a dark green house with a white door, roses in bloom out front. I know I'm here only because I'm not thinking very clearly. I get out of the car before my brain can catch up. My heart beats fast after I hit the doorbell.

It occurs to me, in the few long seconds before the door swings open, that I could have driven to Swapna's instead. Or even Julian's, or Lani's, or the home of anyone else from Knowledge Bowl. Or some of my friends from band, if I knew where any of them lived. It would be weird, showing up unexpectedly at any of their doors, but I know Knowledge Bowl still needs me on the team. I have a good chance of making first-chair flute next year. They probably wouldn't hold it against me.

"Penny?" Lía raises her eyebrows.

"Hi." I clear my throat. "Is Mateo home?"

"Yeah." She tilts her head. She looks beautiful, wearing a cool floral blazer over a crop top and jean shorts. Flawless makeup, dark hair up in a sleek, high bun. Like she's about to go out. Belatedly, I realize it's Friday night. "Do you have another driving lesson tonight?" she asks.

My brain stutters over what to say. "Maybe."

She smiles. "I'll go get them."

I contemplate running away once she disappears into the house. Instead, I turn away and press my thumb into the inside of my wrist until I can feel my pulse. I count the heartbeats and try to think about nothing at all.

"Penny?" I turn to see Mateo step out onto the porch, closing the door behind them. They tilt their head at me exactly like Lía just did. It makes me want to give both of them a hug. If I were close enough to either of them to do such a thing.

"Hi," I blurt out. Mateo's wearing a sweatshirt and athletic shorts, a pair of slides. "Do you want to go for a drive?"

TWELVE

College Fund: $1,126

Mateo turns on the engine of the navy truck as I'm clicking in my seat belt, and I'm thrown back against the seat by the volume of the stereo.

Which is blasting "We Don't Talk About Bruno."

Mateo rushes to turn it down. "Sorry!" They hesitate before clicking it all the way off. "Um." They run a hand through their hair, exposing the tips of their ears, which have turned a dark pink. "I was listening to my theater-nerd playlist earlier."

"Earlier? You were driving the truck earlier?"

"Yeah." They swallow before continuing. "My dad wanted to see how I'm doing."

"Yeah?" I turn my head toward them, any bizarre jealous feelings that may or may not have arisen about someone else driving with Mateo fizzling away. "What did he say?"

The tiniest of smiles as Mateo adjusts the rearview mirror, but it doesn't reach their eyes.

"He, uh, was really pleased."

"Mateo! That's great!"

They shrug. "Yeah. I guess. Thanks for that. Anyway, I'd actually been wondering where I left my phone." They pick it up from the center console. "I can change—"

"No!" I reach over to turn the volume back up and motion for them to press play. "I like it."

Truthfully, I probably won't know most of the songs that are on a theater-nerd playlist, but at least they won't make me feel the way the pretty music Mateo played after our first driving lesson made me feel. Probably.

Mateo gives me an uncertain look but presses play and drops the phone back into the console.

"Wait." They pause as their hand grips the gear level, and I practically see the light bulb switch on in their eyes. "Your brother—"

"Is named Bruno. And he has listened to this song every day since he was three, yes. Actually, maybe we skip the rest of this one, if that's okay."

Mateo laughs and hits next on their phone; the bold opening beats of "Alexander Hamilton" blast through the truck.

"Ooh!" I practically shout. "Don't skip this one. I know this one."

Mateo smirks, but they leave the phone alone and shift into reverse. "I think everyone knows this one, Penny."

"I know."

The truck barely stutters as they slowly glide down the drive. I bite my lip to keep from cheering for them. And because I'm feeling lighter than I have all day, I decide to keep talking.

"My mom and I used to listen to this soundtrack *all* the time when I was in fourth grade." A pang of nostalgia hits me for that summer when it was just me and Mom and Alexander Hamilton. She'd already started dating Mama D then, but it was the last summer before the triplets came.

"I still like it," I add. Because when the ensemble starts purring together about how you can be a new man in New York, I have to ball my fists to keep from dancing in my seat.

"Yeah," Mateo says as they slow for a stop sign at the end of their street. "Me too. Obviously."

They roll through the intersection right as the chorus of the song crescendos, and I can't help it. I yell:

"Mateo! Oh my God, you're doing so good!"

They laugh.

"I have conquered second gear on an empty street. You're right. I deserve a medal."

"Maybe you do."

They shift into third, still smiling. "I bet you know all the words to 'Satisfied.'"

I puff up my chest. "I do my best."

They nod toward their phone. "Find it. Do it."

I hesitate. My heart thuds in my ears again.

"I want to hear it," they push.

"Will you rap it with me?" I ask, picking up their phone like it might be radioactive.

"Oh, hell no."

"Mateo! You're the one who's actually in theater!"

They laugh again. "I am on *crew*. Big difference."

I bite my lip and put the phone back. "Maybe later."

Mateo frowns, disappointed, but they let it go.

And then we reach Route 72.

"Uh," they say, stopping at the red light. "Where are we going?"

Oh. Right.

I remember, suddenly, that this was not planned. Maybe it was easy to forget because Mateo went along with it so easily. They haven't even asked what's going on with me, like this is normal.

"Uh," I say back, staring at the red light.

Where *do* I want to go?

The light turns green.

"Go right," I say, fast and impulsive. Mateo turns right. The truck stutters for a second but then continues easily through the turn. They release a small sigh of relief.

"Okay," they say a beat later. "Where are we going *next*?"

I bite my lip again. "Would you . . . want to go to Silver Falls?"

Mateo is quiet for a moment, eyes focused on the road. "Like the state park?"

"Yeah."

"That's all the way on the other side of I-5."

I take a deep breath. For the first time all day, I feel it from deep in my lungs. My pulse is thrumming again; I am making *bad decisions*. I have possibly lied to my parents. My stomach is full of nerves.

But I don't feel anxious anymore.

"I know." I tilt my head toward the window, looking up at the sky. "Do you think we could make it there and back before it gets dark?"

"We could make it there, for sure. *Back* before it gets dark, I don't know."

I'm still looking out the window, staring at the clouds. Thinking.

"We can just stop at North Falls," I reason to Mateo, to myself. "We don't have to drive all the way through the park. North Falls is my favorite one anyway. I just want to be around some trees for a while." I straighten and look at Mateo's profile. "If that's okay with you."

"Sure. Except—" My stomach sinks. "The roads are kind of intense there. You're definitely taking over at some point."

I grin. "I don't know. I think you could do it."

"Nope." They shake their head. "I'm not stalling out on those curvy little death traps. You're taking over for sure once we pass the highway."

"Okay," I acquiesce. The word travels through me, tingling in my fingertips.

Okay.

A new song starts. Mateo turns it up.

"Do you know *Heathers*?"

I shake my head. It's a loud song, the beats hard and fast.

"It's my favorite," Mateo says. They pound their palm against the steering wheel in rhythm with the beat. We're cruising farther away from Verity, past the stop-and-go lights of Route 72, toward the farms and the forests. It makes me happy, seeing Mateo so at ease behind the wheel that they can unclench their fists for long enough to drum along to a favorite song. This is what driving should feel like.

It makes me happy, being in Mateo's truck on the way to a place I love.

Being *out*. Not at home, not at school, not at Delicious Donuts. Just . . . out.

Outside of my own head for the first time all day.

How often do I let myself be just out?

The chorus of the song slows, gets quiet and vulnerable after the aggressive verses. It takes me a few seconds to realize Mateo is mouthing the words. Their lips are barely moving, but they are totally singing along, even if it's silent. It is kind of dorky.

If I weren't here with them, I bet they'd be singing out loud.

I knew Mateo was a theater kid, but seeing this version of them feels so . . . different. From how I had gotten used to seeing them. Frowning at me in class, avoiding my eyes in the halls, scowling at me over their sketchbook. Things had been better this summer, yes, as we had awkwardly and vaguely maybe established. But kind-of sort-of friends or not, they were still on a different level than me.

Until, possibly, right now.

A feeling that is only accentuated by the next song that shuffles onto the stereo.

"Oh," Mateo says, reaching for the phone, but I'm faster.

"Eyes on the road!" I shout as I snatch the phone from the console, my fingers brushing against theirs. The grin explodes onto my face as the screen confirms it. "You have the *Tarzan* soundtrack on this playlist?"

Because *Heathers* sounded cool, even if Mateo lip-synching to it felt surprisingly soft. But even I know Phil Collins isn't cool.

Mateo blows out a breath, making the hair around their face flutter. The color is starting to grow out a bit; their dark roots peek out at the scalp.

"Listen, I watched this movie all the time when I was a kid. And it's a really fucking good soundtrack. Totally underrated in the Disney discography."

I laugh. "Okay."

"What's *your* favorite Disney soundtrack?"

"Um." I rack my brain. "I don't think I have one?"

Mateo gasps, a hilariously dramatic sound. "I don't believe you."

"I'll think on it," I offer.

Mateo just shakes their head. And then they appear to make a decision.

"You know what? Whatever. This song kicks ass." They turn the volume up even higher and glance toward me, a look on their face I once again can't decipher.

And then they roll down their window and belt out the chorus.

My mouth hangs open in shock. I'm sure they rolled down the window in an attempt to mask their singing, but even over the wind—we are cruising pretty fast now; my hair flies around my face—I can make it out. Mateo shouts about wanting to know about strangers like them—*Can you show me?*—and their voice is . . . atrocious. I start laughing so hard I can hardly breathe.

"Oh my God." I gasp when the chorus ends and Mateo's mouth snaps shut. Their ears are pink again—I can see them because the wind is also making their hair go everywhere—but they're laughing too.

They roll the window back up.

"There," they say. "Now you have to do 'Satisfied.'"

A thought occurs to me. Is Mateo trying to cheer me up?

It sinks in again, the reality of what's actually happening. I randomly showed up at Mateo's doorstep, probably looking a mess, and they just went with it. They said *Sure*.

My laughter fades in my throat; it curls into a little ball and gets stuck there, right above my chest.

"I'm going to need some time to recover first," I force out, voice reedy.

"Fair." They're smirking, but I think for once they're smirking at themself, not me. "See? Told you I'm just crew."

"That was amazing," I loud-whisper. "It *is* a good song, though."

"Right?" I can't remember if I've ever heard Mateo sound so excited to agree with me. Although I guess I agreed with them first. Still, it makes me feel like—like at least for now, maybe I don't need the other halves of the answers Mateo hasn't given me. Maybe I don't need to understand everything about our past. Because right here, the landscape blurring by, the sun traveling lower in the sky—this feels like friendship.

Real friendship. The kind I haven't been able to grasp in so long. It feels essential, something knowing in my bones, that I hold on to it while I can.

Maybe I don't overthink something for once.

The playlist jumps to another song I don't know. A glance at Mateo's phone screen tells me it's from something called *Tick, Tick . . . Boom!* There's a lot of fast piano and drums happening, and it makes me want to jump across rooftops or dance through busy city intersections or whatever people in musicals do.

Mateo clicks on their blinker, pulls into a huge truck stop just off I-5.

For a half a second, I think Mateo's on the same page as me, and we're about to jump into a musical. At least, the Verity, Oregon, version of one. We'll leap out of the truck and run through the grass seed fields. Climb to the top of the towering oak in the distance. Do a dance number in the middle of the Flying J.

But Mateo only tosses me the keys. "Your turn," they say, and I remember. "I'm gonna go grab some snacks."

They return a few minutes later with sour gummy worms and Doritos, strawberry milk, a pink concha wrapped in plastic.

"Strawberry milk?" I raise an amused eyebrow as I navigate us back onto the road.

"Listen," Mateo says as they crack it open, "it's freaking delicious."

"I am learning so much about you on this drive."

Mateo doesn't respond. The landscape gets quieter, the road narrowing as I navigate us toward Silver Falls. They haven't turned their playlist back on, and the silence stretches until my stomach starts to grow uneasy.

"Penny." Mateo clears their throat. "Why did you show up at my house tonight? I mean," they add quickly, "you don't have to tell me anything if you don't want to."

I breathe in through my nose. Exhale slowly, count the beats. Wish for a fast song from a musical again.

It's not that I don't want to talk to Mateo. It's that I don't really know the answer to their question.

But I know they deserve something.

"I get overwhelmed sometimes," I eventually start. "About a lot of things. Mostly when I think too much about climate change. Nowhere is safe from it, you know? Even if every country in the world cut their greenhouse-gas emissions right now—" We're approaching a sharp curve on a steep hillside; the engine whines as I decrease speed. I shift downward, feeling Mateo's gaze on the side of my face. I swallow, mind buzzing too loudly from the force of it, the sudden swelling of all the things I get overwhelmed by inside my head: genocide, overfishing, guns, the impending Cascadia earthquake, voting rights, factory farms, biodiversity loss.

"You know my siblings you met the other day?" I say after a long, long beat. I sense Mateo's nod in my peripheral vision. "The tiny one with the blond hair, Nikki?"

"Yeah," they say out loud, and somehow the steadiness of their voice helps me keep going.

"When they were all born, Bruno and Emma were okay, but Nikki's heart wasn't fully formed. She was in the NICU for sixty-four days." I swallow again. "It's called hypoplastic left heart syndrome."

"Okay," Mateo says, just as steady.

"She's had a bunch of surgeries, and she's okay, but . . . it's possible she might not be okay one day. She might have further complications as she grows, or she might need a heart transplant."

"That's . . . stressful."

"Yeah. She probably won't . . ." The truck whines around another curve. It's hard for me to say this part. To even think this part. "Won't live as long as other people. Anyway, she has a heart specialist in Portland she goes to see, and she's been doing well, all things considered, but she had an appointment up there today and my moms didn't tell me about it. I just like to know when things are happening, you know? So I can be ready." I grip the wheel, my heart starting to beat faster again, my throat getting tight. Does this sound dumb to Mateo? I don't know. I don't know if any of this makes sense. "I like to *know* things. And I just . . ."

"Penny?"

"Sorry." I blink, focusing on the road, knowing I trailed off for too long. "I just hate not knowing what's going to happen to Nikki."

"Yeah. Hey, do you want to pull over somewhere? I can take it from here if you want."

"No, no, it's okay. I'm sorry. We're almost there."

And we are. Five excruciatingly quiet minutes later, I navigate into a spot at the trailhead.

"Was everything okay today?" Mateo asks once I turn off the engine. "At the appointment?"

"Yeah. Yeah, it was, or at least my moms said it was." I turn away, staring out the driver-side window, swiping away some tears that have infuriatingly broken free. "Which is why it's dumb that I'm spiraling out so much."

I don't talk about Nikki a lot—or at least, not about Nikki's heart—to anyone other than Hannah. Maybe because *this* is what happens when I do, and it's so selfish, because I'm not the one with the heart defect. I'm not my moms, going bankrupt over medical bills. I'm just the older sister with an annoying brain.

"It's okay, Penny. I'm sorry your moms didn't give you more warning about the appointment. It sounds like they should know, right? That you like having more warning."

"Yeah. They've been stressed lately. I know it just slipped their minds. It's okay."

"You can still be mad about it, though," Mateo says quietly.

"I don't like being mad," I admit just as quietly. "Let's go look at some trees."

"Sure," Mateo says, voice easy again, like I'm not crying in their dad's truck. "One sec."

Suddenly, Mateo's shoulder is in my face. The fabric of their T-shirt brushes against my cheek and I lean away, sucking in every available molecule of air in an embarrassing hiss.

Mateo lands back in their seat, a flashlight in hand, procured from the back. Waving it with a grin, they say, "Safety first. Just in case." And then they jump out of the truck.

I close my eyes, breathe out. Unclick my seat belt. Our slammed doors echo in the quiet lot.

They're right about the flashlight, of course. The sun is lower in the sky now, the horizon going orange at the edges, and it's always darker in the forest.

I check my phone before sticking it in my back pocket, making sure we have service out here in case anything goes wrong. A couple of missed texts from Swapna light up my screen.

Swapna: TOMORROW!!!
Swapna: thank the gods, why is summer so boring 😩

I had almost forgotten. Knowledge Bowl Goes Bowling is tomorrow night.

And this is why Swapna gets me. I bet she hates July too.

"Penny? Everything okay?"

I text Swapna back a quick YES and i knowwwww and hustle after Mateo.

"Yeah," I say, trying to remind myself again. "Everything's okay."

We start down the trail, and I feel it within the very first steps: a certainty, a clicking into place when something you want somehow actually *happens*. The knowledge that my agreement with Swapna a second ago wasn't completely true.

Because this July doesn't feel very boring at all.

It hasn't rained in a while, so the track down to the falls is relatively dry. Silver Falls is the largest state park in Oregon and often crowded, especially in summer; it's known for its trail through a system of ten waterfalls. But when we approach North Falls, we're the only two hikers on the path, our surroundings quiet. Ferns brush our ankles; patches of prickly salal tickle our sides; hemlocks and maples surround us—the rustling, darkening cocoon of a Northwest forest.

It is an abrupt change of atmosphere from Mateo screaming lyrics inside a moving truck, from the wind tousling my hair, from the tension and tears of the past ten minutes. But my body immediately accepts the switch, sighing happily into the quiet of the trees. Like a dog welcoming its owner home after a long day of work. Like the way Nikki always hugs my leg and the way Emma's brain focuses on a new Lego set. Something that will always be true.

"Hey," I call to Mateo, who's walking in front of me. They turn as I snatch a few golden berries from the bush next to me. "Salmonberry?"

"Sure." My fingers brush their palm as I pass off the berries; a shiver creeps along my skin. Their fingertips, the side of their pointer finger, are gray with smudged graphite. I wonder what they were drawing before I interrupted their night.

Their hair bounces along their shoulders as they resume their steps, the thunder of the falls increasing in volume as I follow. It's not truly dark enough yet to need the flashlight, but even if it were, I wonder if maybe their hair would be enough. Even in the fading light, it shines.

It takes about fifteen minutes to reach it: a powerful column of white water pouring over a basalt cliff into a small pool below. North Falls. We inch along the trail that hugs the cliff until we're underneath it—both the rushing water and the rock, which stretches behind us into a deep, dark cave.

It's a little creepy, if I'm being honest. And also really freaking awesome.

I've been here lots of times over the years with my moms, though we normally start at the more popular South Falls. But there's something reverent feeling about being here by ourselves, just me and Mateo, the rumble of the falls and the coolness of the stone. It's dark in the cave, the ground wet from the splashing of the water, a mist that clings to our skin. We creep along until we silently, mutually agree that we are perfectly behind the falls, and we stop.

The sound and the feel of it pounds in my chest, the inside of my skull. It steals my breath, drums in my fingertips. It's overwhelming in a different way than the thoughts that often invade my head; it cleanses, pushes anxiety and stress out, leaving only the water and its echoes through the deep green.

After several minutes of letting it fill me up, I look over at Mateo. They're staring toward the top of the waterfall where it begins its cascade, far above our heads. It's hard to see, but the thundering water catches the light, amplifies it in front of us. They turn to meet my gaze. Lean down to shout into my ear.

"You really love this, huh? Being in the woods."

"Mateo," I shout back. "I love it *so much*." And when they

only grin at me, I say: "Don't you?"

They shrug, their smile deepening. "It's okay," they say, and I want to explode.

"Mateo!" I wave my hands in front of us. "Look at this!"

"I am." They look around the cave. I watch the curve of their neck as their chin stretches upward. "Feels like a good place to be murdered," they yell once their face is level with mine again.

I roll my eyes. "Whatever," I say. And then, without thinking: "This is what I want."

Mateo's eyes turn serious. "What is?"

I look out at the curtain of water, trying to process what I just meant.

"I want to always be surrounded by places like this," I say, trying to project my voice over the sound of the rush. "I want to go to college and learn how to save them."

The smile returns to Mateo's mouth. The small, gentle one I like seeing most.

They lean toward my ear again.

"Where do you want to go?" they ask. "What's your dream school?"

My brain stutters. I stare at the strings of Mateo's hoodie lying against their chest, one slightly higher than the other.

I usually try not to think about this question.

"I'll probably go to Oregon State," I eventually shout up at their face. "If I get in."

They frown, hunch toward me again.

"You'll get in, Penny. But is that really your dream school?

It's only, like, twenty minutes from Verity."

"They have a good environmental science program," I volley back. And it's true. They have a ton of field-based classes and internship opportunities. I could take classes with Dr. Petroski. The campus is great.

And maybe I still won't be able to afford it. Maybe I'll have to take classes for two years at Benton Community College first. But in-state tuition at Oregon State is at least more of a realistic goal than tuition . . . anywhere else.

"Sorry," Mateo says. "It's okay if OSU is your dream school. I just"—they raise their head an inch to look at me—"like picturing you at Stanford or something."

My heart thuds.

I blink away from their gaze, then raise my chin to meet it again a second later.

"I'm not actually that smart, you know." It's a little ridiculous, shouting this conversation in this loud, echoing cave. But a part of me likes it each time Mateo has to lean down toward me. How close we have to stand to hear each other. "You're just as smart as I am."

Mateo was such a good sparring partner in US History because they knew their stuff as well as I did. It was different than arguing with someone who came from a place of ignorance. It was arguing with someone who wanted to push you to think harder.

Mateo's eyes turn serious again. It's increasingly dark in here, increasingly hard to read them, but I can't shake the feeling that Mateo is looking straight into my soul somehow.

Straight inside my chest, where I want to see myself at Stanford too. Where all the selfish, overwhelmed feelings tumble and grow.

"You care," they say, the force of their voice lower than a yell for the first time in ten minutes, and somehow, even as I strain to hear them, it makes the words hit harder. "You try."

I don't know what to say to this.

I want to tell them how often I wish I could care so much less. That always needing to try sometimes makes me feel like an idiot.

They keep looking at me, quiet and steady, and I look back at them, words stuck in my throat, until my heart flutters, my stomach swooping and uneasy, just like it was that first night in their car when they played the music my body didn't know how to process while sitting beside them. Like I'm inside a conversation I suddenly don't understand.

"I think we should get a food truck," I shout.

Mateo blinks.

"Well, I think *Elen* should get a food truck," I clarify, taking the tiniest of steps away. "I've been thinking"—I try to steady my heart, clear my thoughts—"that I can't make the town of Verity spend more time on Main Street, you know? So maybe what Elen needs to do is bring Delicious Donuts to *them*. She could set up at festivals and the farmers' market, and even at Verity High during football games, you know? Or, like, any sports games throughout the year, really, if Verity ever decides to fully support something other than football."

I look back up at them, and it's like their whole face has

shuttered. They don't say anything, and my heart starts racing again. They just told me, in what I thought was an affectionate tone, that I try. I don't know how to save the whole earth yet, but in some strange way, being here at Silver Falls has deepened my need to save Delicious Donuts. Because fine, whatever, maybe I *do* want to leave this place, maybe I dream about exploring the coasts and forests of Costa Rica, Nicaragua, Belize, the reefs of the Pacific, the Sitka firs of Alaska. Maybe all I want is to experience new things, see different corners of the world.

But *this* corner of the world, right here, right now, is special too. From Main Street to Silver Falls. There are always things to fight for, right in front of you.

Mateo's eyelashes flutter against their cheeks as they stare at the wet stones underneath our feet. The mist from the waterfall has darkened the tips of their bright hair, frizzing the rest of it around their face. It's visceral, how much I miss seeing their eyes, a strange yank behind my belly button.

"I thought you said you were going to help," I shout after a second, the silence making me feel insecure. And then, quieter: "I thought it was a good idea."

Mateo sighs; I watch their shoulders rise and fall.

"Sure, Penny," they say, barely audible over the falls. They turn and walk away from me.

I follow their bent head the whole way up the trail, back the way we came, until the forest is quiet again. My throat constricts, my breath reedy from the climb, from the tension radiating off Mateo's back.

When we reach the parking lot, Mateo tucks themself into the passenger side of the truck without a word.

They put on a playlist that's full of neither musicals nor too-pretty songs; they're all ones I've heard before, on the radio or TikTok. Every one somehow makes me sad, a sinking feeling deep in my chest, worse than I felt before.

We don't say a thing the whole drive home.

THIRTEEN

Lanes at Verity Bowl: 10

"This is taking entirely too long," Blake complains. But Blake always complains.

"Listen, it's hard!" Swapna snaps from her seat at the monitor. "Working with technology from 1972 takes time!"

A second later, JULIANNN pops up on the boxy, curved TV screen over our heads, joining SWAPNAAA and PENNYYYY above it.

"Hey, that's me!" Julian grins and tosses a piece of popcorn into his mouth.

"Do me next, at least," Blake says.

"Sorry, Blake, you know I'm ace," Swapna replies without looking up. Blake groans.

"Don't be gross."

"You asked for it."

BLAAAAKE pops up on the screen. Blake brightens.

"Oh! That's good. I was all ready to criticize BLAKEEEEE."

"Always one step ahead of you, Blake-ee."

Blake returns to frowning.

"Me! Me! Me!" Lani chants. LANIIIII is soon followed by CARMELLO, which, sadly, takes up the maximum number of spaces by itself.

"We could call you Carmelloooooo the rest of the night anyway," Lani offers.

"You know, I think I'll pass."

Swapna stands with a clap of triumph. "Let's do this thing!"

She chucks her neon-pink ball down the lane with a bone-shuddering *thud*. It slams into the gutter halfway down.

Knowledge Bowl Goes Bowling is officially underway.

"Okay, everyone!" I stand with my back to the lane before I take my turn. I wave my phone in the air. "Instagram time!"

Everyone groans.

"Your fault for not listening to me before!"

"We were literally in the middle of getting our shoes and you were shouting instructions at us. You chose chaos!" Blake complains.

Blake has a point here.

"Fine. But now you're focused, so you can all go follow at verity.deliciousdonuts." I open my own app. "On TikTok too. I will bug you all night if you don't."

"Aww, look at that cute donut on the sign!" Lani says. I force a smile.

"Like every post!" I add. "There's only five; it's not hard!"

"Are you getting paid for this?" Blake asks. "You should be getting paid for this."

"I am being paid in your friendship. Please and thank you."

"I do love my friendship being forced and threatening," Julian says.

"I knew you'd get it." I stuff my phone in my pocket once the notifications have all pinged through. I twirl and grab my ball from the trough thing. I chose a black, sparkly ball tonight. It reminds me of Mateo's nail polish.

I get a spare.

My team cheers.

I plop back into my seat, forcing another grin on my face.

Knowledge Bowl Goes Bowling is the best, and I'm trying very hard to remember that. I know, logically, that I am having fun. Maybe. I know I *should* be having as much fun as I had last summer at Knowledge Bowl Goes Bowling, as much fun as I had when we traveled to Portland this spring for the state tournament. Swapna and Carmello made up a bunch of ridiculous games for us to compete in at the hotel—very Office Olympics from *The Office*—and we got in trouble with the front desk for being too loud. Our adviser, Mr. Jacobson, tried to be stern with us, but Mr. Jacobson is superbad at being stern. We all collapsed into giggles afterward.

I know I should be hanging on to this, appreciating every minute. Because whenever I'm with the Knowledge Bowl team or friends from band or iTuna, it always *feels* natural. Friendship, that is. I just don't know how to, like, sustain it. Because I'm sure that tonight, just like last July, after the last pins have been knocked down we'll all go home and proceed to barely talk the rest of the summer. I can't stop that truth from seeping into my head now, keeping me from being fully present at the exact moment I should be reveling in it.

At least, it's *one* of the things messing with my head.

I'm back to my original thesis: July is the worst.

I should state for the (increasingly long) record that I have understood friendship before, at least back in elementary school. It felt natural, finding real friends, the ones you hung out with all the time, the ones you told everything to. When I was a kid, it was easy to spend every afternoon with Nathan, my neighbor across the street, to have my moms drop me off at the houses of my friends from Girl Scouts for sleepovers. I didn't spend all my spare time wondering whether my friends secretly thought I was annoying. I didn't worry about who did or didn't follow my social media accounts, who was or wasn't judging my posts.

But then Nathan moved to Bellingham, and my friends from Girl Scouts all joined soccer instead of band, and everything just kind of fizzled away.

I don't know if it's just a natural-part-of-getting-older thing, my increasing levels of confusion about friendship, or just a my-brain thing. It would be really helpful if the universe assisted me in differentiating between the two a little more.

I bring out my phone again as Blake takes his turn. I instruct everyone to lift up their feet for a bowling-shoe photo and post it to my personal Instagram to have documentation for future Penny that this night happened. That these friendships, at least when we have it together enough to plan a night like this, are real in the moment.

Two rounds of bowling later, as I'm minding my own

business, absorbing the activity around me—Lani and Julian are discussing some epic fantasy show I've never watched; Carmello and Blake are betting on the likelihood of us beating Lake Oswego next Knowledge Bowl season—Swapna ambushes me.

"So." She's sitting two seats away; she turns to prop her knee onto the empty seat between us and takes a loud slurp of her soda. "You're working with Mateo della Penna this summer."

I choke on air and pretend I didn't.

"I am," I confirm.

She waggles her eyebrows at me. "That's interesting."

"Is it?" I attempt to sound neutral. An eyebrow waggle is not to be trusted. An eyebrow waggle makes me feel, irrationally, like Swapna somehow knows I have spent the past forty-eight hours obsessing over my and Mateo's painfully silent ride from Silver Falls. Like she knows it has upended everything I was just beginning to trust about Mateo and me this summer. Like she knows that even now, in the middle of bowling night, I can't stop thinking about it.

"Um," she says, "it is only about the most interesting thing to happen to me, personally, this entire summer."

"You haven't even been in to get a donut!" I frown at her.

"Who cares about donuts?" I open my mouth to protest, because I find myself actually caring rather a lot about donuts these days, but Swapna pushes on. "I care about the slow burn of the century. I had to watch you two be all weird and huffy around each other for the entirety of the last school year and now you're *working* together?" She throws her head back and punches her fist against her chest. "It's too good."

I frown harder. "What are you even talking about?"

"Your great love story, obviously."

My frown is wiped off my face as my mouth drops open. "What?" I yell loud enough that the rest of the team stares at us.

"Oh, yeah," Swapna goes on. "You and Mateo. *Big* enemies-to-lovers vibes."

"What?" I say again, because what the hell. Swapna *knows* us. I add, annoyance flaring, "We are not *enemies*."

"Have I contemplated writing fic about you two before?" Swapna tilts her head. "Yes. Have I actually written it?" She lifts a finger in the air. "No. I do have boundaries. You're welcome."

"Swapna," I say, before my returning frown eats my face in half. "Stop saying nonsense words. Explain."

Swapna drapes herself across the seat between us.

"I really put my finger on it during the Electoral College debate in history this year."

"What?" Because oh my God. What?

"I've had quite a few classes with Mateo, too, Penny, and does Mateo care about politics? No, no, they do not. They care about their sketchbook, and theater, and Spicy Sweet Chili Doritos, which is unfortunate, as that is the worst flavor. *But*"—Swapna raises a finger again—"they were, like, *super* into states' rights that day you ranted about abolishing the Electoral College."

"Because it's ridiculous!" I screech before I can stop myself.

"We can barely call ourselves a democracy! The Founding Fathers could never have predicted the way—"

"Penny. Stop. It's bowling night; no one wants to discuss the Electoral College. I'm just saying, Mateo's normally pretty quiet in class, unless they get to argue with *you*."

"I know!" I practically shout. "It's annoying!"

Man, now I'm feeling riled up about the Electoral College.

But as much as this conversation is making my brain melt, I feel gratified that Swapna noticed this too, about Mateo arguing with me in class. That it wasn't just me.

"Because they're in love with you. Obviously." Swapna chomps on a nacho.

"That . . . doesn't even make sense." Part of me wants to walk her back to the beginning, explain Mateo's old *Penny is the worst* stance. Which I didn't think they felt anymore, but—do they? *God*, what do I know! Does anyone know what the heck Mateo is ever feeling? Well, I bet Talanoa does, and Lía, and even Candace. Whatever! It's fine!

"Penny, do you consume *any* pop culture? Come on. We are members of a club that's exclusively about knowledge. You two are always staring at each other. You should be able to see the signs here."

"We do not—" I sigh. I only glared at Mateo so much during this past school year because they were always glaring at *me*! "Mateo isn't in love with me."

Because *Maybe at times not thinking I'm the worst anymore* and *Being in love with me* are very different things.

And anyway, I don't know if Mateo is even into girls. It's

possible Swapna literally has no idea what she's talking about. The only person Mateo's ever dated, as far as I know, was Kevin Swanson in freshman year. At least I assumed they were dating; I saw them holding hands a few times.

Not that that means Mateo *isn't* into girls.

Not that Mateo's preferences are any of my business in the first place! Like, at all.

"Okay. Counterpoint." Swapna raises a brow. "You're in love with Mateo."

"I—" I cannot believe I'm even having this conversation. I cross my arms over my chest. "I am not."

"Mm-hmm." Swapna sucks on her soda straw and raises both eyebrows at me.

"I'm going to get my own nachos," I declare. And I leave.

Because there is no good way to end this conversation and because, damn it, Swapna has made me want nachos.

It's a relief when Julian steps up next to me at the snack counter. I need a distraction from the five-alarm blaze that has been my face for the past ten minutes.

"Hey!" I smile at him, trying to erase Swapna's words from my mind and get back into the swing of the evening. "You were able to get the night off from younger-sibling duty, huh?"

Julian is one of my favorite people. He's super-easy to talk to, and he has a big family too, way bigger than mine—he has *five* younger siblings, and one older—so he understands the constant-babysitting lifestyle even more acutely than I do. Except I think his family is so large because his parents are, like, super Catholic and don't believe in birth control.

Which is a little different from having two queer moms who accidentally had triplets, but still, it's nice talking to someone who gets it.

Julian lets out a breath. "By the skin of my teeth."

I laugh. "I hear that."

Mom actually made a big deal about tonight. She mentioned how happy she was about it like five times in the past twenty-four hours. Which was nice, I guess? But it also made me feel kind of weird, like I should be grateful for getting to go out with friends on a Saturday night. Like it was some big thing. Which, don't get me wrong, I *am* grateful for; I just . . . I don't know.

Julian orders fries and a Cherry Coke. My nachos arrive, and I'm about to go back to our lane when Julian clears his throat and taps his fingers on the counter.

"Uh," he says, staring at the menu on the wall, "I couldn't help overhearing what you and Swapna were talking about. Because, you know, Swapna was being loud."

"Right?" I lean against the counter and pick out the gooiest nacho from the top of my stack. "It was embarrassing." I stuff the chip in my mouth, suddenly thrilled to have a sane person to talk about this with. "She was being ridiculous," I add, somewhat inelegantly, being that I'm speaking through processed cheese.

"I don't know," Julian says. His fries arrive; he takes the basket in his hand but doesn't move to leave the counter. "Was she?" He turns to look at me. "Do you like Mateo?"

Something dies in my throat at this unexpected direct

question—my intended protest, my embarrassment. Maybe because Julian's the one who asks it. Julian, who I always feel comfortable talking to.

I think for the millionth time in the past two days about Mateo leaning down to talk in my ear underneath the waterfall. About them singing along to Phil Collins, the wind blowing through their hair.

"I don't know," I say.

Julian nods. He looks down at his red-and-navy bowling shoes. "Well," he says slowly, before he looks up again, "I think Mateo would be really lucky. If you did."

I blink.

Julian walks past me, back to our lane.

I have only a few seconds to stand there and process what Julian just said. Blake's calling my name, telling me to hurry up. Everyone's waiting for me.

My next turn is a blur. My sparkly black ball hits the gutter on its first roll; I knock down one wobbly pin on the next. I slump back in my seat.

Was Julian just being nice? A supportive friend? Like, *You go, girl!*

Or . . . does Julian *like* me? Was that what he was implying by saying Mateo would be lucky? The idea makes something hot spread through my gut, even though I've never really seen Julian like that. It's more just the idea that I'm a person who could be *liked*.

I feel, suddenly, like a fish out of water. Has Julian ever

given me any signs? Has *Mateo*? Have *I* given signs to either of *them*?

I've never given much thought to this kind of stuff before. I'm simply so *busy* during the school year that there's not a lot of time to contemplate dating. It almost makes me want to laugh, even thinking the word. *Dating.* There are so many other things to worry about anyway, like my tuition fund and the melting of the polar ice caps.

Except—

Okay, no. Fine. Fine! I *would* like to go to Stanford, and occasionally I think about romance!

Like . . . I think about it all the freaking time.

It's just that, if I'm honest, I never thought anyone would like me like that. At least no one in Verity. Considering I know everyone here, and no one's ever shown any interest before. My loneliness is something I've always shoved down deep, under schoolwork and extracurriculars and planning for the future and anxiety and my family and . . . it's something I hold on to only when I'm alone. When I'm trying to fall asleep. The idea that one day, if I'm able to escape to Stanford or the University of Chicago or Chapel Hill or Boston or NYU or . . . maybe I'd find someone there. Someone who would think I was interesting, who wouldn't mind my weird lip freckle. We'd have deep conversations late at night in some hole-in-the-wall restaurant in a city I've never been to, and they'd look at me like I was the only person who existed. We'd go to concerts and scientific lectures and learn new languages together, and it sounds so *dumb*, putting it into words, acknowledging any of these fantasies, but maybe falling in love would make everything else feel easier.

But maybe—I guess? Possibly I'd been clinging to my future imaginary world so hard that I'd missed the signs. That there are people who think I'm interesting already. Here. Now.

My heart is thudding fast in my chest.

Or maybe Swapna is just making stuff up. Maybe I'm overthinking that conversation with Julian. The way I overthink freaking *everything*.

Maybe I am simply inept at understanding human interactions.

Would Hannah be able to help me get better at it? No, I can't talk to Hannah about this. I already spend half my therapy sessions feeling self-conscious; if I started my next session with *So, highly trained mental-health professional, how exactly would you define a crush?*, I'm pretty sure she would tell me to, like, go get a diary like a regular sixteen-year-old.

No—no, she wouldn't. I know she wouldn't. She would be so nice about it, like she's nice about everything, which would be ten times more embarrassing.

An indeterminate number of minutes later, the lights go out.

For half a second, the bowling alley is submerged in total darkness. Which is helpful for me, as I was having a hard time making eye contact with Julian. And Swapna. And everyone.

But then neon strobe lights dance across the lanes, and loud music pumps from the speakers.

Blake groans. "I hate Night Bowl," he complains. "It's so corny."

"Oh, stuff it," Swapna says. "Give in to the Night Bowl, Blake. Also, it's your turn."

Soon after, it's my turn again, but I've stopped caring about the score. The darkness and the swirling lights make me dizzy as I toss my ball down the lane. I actually sway for a second after I release it from my fingers but catch myself before I fall over. I barely even aimed the thing.

I get a strike.

The team whoops and hollers behind me as the pins all clatter to the ground and get swept away. Maybe *I* have unintentionally given in to Night Bowl, but I hear myself laugh out loud.

Maybe Swapna is being ridiculous. Maybe she isn't.

Maybe life is just ridiculous.

There's something peaceful about that thought. That maybe I can just laugh about everything for once instead of focusing on all the awful parts.

When I turn to go back down to our seats, the song changes. I hadn't recognized what was on during my turn, some loud screechy oldie. But I know "Bohemian Rhapsody."

Julian's up next; the little triangle on the screen blinks next to his name. But he doesn't move to get his ball. He stands on his seat instead. Carmello immediately jumps up next to him. And they start singing.

Swapna and Lani scramble onto their chairs next. Even Blake doesn't protest; he climbs up too. I'm a second behind everyone else, but my feet find purchase on the hard plastic by the time Freddie Mercury is singing about murdering someone. Which has always felt pretty bleak to me—like, not the kind of lyrics you take joy in singing along to—but that's what we do anyway.

Ridiculous.

Julian catches my eye and grins.

Maybe I'm only projecting what I want to see, but it feels like a *We're okay* grin.

I needed to see that grin.

I smile back, and something in my chest releases, some chamber I'd been holding tight.

Even if we see each other only once a summer, even if we're not text-each-other-in-the-middle-of-the-night friends, I still really need Swapna and Julian.

We get more into it as the song progresses, dancing, laughing, making dramatic flailing gestures with our arms. Blake's right. It is corny as hell.

And it's the most fun I've had in months.

When my friends first leaped onto their seats, I worried someone would come over and yell at us to get down. But it never happens, because half the other lanes are doing the same thing. It feels easier not to be self-conscious when you're in the dark among a mass of other people being as embarrassing as you.

I can't help but think, again, about being in Mateo's truck. Their surprising playlists, the horrible croak of their voice shouted into the wind.

I can't help but feel it, deep inside myself, right now:

I wish Mateo were here.

We sink back into our seats once Queen is done. Julian picks up his ball and chucks it down the lane. The game resumes.

I wait until my next turn has come and gone, then I sit back down next to Swapna. Stick my hands underneath my thighs. Lean in close so she can hear me over the blaring music.

"I don't think I like enemies-to-lovers," I say. "I want . . ."

I bite my lip, trying to think about what I would want if I allowed myself to want it.

"I want, like, *Heartstopper* leaves, you know?" I gesture with my hands, fluttering around my face. "Pretty and cute and happy."

I fall back against the hard seat. I feel embarrassed again. But I'm trying not to be.

Swapna nudges my shoulder with her own.

"Well, then, Penny," she says with a grin, "go make your own *Heartstopper* leaves."

FOURTEEN

College Fund: $1,411

"Hey, Elen," I say two mornings later. "Have you ever thought about having a food truck?"

She arches an eyebrow while she clears a steam wand.

"A food truck?"

"Yeah." I've been trying to regroup the past couple days. It's been . . . difficult, for a variety of reasons, including Verity suffering through a rough heat wave. No one's particularly in the mood for a donut; the shop has been slow, the customers grumpy. Even my own overheated stomach feels a little queasy when I look at all the sweet treats. Their colorful icing melts bit by bit throughout each day as our AC struggles. "I know it'd be a hefty initial cost, but I don't think we'd even need one with a full-functioning kitchen, just something to help transport the product. And I think the return on investment would be more than worth it."

I allow myself a mental pat on the back for using this phrase, *return on investment*, so smoothly. It's possible I've been googling small-business things.

"You could bring Delicious Donuts anywhere—to fairs, the farmers' market, private events, sports games. It would be like bringing Main Street to the whole town, and in return, it'd remind people to come to Main Street more. Like a"—I tumble my hands in a circle—"positive-feedback loop."

"Penny," Elen says, and even though I expected this tone of voice, and even though it's not unkind, it still makes me wince. "You sure you don't want to major in business?"

I shake my head. This is now the third time we've had this conversation; the second was last week, when she helped me order the stickers and then let me set the price points.

She shrugs a shoulder. "I'm just saying, a lot of environmental activism is about fighting against business, right? It could be helpful for you to learn more from the inside. Make you a kind of"—her eyes narrow as she thinks of the right words; she throws a few fake punches my way—"double threat."

I consider her over the row of cups that separates us. "Are you saying no to the food truck?"

Elen drops her fists and smiles, but it's sad. "Yeah, Penny. It's a good idea. But I don't have the cash or the manpower for any offshoots of the business right now, plus there's a ton of licensing that goes into running something like that. But—"

She steps closer to me, picking up one of the stickers that now live by the front counter.

"These have been popular." Her brown eyes flick to mine again. "You still think more Delicious Donuts merch is a good idea? That people would buy T-shirts with these designs on them?"

Part of me knows she's just trying to let me down easy, soften the blow from the food-truck rejection. But the other part of me says—"Yes! Absolutely."

She smiles, and it's an inch less patronizing this time. "Look up some vendors and get some quotes for me, okay? A small run to start with."

I nod fervently. Some vendors and quotes. I got this.

The door chimes, and Mateo walks in.

They glance our way, give a quick wave, and disappear into the kitchen. I swallow, staring at the counter.

"Great." Elen's already untying her apron. "Now that Mateo's here, I'm going to go finalize next week's schedule and then head home. Text me if the Big Boy gives out, okay?"

Our bestseller this week has undoubtedly been iced drinks, and the ice machine in the kitchen—which Elen calls the Big Boy—has been groaning like a fracturing iceberg from the stress of overuse.

Mateo walks behind the counter just as Elen exits. I immediately turn and fiddle with Mr. Bun-Bun, praying for a customer.

The shop being slow—and everyone being sweatier than usual—does not help the fact that, ever since Knowledge Bowl Goes Bowling, I feel like there is a spotlight on Mateo in my brain. Everything about them is brighter, every movement noticed in precise detail by my annoying eyeballs.

They're wearing half their hair up in a ponytail to keep it out of their face today, as they've started doing in the heat. This has led to two intriguing discoveries: One, the baby hair around their temples curls in humidity, and two, this look exposes more of the dark roots that are continuing to grow underneath the neon dye, and somehow I like this combo—pink, purple, dark brown—even more. And how is that possible, that your roots growing in makes you look even cooler? What the hell. How does Mateo della Penna exist?

They've also been constantly lifting the collar of their T-shirt and using it to wipe the sweat off their face, so I've learned they wear a worn brown leather belt, which I did not particularly need to know, but now it's implanted in my memory forever probably.

Other fully unnecessary things in my memory bank: They have a scar on their left hand, a mole on the back of their elbow. Their right Converse is more scuffed than their left. I could write an essay about the bracelet around their right wrist.

I'm jumpy anytime they're near. I attempt to avoid any and all eye contact, even though I am positive I am staring at them 45 percent more than is normal.

Which is all even more ridiculous because it's also obvious that they are still, for some unknown reason, pissed at me.

I have no clue what I did at Silver Falls that so thoroughly erased all the progress we'd made this summer, but at this point, I'm too pissed in return to care. A few days ago, after the hope my bowling outing infused in me, I thought that maybe I had overblown the awkwardness of the ride home that night. Maybe Mateo had just gotten tired; maybe I'd pushed too hard about a campaign they were lukewarm about from the start. Maybe we were still at least friends.

But each painful shift at Delicious Donuts since then has proven me all the way wrong.

I hate that I'm more aware of them than ever.

I hate that they haven't smiled at me in four days.

Heartstopper leaves! What was I thinking? Swapna and Julian blew a bunch of smoke up my butt and made me delusional, clearly.

The door jingles, and I turn toward it in relief. A genuine smile jumps onto my face when I see who walks through it.

"Julian! Hi!" As if I conjured him with my thoughts.

He grins in return. "Hey, Penny."

He's followed by three adorable mini-Julians, who race toward the glass counter in much the same fashion as my own siblings did a couple weeks ago.

"Only in charge of three today?"

"Yeah, Raquel's watching Max and Santi right now. This is Alejandro, Gabi, and Miri. Alejandro, Gabi, Miri, say hi to Penny."

Julian bops them on top of their heads as he names each one. They all shout in unison, as if they rehearsed: "Hi, Penny!"

I laugh. *God*, it feels good to laugh.

"How's your summer going so far, Alejandro and Gabi and Miri?"

They all answer at once. Pure chaos. I barely catch some shouted information about Pokémon. Their faces are shiny with sweat. I can't stop grinning at them.

"Okay, okay, good summaries! Excellent job! Let's wrap it up!" Julian bops their heads again, and again in unison, they stop.

This is an incredible move. I'm going to have to get pointers from Julian on its execution.

"We don't have AC at home," Julian tells me. "We're basically roaming the town looking for places we can hang that have some."

"Oh God. Ours is barely working here. Are you going to be okay? I think there are some cooling shelters open in—"

"Yeah, no, we'll be okay," Julian says quickly. "The little ones just get restless when they're this warm."

"Yeah, of course. I think we all do."

"Seriously. How's working here going, by the way? I didn't get to ask you the other night."

Julian's eyes slide to Mateo and then back to me, as if he's remembering what we *did* talk about at bowling night. I wish I could widen my eyes and mime a *No, nope, no* slitting-my-throat gesture at him without it being obvious.

"It's good," I say. "Well, other than when it's—"

"So are you guys going to get donuts or what?" Mateo suddenly talks over me. The end of my sentence gets jumbled with theirs.

I shoot them a look. They're normally good at customer service, but they just sounded . . . rude. And why in the world would anyone want to be rude to Julian, of all people?

"Oh, yeah, sorry!" Julian smiles, either oblivious to Mateo's tone or polite enough to ignore it. "Didn't mean to hold up the line." Even though there *is* no line, and we all know it. I shoot Mateo another glare for good measure. Julian looks down at his crew. "You can each choose one, okay? I'll take a plain glazed and an iced tea, if you have it."

Woodenly, Mateo turns to get the iced tea.

I hold in an eye roll at them and grab donuts for Julian and his siblings, catching up a bit more. We both agree the Knowledge Bowl team should do something else before school starts again.

But just mentioning school starting again leaves me feeling a little off-kilter. Which is strange, because school starting again is normally what I look forward to all summer. But there's still so much left to do to help Delicious Donuts before the end of August rolls around.

I twirl to face Mateo as soon as Julian and his siblings leave. I cross my arms over my chest. "Mateo," I say, trying to settle the annoyance in my voice, "you okay?"

"Yeah." They blow out a breath. "Yeah, I'm good."

And they turn and disappear into the kitchen.

I'm holding in a scream when the door chimes again.

And I'm thrown even further off-kilter when Roman Petroski walks in.

I shouldn't be surprised to see him; he's stopped by the shop a bunch this summer. I should be thanking him, actually, for his continued patronage of Main Street. But seeing Roman always feels like a surprise. Maybe because he's always wearing so little clothing. Those shorts are . . . short.

"Penster!" His golden curls fall against his golden forehead as he looks around. "Della Penna not here?"

Before I can answer, Mateo walks back onto the floor. And when Roman spots them, his face veritably lights up, like a heat lamp turning on. As if we need heat lamps in this climate-change July. "Della Penna," he says, and I scowl.

"Hey," Mateo says, already scooping up a plastic twenty-ounce cup. "Iced latte with caramel?"

Roman follows Mateo to the espresso machine; he leans against the other side of the counter as they chat. I ring up Roman's drink and leave the transaction open at the register while they gab about whatever. Roman's vacation to Maui last week; if Mateo had heard about so-and-so hooking up in so-and-so's dad's garage. Mateo smiles as they pour the milk.

I stomp into the kitchen, scooping up the bucket we use to haul ice from Big Boy out onto the floor. Let Mateo finish the transaction. I can still hear the sound of their low laughter over the crash of the ice and the wobbly grumble of Big Boy's motor. Maybe Mateo will just give the drink to Roman for free. Maybe they'll make out later. Who knows! Who cares!

Roman's still there, sucking his latte through his straw, when I lug the bucket to the ice freezer at the back counter by the espresso machine.

"I should take off," he says, "but you're both still coming to my party next month, yeah?"

My hands freeze around the bucket handle.

"Yeah," I hear Mateo say behind me. "Of course."

"Sweet," Roman says without waiting for my response. "See you guys later."

The door jingles. I dump the ice down with a crash.

I had almost forgotten about Roman's party.

A different kind of Penny summer.

But will I know anyone there, other than Mateo?

And if Mateo's not even speaking to me . . .

I turn to see them lifting the collar of their shirt to wipe their face again. A slice of stomach appears.

I stomp back to the kitchen for more ice.

When ten more minutes have passed without a single customer appearing, something in me snaps.

"Listen," I burst out. "You don't have to keep doing any of this with me."

Mateo, who is leaning against the back counter doodling on a piece of receipt paper, looks up. "What?"

"Trying to save the store," I clarify, motioning around us. "I know you've never been super into it. And you're pretty good with driving on your own now, so—"

"Penny, I'm sorry, but what the fuck?" They're not leaning anymore. They're suddenly in my space, standing at full height, sweaty face etched with anger. "Not super into it?"

They reach around the register and grab a fistful of stickers. "You know how long I spent on these dumb designs, right? How long I spend on your dumb sign every week?"

"Don't bend them," I mutter, grabbing the stickers from their hand. My fingers brush their palm. "And if you care, stop calling everything *dumb*."

"And I'm *not* good with driving on my own. You saw me not being able to drive all the way to Silver Falls. And driving in the dark scares the fuck out of me."

"No." I actually stick a finger in their chest. Their T-shirt is soft. I regret the gesture immediately. "I didn't *see* you being unable to drive to Silver Falls; I heard you *saying* you couldn't, which is a totally different thing. It clicked for you that very first day at Walmart; I *saw* that. And driving in the dark scares everyone."

Their nostrils flare. My blood is racing in my veins now that we're talking about that night, acknowledging it existed.

We're standing close enough that I can fully see the new addition to Mateo that I've been trying to not study all shift: little metal trans flags, shiny and pastel, in their earlobes. I don't remember them ever wearing earrings before; I want to ask if they just got their ears pierced. Where they went, if Talanoa or Lía went with them. If it hurt. What their dad thinks.

"I still stall all the time."

"Who cares," I snap. "Come look at food trucks with me."

Their nose wrinkles. "What?"

I blink and try to recover, pretend the idea hadn't shot out of my mouth before I truly processed it.

"There's a place outside Salem that sells them. We could go look, see if there's one that might work for Delicious Donuts."

Elen said no, but it was just a first no. Maybe, with a little more research, I could nudge it toward yes.

Mateo stares at me for another beat until they sigh.

"It'd have to wait a few days. I'm leaving tomorrow to go camping with my family."

"You are?" The fire within me wavers for a second; I'm thrown somehow by this news. "For how long?"

Another sigh. "Four days. But I'll go to the lot with you when we're back."

"No." My voice surprises me once again. Mateo's eyebrows lift. "Tonight."

If I wait any longer, I'll let Elen's first no sink in too deep and I'll start to doubt myself. I don't want to wait four days. Who will be covering Mateo's shifts while they're gone? DJ, probably. Ugh.

"Okay," Mateo acquiesces, stepping away, and something in their voice makes my stomach hurt. Like they're so tired of me. "Tonight."

"You can meet me and Dolly there," I add. "I'll text you the address. You should drive yourself."

Their head shoots my way again.

"You can do it." If they're not going to be confident in their own abilities, I will be for them.

The door chimes with a group of overheated customers before they can argue.

FIFTEEN

@Verity.Deliciousdonuts Follower Count: 213

I pace in front of the chain-link fence, hating myself.

Reason one: I forced Mateo to drive here by themself. Why? I can't believe I purposely put them in possible danger. Plus, the drive out here was not insignificant, and that truck is probably less fuel-efficient than Dolly. I have chosen to waste fossil fuel.

Reason two: In my spontaneous plan-making several hours earlier, I neglected to research the actual operating hours of the food-truck lot.

The food-truck lot that is apparently . . . closed for the night.

But I only discovered this fact five minutes ago, and presumably Mateo's already on their way here, so I can't—

A navy truck rumbles in and parks behind Dolly. Mateo tumbles out half a second later and marches up to me, face even sweatier than it was a few hours ago, chest rising and falling fast.

"Few things I thought about on the way," they say, and I am so *relieved* that they made it, alive, that they are here and *talking* to me, that I'm almost breathless when I respond.

"Yeah?"

"Number one: Do we think the owners of this lot are even going to talk to two kids like us?"

To prevent them from turning and leaving as quickly as they arrived, I brandish the card from my pocket. "Answer to number one: We'll tell them we work for the shop and are doing a preliminary look around for Elen."

"Elen has business cards?" Mateo takes the card from my hand, frowns at it, and hands it back.

"Of course she does. They're right next to her computer." I don't tell them that the whole stack was a little dusty when I grabbed one today. "Also, can you stop referring to us as *kids*? You are weirdly into infantilizing us."

A corner of their mouth quirks before they smoosh it back down.

"What?" I ask, hackles up.

"I've just never heard another human use that word before."

"What, *infantilizing*? That's a totally normal-usage kind of word."

The mouth quirk returns and is just as quickly smooshed, but less effectively.

"Sure." And then they meet my eyes, their own soft for the first time in a week. "Smart" is all they say. I blush and look back at the food trucks.

"Anyway," I say before they can mention what else was on

their mind, "I should tell you that the lot is closed."

"What?"

"But it's okay, because I think we can maybe squeeze in over there." I motion quickly toward the end of the stretch of fence we're standing next to, where it seems to disappear into the line of trees that border the back of the lot.

"Penny Dexter." When I look back at Mateo, their mouth hangs open in shock. "Are you suggesting breaking into the food-truck lot?"

"Just quickly." I try to sound calm even though my heart's pounding against my rib cage. "Come on, let me show you." I turn and walk toward the trees, praying Mateo follows me.

It's not that breaking the law necessarily fits into a different kind of Penny summer, but I can't accept another failure. I can't accept making Mateo drive all the way out here for nothing.

Making them even angrier with me.

But I'm definitely not brave enough to break the law *alone*.

"This section of fence here." I push gently on it, welcoming the shadows of the trees. "I think we could squeeze through and then run for"—I point toward a truck not too far away—"that one."

I noticed it as soon as I parked. It's—well, it's dusty pink. It's a touch smaller than most of the others, with a cupcake painted on the side. I can only imagine that whatever needs a cupcake shop has would apply to donuts too.

Mateo's shoulder brushes my own.

"You don't think there are security cameras around here?"

I glance up to see their throat bob as they swallow and look toward the top of the fence.

"There's one," I admit, "by the office. At least, that's the only one I've been able to scout out. But the office is all the way over there, and if we're quick—" I pause over my own swallow. "I think it'll be okay."

"And what if the truck's locked?"

"Then at least we'll have tried."

Mateo's quiet. The sun is beginning to bend toward the horizon, the shadows lengthening around us. I start to hope they'll call my bluff, that they'll shake their head and tell me they can't do it. We could get *arrested*. This could go on our permanent records. Can we really fit through the fence here anyway? God. Who even am I this summer?

"Okay," Mateo says.

And before I can process it, they're pushing the chainlink fence away, squeezing through, muttering a curse, and running.

My feet scramble after them.

"*Shit*." My own curse strangles out of me, breathy and embarrassing, as a jagged edge of metal scrapes my cheek. My sneakers thud against the dry, uneven dirt after Mateo's, my vision tunneling in on their form in front of me, which is yanking on the dusty-pink door, and—

And oh my God—jumping into the truck.

Their hand shoots out from the dark to help me up; I automatically take it.

"Oh my God," I say out loud. "I can't believe it was open."

Mateo's soft laugh, still rough at the edges through their rapid inhales, rolls toward me.

"I know."

It's too dark in the back of the truck for me to see them, to see anything. Cautiously, I shuffle toward the light filtering through the windshield and side window. Dust greets my eyes; I sniff and am pleased to discover I can smell a hint of sugar, like if the Delicious Donuts kitchen spent a few months trapped in an attic.

So abandoned-looking, but still recently used. Still possibly viable.

I spin in place, trying to take in more details in the better light.

"This could work, right?"

Mateo opens a cabinet above the back counter. I examine the space behind the serving window.

"Yeah," they say. "It could potentially work."

"Potentially!" I swerve toward them in accusation. They laugh, holding up their hands.

"Yeah, potentially. Like, if the engine still runs, and Elen actually wants to buy it."

I swallow.

"She should buy it," I say. "We could make it so cute."

Elen said no to this earlier today, but I haven't seen any paperwork regarding Northwest Donuts in weeks. She hasn't mentioned anything about the buyout either, and she's been more and more encouraging of my ideas, letting me in on more of her business decisions.

Our social media followers increase by the day.

Like, slowly, but they're still increasing.

This would be a *good* investment. Candace would love it; I can already picture her hanging out the window, calling to anyone who passes by wherever we park it.

"I should take pictures to show her." I grab my phone from my pocket.

"Pictures to document our crime, you mean?"

I scowl at them as I swipe my screen. "It's a very minor crime. We're not here to steal or hurt anything."

Mateo laughs. "Penny, I don't think—" Their laugh dies, replaced by a concerned furrowing of their brows. "Penny," they say again, stepping toward me. "Your—"

I step back out of instinct as their hand reaches for my face, but it's not exactly roomy here in the dusty-pink cupcake truck, and my back hits a counter almost immediately. There's no escape from Mateo's fingers brushing against my cheek.

"Did you scrape it on the fence? And shit"—they yank their hand away—"my hands are so dirty from that door."

I see, in the light from my phone screen, streaks of blood against their fingertips.

"It's okay," I say, even though my cheek stings; I just forgot about it in the adrenaline rush of getting into the truck. It's a sting that's suffused now, confusingly, with the warmth Mateo's fingers left behind. "I've had my tetanus shot."

"It's not okay, Penny." Mateo breathes out, frustrated. "We need to get out of here and get you cleaned up before it gets infected."

They're not frustrated, I realize. Or maybe they are, maybe they're annoyed by this entire situation, but it's not just that. The intensity in their eyes I'm able to see even in the dim light—

They're concerned. For me.

The question bursts straight from my gut:

"Why are you so hot and cold with me?"

Mateo's eyebrows somehow scrunch even closer together. "What?"

"This last week, you barely talked to me. And now"—I flap a hand toward my face, but I forget I'm still holding my phone and I almost smack Mateo in the chin with it—"you're worried for my health?"

Mateo's eyebrows unfurrow.

"Me," they say, deathly slow, "hot and cold with *you*?"

"Eighth grade," I spit out, suddenly unable to keep it all in. "I had a really good time getting to know you your first day of school, and ever since—"

"Hold up. We're standing inside a creepy food-truck lot about to get arrested, and you want to talk about *eighth grade*?"

"*Yes.* You ignored me the rest of the year, and I never understood what I did wrong. And then—"

"Penny." Mateo's nostrils flare as they breathe in and out. "I was angry as shit that entire year. Like, *so* angry. I didn't want to be here, I missed California like hell. I *still* miss California like hell. I was trying to figure out all this shit about myself; Lía and my dad were fighting all the time because *she* didn't want to move here either, and then she stopped going to church . . . look, it had nothing to do with you. You were the nicest person I'd met here; you've *always* been the nicest person here, but I didn't think you'd actually want to be friends past that one day when you were, like, legally obligated to be nice to me as my tour guide, you know?"

"Well." I hug my arms across my stomach. "I did."

"Well," they say back, "I didn't know." And then, some of the fire leaving their voice: "It bothered you? That I didn't talk to you in eighth grade?" Their eyebrows scrunch back together.

"Yeah. I thought we . . . I don't know." My pulse is still racing too fast, but something does settle in my chest as I process Mateo's words. Eighth grade makes sense now. At least one puzzle piece has clicked into place. "I'm sorry it was a hard year for you."

They audibly swallow. "Me too."

I'm contemplating how to bring up everything else when they speak again, getting there first. Their eyebrows have smoothed, but when I meet their eyes, their gaze is dark and fierce.

"Penny. Maybe I was a bitch in eighth grade, and maybe I was hot and cold with you earlier in the summer when I was trying to feel out how to get through working together after we'd been at each other's throats all school year. But, Penny, *you* showed up at *my* house out of the blue last week. *You* took me on some enchanted-forest walk and opened up to me about your life. That was, like, the most romantic night of my life. I thought—" They pause, hands shifting to their hips. Their chest rises and falls as they clearly struggle for their next words. *Romantic* pings around in my brain like a word I've never encountered before, mysterious and strange. "I thought we were going to make out."

"What?" It escapes my lungs in a whisper. Oh my God. Swapna was right.

Maybe? I can't quite capture any thought in my head; everything in the universe suddenly feels slippery and opaque.

"I told myself for a long time to forget about . . . *you*, about pursuing the possibility of something with you, but then this summer happened, and then the moment was *right there*, we were literally under a fucking waterfall, and then you started talking about the store! *Again!*"

"What?" It comes out louder now, but it's still embarrassing, almost a sob. "You agreed to help with saving the store."

"I know I did, Penny!" They *are* frustrated with me now, and I'm still struggling to catch up with everything they're saying; I'm so behind and confused. "I'm *fine* with helping save the store! You're so fucking *cute* with all your ideas and your passion and—"

Mateo blows out a breath, sinking their face into their palms.

"I just didn't want to talk about the store *then*. Sorry if I've been cold since that day, but you rejected me pretty hard, Penny. It sucked."

"You—" I try to take a deep breath. I blink furiously, looking away from their gaze, pressing my thumbnail into my cuticle. "You wanted to kiss me. Under the waterfall."

I glance over quickly to see their eyes soften.

"Yes, Penny. I did."

"And that wasn't the first time you'd wanted to—" I can barely form the words. "You said you'd—you'd told yourself to forget about . . . having something with me."

They nod, slow but sure. Their eyes are still gentle, not frustrated anymore, and it gives me the tiniest bit of courage to keep going.

"Why?" I make myself ask. "Why did you tell yourself to forget?"

They finally break eye contact; they scratch at their temple before hugging their elbows across their stomach.

"Because I've spent every second since we moved to Oregon being a total mess, Penny. Things are slightly better now, but you . . ." They scrunch up their entire face this time. "You're like everything good about Oregon to me, other than Talanoa and theater sometimes, but I just—didn't think I deserved you, and we run in completely different circles anyway and eventually I figured it'd be easier to put you out of my head since I'm going back to California as soon as I can. But then I *couldn't* put you out of my head last year because you were *always there*, and then this summer . . ."

They blow out a big breath. Their sentence hangs in the air, unfinished, as if they simply ran out of words.

"But," I make myself say, voice small and tinny inside this hot metal box, "but you said I was the worst."

"What?" The plate tectonics of their forehead smash together.

"The first day of school last year. You were at our lockers with Talanoa and you said—you said I was the worst. And then Talanoa laughed."

Their mouth drops open. "Penny. I have literally no memory of saying that. Maybe . . . maybe we were talking about the situation of you being in all my classes, and Talanoa was giving me shit because he *loves* to give me shit about you—"

"You talk to Talanoa about me?" But then I remember when Talanoa brought up the idea of me teaching Mateo to drive, how I could tell they'd already had a conversation about it.

"Yeah, Penny, I mean—" Mateo throws up their hands, letting out a little unhinged laugh. "I feel like I'm being as clear as I can here; I've *been* obvious. I—wait." They drop their arms and look at me with horror. "Is that why you said the thing about us not being friends? After you heard me and Talanoa say whatever you thought we'd said?"

I hug myself tighter.

"Yeah. I—I don't know. I thought it'd be easier." My voice is so small, I can barely hear it. "To protect myself."

A look of anguish passes over Mateo's eyes, and they cover their face with their hands.

"Penny," they mumble through their fingers. "I'm sorry."

My chest feels too big for my body. "Me too," I whisper. And then, "Could I have a do-over?"

Mateo's face reemerges from their palms. A wry smile tugs at the corner of their mouth. "Of sophomore year? I wish."

"No." I shake my head. "Of the waterfall."

The smile fades from their face. They lick their lips, glance at mine. I feel like I am outside my body. Like the world has tilted.

"Um," they say.

I step forward and kiss them.

I think Mateo helps me out, meets me halfway. It's a bit of a blur. All I know is that somehow, my lips are on Mateo's, my hands on their cheeks. Their skin is soft, their lips softer. Their hands are on my back, pulling me closer to them, and then we're stumbling until I hit the counter again and—okay. Okay.

Okay.

I get it now.

Why people are so into this.

I am a big fan of this.

I could do this for a long time.

But eventually, Mateo pulls their mouth away.

"Penny." They pull their hands away too, sticking them in their hair. "Is this—are you—"

"Yes," I say. "Good. Are you?"

They nod. I can feel their breath against my face, smell their roses everywhere, mixed in with the sugar and the dust.

I kiss them again, while their hands are still in their hair, because they look very cute like that, and because I want to. When their hands drop to my neck, it feels oddly natural. This is the most intimate thing I have ever done, and I'm doing it with Mateo while maybe possibly breaking the law, and it all feels *right*. Seamless. Like I could sink into it forever and feel happy for the rest of my days.

"Penny." Mateo drags their lips from mine and rests their forehead in the space where my neck meets my shoulder. One of their hands still rests on the other side of my neck; their thumb swipes back and forth along my jaw. They are . . . so much, so warm and solid against me, and it's hotter inside this truck than ever, and I can't quite breathe, but for freaking *once*, I don't mind all that much. "You're bleeding."

"Huh?"

"You're bleeding," Mateo repeats, and I feel it vibrate against my skin as much as I hear it in my ears. What a sensation. I wonder if there's a scientific catalog for these kinds of things, some kind of classification system. *Epidermis oscillatory mateo, acute.* "And it's possible the cops are on their way to kick us out. We should . . . go."

"Yeah," I say. But my fingers are now exploring the feel of their T-shirt, the muscles of their back as they shift underneath it, and I can't seem to make myself let go of that. *Latissimus dorsi tension, subclass cotton.* "We should go."

Their head shifts just enough to run their lips over my neck, and I full-on shiver. Their mouth moves against my skin, and I think they're smiling. I think Mateo is smiling into my skin. I could explode.

"Dexter," they whisper just below my ear. "I—"

A siren blares.

SIXTEEN

Photos Taken of the Food Truck: 0

I don't know which one of us moves first; all I know is that we are running. I barely remember stumbling out of the truck. Belatedly, as the fence comes into focus, I hope Mateo closed the door behind us to reduce the evidence. Even though our fingerprints are all over fucking everything. Mateo's fingerprints are all over *me*. I'm thinking in curses, which doesn't normally happen. None of this normally happens.

"Watch your fingers," I whisper as Mateo stretches open the broken span of fence for me, hoping they don't catch the same ragged edge my cheek did a half hour ago. Has it been a half hour? Maybe it's been weeks.

"Watch your *face*," they reply just as I'm slipping through, and something about it throws me into uncontrollable giggles.

And then we're tumbling behind Mateo's truck, hiding, on our knees, Mateo's finger pushed against my lips. "Shhh," they admonish, but their mouth is trembling with the effort of keeping their own laughter in. A nearby streetlight turns on;

I'm so startled I fall back onto my ass, then flat on the ground, my skull almost hitting the bed of the truck. An inch closer and I would have cracked my head open.

"Penny! Penny, *shh*." Mateo crawls over me, their palm chasing my mouth, but I'm already there. I cover my face with the crook of my elbow, trying to keep every unhinged bit of sound in, but I can't help it. My mind is no longer in control of my body. Everything is too much. Even if we do get arrested, the only clear thought in my head is that it was worth it.

Except . . . there are no sounds other than the huff of our breath and the rush of traffic from the road. Not a siren to be heard, no nearby footsteps. Eventually, my giggles die down. I realize gravel is digging into the stretch of my back where my shirt must have ridden up, and Mateo is still hovering over me, their palms flat against the ground at my sides.

Their laughter dies half a second after my own.

And then they retreat, falling back on their haunches, and I scramble to sit up and pull my shirt down.

"I think . . . no one's here?" Mateo says, voice scratchy. I look around us, taking a breath.

"It must have been a passing ambulance or something."

Mateo's mouth cracks into a grin. "You must be a good-luck charm or *something*, Dexter."

They stand before I can reply, holding out a hand to help me to my feet.

"My dad probably has a first aid kit somewhere in here—"

"I have one in Dolly."

"Of course you do," Mateo says to my back as I walk toward my old yellow friend, hands shaking as I fumble with my keys. I can hear the smile in their sentence, this pleasure in my being prepared, and I've never felt so good about myself in my life.

As soon as I retrieve the kit from my trunk, I hand it over to Mateo, not trusting my hands with anything right now. Mateo's are steady, though, as they find what they need, rip open a tiny package, swipe the sterilizing wipe across my cheek.

I wince at the sting; they wince in tandem.

"Sorry," they whisper.

I watch them as they open up a Band-Aid and press it onto my face, then open another, and another. They apply each one so carefully, their nose wrinkled in concentration, the streetlight making their hair a cupcake-colored halo.

"You okay?" they whisper as they spread out the last one, fingertips tickling close to the corner of my eye. "You're being too quiet."

I know I am. It's hard to believe I was just laughing a few seconds ago. I can barely breathe now, sandwiched between Dolly and Mateo.

But all I can see, all I can feel, are *Heartstopper* leaves.

"I like your earrings," I whisper. "I wanted to tell you earlier."

A self-conscious pull of their lips as they stuff the trash from my wound repair into their pocket.

"Thanks. My dad hates them, obviously. I thought I'd

just wear them at the shop, so he wouldn't see them . . . but the place said if I take them out for too long, the holes will close up."

They lean back an inch, worry the beads on their bracelet.

"It's just tiny holes in your ear," I say, voice still barely above a whisper. "If tiny holes in your ears are a big deal to anyone other than you, then fuck them."

A squishy feeling enters my stomach as soon as I say it. Mateo's dad is still their *dad*. I've never even met him. Maybe I shouldn't be out here throwing around *fuck them*s.

Even if I meant what I said.

It's hard to read Mateo's face; it's getting darker by the minute, and their expression hides in the shadows.

I breathe out when they finally speak.

"I'd actually like to get, like, dangly ones?" They touch their ears with care, and I wonder if they're still tender. "I don't know."

"You should try different ones out," I say. "See what feels best."

"Yeah." Their gaze meets mine again. "I can't believe I won't get to see you for four days."

"What?" But as soon as I say it, I remember. "Oh. Camping." I swallow down my disappointment. "Where are you going?"

"Just Cascadia."

A small gasp escapes me. "I love Cascadia!"

This earns me a full-blown smile. "I figured you did."

"Do you *not*?"

"I'm going to tell you something that I hope doesn't make

you regret kissing me." They lean down to whisper in my ear: "I hate camping."

I shake my head, fighting back my own smile. "I mean, I already knew you had a lot of bad opinions."

They lean back again and frown. "Like what?"

"Well, the Electoral College, for one thing."

The smile that spreads across their face feels new. Special. Just for me.

But maybe that's only how it'll live in my memory because it's what appears a second before they kiss me again.

I want to catalog this too. I have always wanted to catalog Mateo's smiles.

And *The smile before they kiss me* has to be the best one yet.

It's a gentle kiss, not as intense as it was inside the food truck, but somehow it feels more intimate. More real, out here in the twilight. Hushed. Purposeful.

"You have no idea," they say when they pull back, "how long I've wanted to kiss this."

They place a finger on my lip.

When I realize what they're touching, I cry, "Oh my God," totally breaking the magical chrysalis of our embrace. "My *lip freckle*?"

"Yes." Mateo's voice is painfully sincere. "I am *very* into your lip freckle."

"I *hate it*," I say with equal passion. Because they have *got* to be kidding. "I hate all of it." I cover my face with my hands as if I could make it disappear.

"Penny. Do you know how many times I've drawn this

face?" They pull my hands away. I blink back at them.

"You've drawn me?"

"All the time." They touch my lip again, then draw a map around my face with their fingertip. "No one else looks like you."

They kiss me once more. Brief, sweet but firm. A closing argument.

They step back. "Bye, Penny."

"Bye, Mateo," I whisper, everything inside me quiet again. *Quiet* doesn't feel like the exact right word, though. Everything's quiet and loud all at once.

I get inside Dolly but wait for Mateo to leave first. To make sure their truck starts okay, that they get to the end of the street and turn left without a hitch.

Then I keep sitting there, hands on the wheel, fingers tingling, trying to get a hold on the quiet and loud feelings. I turn the ignition only when I can put a name to it: It's like a hive of bees has taken up residence in my chest. Buzzing away, full of honey.

I drive home slowly, listening to their hum.

It's not until later that night as I stare out the window of my bedroom, after hours of attempting and failing at sleep, that the hum starts to dim. That I start to feel the prick of my bees' stingers.

We run in completely different circles . . . I figured it'd be easier to put you out of my head since I'm going back to California as soon as I can . . .

The questions I should have asked Mateo before they drove away pile up in my head.

Are we *dating* now?

Everything that happened, everything that was said happened so fast and—I feel like a totally different person. I ran into my room as soon as I got home, worried my moms would see it on my face. Well, Mom, anyway; I didn't see Mama D's car in the drive.

It's just so *unexpected*, so weird, suddenly transforming into a new person, that I'm not sure how to adjust to it. How did I even know how to kiss someone? I didn't even think; I just—

Bodies are magic. In, like, a kind of terrifying but incredible way.

Also: How does one date, exactly?

Related: Is dating the worst idea in the world if it has a specific end point?

Because I don't know where I'll end up after I graduate from high school in two years, but I *do* know that earning minimum wage at a donut shop isn't going to cover out-of-state tuition. I am not destined for California.

But I remember how sure Mateo sounded about it when they told me they were.

And even though I know they must like me, because I *know* how they kissed me back, how they took care of my cut, how they said *You've* always *been the nicest person here*—now, in my bed in the middle of the night, away from the reassurance of them next to me, it's hard to fully believe it.

Maybe I don't know how to handle a hive of bees. It's too many bees, you know?

I've been trying to avoid my phone because it never makes me feel better when I'm like this, but I reach for it now and google Northwest Donuts.

I need to remember why I drove to the food-truck lot in the first place.

I just need to focus on a goal I understand.

Northwest Donuts started in Seattle in 1995 and has since branched out to locations throughout the West Coast, British Columbia, and Idaho. When I zoom in on the map on their website, I notice they even have a few locations in Arizona and Texas. Texas! *The Northwest's Favorite Local Donut Chain*, my ass.

I can't believe I won't see Mateo for four days. And I know from experience how nonexistent cell service is out at Cascadia.

For the first time in my life, I think I hate the woods.

Northwest Donuts doesn't, though; all their stores have the same design aesthetic—all dark greens and browns, exposed wooden beams and crisp white tiles behind the counter, like a Starbucks had a baby with an REI.

Is it an aesthetic that deeply appeals to me? Maybe, okay? *Maybe.*

But it's not Delicious Donuts. Give me a slightly chipped orange laminate booth above sticky brown tiles or give me death.

I know there are only so many additions to Elen's current

business model that I can throw at her, though, before she becomes annoyed with me. Or, like, more annoyed. Maybe I've been going about this the wrong way. It's not that Delicious Donuts isn't good enough as is for our town. It's that Northwest Donuts isn't *right* for it.

I have to dig up dirt on them.

But when I google *Northwest Donuts CEO*, all I get are pictures of a wholesome-looking white guy wearing a North Face jacket on a mountain-top.

Ugh. I know it's 2:20 a.m., but I give in and open my brief text chain with Mateo. Something has to be said.

And what I say is this:

> Penny: Soooooooooo askjdhshgeyurgehjasdhkjasgs

I feel it sums up the situation pretty well.

My heart about leaps out of my rib cage when they actually respond.

> Mateo: lol
> Mateo: i agree
> Mateo: Ok question though
> Mateo: freshman year
> Mateo: you yelled at me when i found you in that band room that one time
> Mateo: like, way before you thought i thought you were the worst

> Penny: I'm sorry!! I was having an anxiety attack! I didn't respond well!!

Mateo: well yeah

Mateo: that was why i followed you in there in the first place

Mateo: you were clearly upset & i just wanted to make sure you were okay

> Penny: Oh

Oh. For some reason it had never occurred to me to wonder why Mateo was there that day.

Mateo: and then you spilled shit on me, like, a weird amount

> Penny: ACCIDENTS, ALL OF IT

Mateo: you lit me on fire

> Penny: THE FLAMES WERE VERY SMALL

Mateo: 😂

> Penny: I'm sorry about your shirt, though.

Mateo: it's ok

I bite my lip.

> Penny: Sorry that I need to just confirm
> Penny: But you really never thought I was the worst?

Mateo: no, penny

Mateo: i swear

It only really sinks in then.

Last year was entirely my fault.

> **Penny:** Last year was entirely my fault
>
> **Penny:** I'm so sorry

Mateo: it's okay

Mateo: honestly, arguing with you in class was kind of fun sometimes

Mateo: your face gets all red and cute :)

> **Penny:** oh my god

Because *oh my God.*

> **Penny:** well I hated every second
>
> of it & I am still very sorry!!

Mateo: i decided to officially forgive you when you stuck your tongue in my mouth

Mateo: so no worries

> **Penny:** oh my god
>
> **Penny:** okay but also
>
> **Penny:** the kissing
>
> **Penny:** We can keep doing that?
>
> When you get back?

Mateo: uh yes

Mateo: please

Mateo: :)

Mateo: i need to be up in like four hours so i should

    get some sleep or tomorrow will be more miserable than it already will be
    Mateo: but I had a nice time breaking the law with you
    Penny: that should probably not be documented in text
    Penny: but . . . me too
    Penny: good night Mateo
    Mateo: night penny 💖

I contemplate what heart to send back for probably too long. It just seems like a big decision. Eventually, I go with a pink followed by a purple, to match their hair. They don't respond, as they are hopefully asleep.

I stare at my phone for a long time anyway.

When I'm tempted to stalk every single one of Mateo's social media accounts back to the year they created them, I chuck my phone onto the nightstand and bury my head in my pillow. But it's useless. This strange feeling of restlessness and exhilaration, exhaustion and adrenaline, is overriding everything.

Eventually, I get up. Maybe I'll make myself some tea and snuggle in with a documentary.

When I'm halfway down the hall, I see a band of light peeking out from Nikki and Emma's room, and it stops me short. It's definitely past their bedtime. I nudge open the door.

Emma sits in the middle of the floor, a headlamp strapped to her forehead beneath her tumble of brown curls. She's surrounded by piles of Legos, deep in concentration over whatever project she's building. Behind her, Nikki snores softly on her bed.

"Hey," I whisper as I crouch down, careful to not disturb any of Emma's neat piles. "It's late."

Emma shrugs without looking up. "Can't sleep."

I settle down across from her and try to remember what I did when I was her age and couldn't sleep. I'm pretty sure I ran whining to Mom every time. She'd sing me Paul Simon songs until I was unconscious.

I watch Emma for a moment, admiring her ability to figure out what she needs on her own, at six years old.

"Do you do this a lot?"

She shrugs again and says, speaking at a regular volume, "Sometimes. You know Nikki can sleep through anything, so."

I glance again at Nikki's snoring form and smile. I do know that.

But I didn't know this, that sometimes Emma can't sleep. That when she can't, she Legos.

It makes sense—everything about this is completely Emma—but it's still a little amazing. That you can watch someone grow for years, from the minute they were born, and still discover new things about them.

"Can I join you?" I whisper. Emma nods.

I study our surroundings in the glow of her headlamp. I start with one of the big, flat green pieces. Begin adding tan bricks. Search around Emma's piles as quietly as I can for some windows. With each piece I add, my mind quiets.

"What are you making?" Emma asks ten minutes later.

"Delicious Donuts." She nods. "How about you?"

"The International Space Station."

I let out a soft snort. Emma, six years old, re-creates the International Space Station. Penny, sixteen, builds a poor imitation of a small-town donut shop.

And you know? It feels right.

"What happened to your face?" she asks. My fingers touch my cheek as if I've forgotten.

"Ran into a fence that didn't like me very much."

She pauses her work to look at me.

"You ran into a fence?" And when I nod: "That's weird."

I snort again. And throw a guilty glance toward Nikki. "Yeah. It is."

I can tell from the look on Emma's face that she's torn between interrogating me more on this and getting back to the ISS. Eventually she chooses the ISS, and I search for brown bricks for my roof.

"Hey, Emma?" I ask after a while. "Do you miss Mama D lately?"

"Oh my God." She says it so loudly and immediately that even she winces; she peeks behind her shoulder at Nikki, who makes only a small sound of disturbance before her steady breathing resumes. Emma looks back at me, lowering the bricks in her hand. "*All the time*," she says at a quieter but just as intense decibel level. "We talk about it all the time."

"Sounds like her work is just really busy," I say because I know I need to say something to soothe her, even if I was the one who brought it up. Because that's my job, to help soothe the triplets. "I'm sure things will settle down soon."

Emma nods and returns to her project.

I stare at her as she works, my own hands still. It's funny—I felt such relief when she first agreed with me, to know I wasn't alone in this feeling. But then—

We talk about it all the time.

I knew the moment I saw Emma and Bruno and, eventually, once she was out of the NICU, Nikki bundled up together after they were born that they would have a special bond. It's been so interesting watching them grow, seeing how different they were even when they were so small, how different they've all continued to become.

But they're still the triplets. They'll still always belong to one another.

And I guess they're old enough now, or I'm just away from the house enough this summer, to have things they talk about without me.

I look down at the tiny donut shop in my hand and blink away the sudden, embarrassing swell of loneliness, despite knowing Mateo likes me, despite feeling more hopeful about my friendships with Swapna and Julian. I will always be on the outside of my siblings' innermost world.

"I should go to sleep," I whisper. "And so should you."

Emma sighs. But she doesn't disagree.

Silently, I help her put our unused bricks back in her meticulously organized bins before I tuck her into bed, kiss her forehead, and slip out of the room.

Emma lets me keep my creation for now, though she'll inevitably need her pieces back. I place it on my dresser when I'm in my room.

I check my phone before I get back under the covers. To my surprise, there are two more texts from Mateo.

> **Mateo:** hey, penny, i'm sorry you thought i thought you were the worst
> **Mateo:** even if it was never true, that must have sucked

I breathe in and out, running a finger over the bright screen. Imagine I'm running my finger over Mateo's wrist instead, giving the beads on the end of their bracelet a light, grateful tug.

> **Penny:** I'm sorry I told you we weren't friends
> **Penny:** I have always wanted to be your friend.

When my head hits the pillow, sleep finally finds me, deep and dreamless.

SEVENTEEN

College Fund: $1,728

The neon sign above Grumpy Toad's Diner is buzzing.

I haven't actually spent much time at Grumpy Toad's, but it seems like the sort of place whose neon sign is always buzzing. It's a mostly nondescript diner at a truck stop off I-5, kind of a weird destination to make a special half-hour drive to. But it's the only business near-ish to Verity other than the Walmart that's open twenty-four hours. Hence a top destination for bored Verity teenagers who want somewhere to hang out in the middle of the night. A good spot, from what I've heard, to nurse a hangover in the morning before heading back home.

But I've never had a hangover, and the only place I've ever been in the middle of the night—aside from building Legos in my little sisters' bedroom—is my own bed. Suffice it to say, standing in the parking lot of Grumpy Toad's at ten o'clock on a Tuesday night is a new experience for me.

"Hey."

I turn. And maybe I should be embarrassed at the way my entire body fills with butterflies when I see them, especially when I've spent the past four days having daily mental doom spirals, and the fact that Mateo's back from camping and smiling at me shouldn't automatically erase all my concerns.

But apparently that's what's happening.

And I can't fully bring myself to care.

"Hey," I reply.

And then we stand there and look at each other like dummies until Mateo leans down and kisses me. Thank *God*. It feels like they have been gone *forever*.

"Thank *God*," I say when we break apart. "It feels like you have been gone *forever*."

They laugh, rubbing a hand over their face. They look tired, bags shadowing their sleepy brown eyes. It makes me want to cuddle into their chest for a long time. Because I'm pretty sure I'm allowed to cuddle into their chest now. Maybe.

"I know we've been texting and stuff," they say. And we have been texting and stuff over the past few days whenever Mateo had service. It's possible I've been glued to my phone. It's possible my moms have given me a hard time about it. "But I think I'm still adjusting to a world where you don't hate me for real. I mean, I started to feel pretty sure you didn't this summer, but—"

"I don't." I am ready to reassure Mateo about this at any point, anytime. "But . . ." I rock back on my heels, stuffing my hands in my back pockets. "Yeah."

Because I'm still adjusting to it too.

Because what happens now?

"Wait," I say, taking them in. I step closer. Bring a hand up to their bare ear. "Did—"

"Yeah," Mateo says, voice quiet. "My dad made me take them out."

"I'm sorry, Mateo," I say, equally quiet.

"Is it okay if I don't want to talk about it?"

"Yeah. Of course."

"Come on."

They hold out a hand, tilting their head toward the diner's entrance. They lead me there, fingers intertwined with mine, with a kind of cool calm I feel incapable of mustering. My head pounds with thoughts about their dad; my body vibrates with the sensations of being close to them. They keep holding my hand as we walk through the door, as we wait on the stained green carpet to be seated. My brain struggles to form complete thoughts other than *Warm* and *Good* and *Okay, then.*

"This healing okay?" Their other hand brushes against my cheek as the waitress grabs menus from the hostess stand, and I nod and think *Yes* and *Thank you* and *Ahhh*.

They release my fingers only when we reach a booth and slide into opposite sides of the table.

"Can I get you anything to drink?" the waitress asks, handing us enormous laminated menus. We both say we're good with water—living on donut-shop wages makes us good with water—and she disappears to check on the next table.

"What should we get?" Mateo opens their menu. "I'm actually not super-hungry; we stopped at McDonald's on the way back from Cascadia, but I'm thinking—"

"Is this a date?" I blurt out. My menu remains untouched in front of me. I can't stop staring at their face. I clasp my own hand underneath the table, still feeling where they touched me.

Mateo looks up from their menu, eyebrows raised. They're wearing a zipped-up black hoodie; their hair is rumpled and tangled from four days of camping. I can't stand how much I like it.

"I . . . do you want it to be a date?" They drop the menu, stick their hands in the pockets of the hoodie. "I'd kind of hoped our first date would be nicer than Grumpy Toad's. I just . . . wanted to see you."

Their text had come through a few hours ago. On our way home, finally. i know it's late, but want to meet at grumpy toad's later?

I'd secured permission from my moms—they said I could go as long as I was back by midnight.

Midnight!

A different kind of Penny summer for *real*.

And then I'd proceeded to spend the next few hours obsessing. Maybe they were asking to meet so they could officially call off the kissing contract now that they'd had some time to think it through.

But each minute in their presence makes my neuroses disappear. My heart swells dangerously inside my body. We're at Grumpy Toad's past my bedtime because they wanted to see me.

I take a deep breath.

"I've never dated anyone before. Just so you know. If that is, uh, what we're doing."

The corner of their mouth twitches. I've seen this before, but now I can officially catalog it: *Trying Not to Laugh at Penny Smile* (affectionate).

"Okay. Do you want that to be what we're doing?"

"Oh my God." I throw my hands in the air. "Stop tossing my questions back at me!"

Mateo laughs. "Okay, okay! I'm just . . ." They stop, shake their head. "So we're dating. If you want. Let's date."

"Thank you." I slump back in the booth in relief. "Good."

And after a second, I repeat their words, confirmation for myself. "So we're dating."

"Glad to be in agreement. This has already been a productive visit to Grumpy Toad's."

"Do you think Grumpy Toad's is named after someone whose nickname is Grumpy Toad? Or after an actual toad?"

"Neither." I almost jump at the waitress's voice, not realizing she'd returned. She flips a page in her notepad, clicks her pen. "Ready to order?"

My mind is still buzzing over this tidbit—*neither!* Then what the hell is it named after?—when Mateo says, "Can I have an order of fries and a slice of chocolate cream pie?"

And when the waitress turns to me, I say, "I'll have the same," because I haven't even opened up my menu, and it sounds good.

Mateo gives me an incredulous look as the waitress walks away.

"What?"

"I can't believe you're not telling me that, like, chocolate cream pie is an abomination or something."

"Of course it's not. It was a solid Grumpy Toad's order." Not that I am, as previously established, a Grumpy Toad's expert, but still. It felt like one.

"Wow." Now Mateo slumps against the booth. "This is going to take some getting used to."

I crumple my straw wrapper with the tips of my fingers. "I'll repeat that I never actually enjoyed arguing with you."

"Sure you didn't. But yeah, I know a milkshake and fries is the classic salty-sweet combo, but I thought—"

"You dated Kevin Swanson, right?" I blurt out. "Freshman year?"

Mateo blinks in surprise. "Uh," they say after a second, flustered. "Yeah. Kind of."

"Sorry." I bite my lip. "I just thought we should know each other's dating histories. Mine's nonexistent. I wasn't sure on yours. But, like, if this is a super-intrusive way to start a first date, you don't have to tell me anything."

I shred the wrapper into tiny little pieces.

"It's okay that you've never dated anyone before, Penny," Mateo eventually says. "I don't think it's that weird. But . . . yeah. If you really want to know. It was only, like, a month, and it's still a little hard to believe it even happened, because Kevin is . . . you know. Really hot. But—"

"Wait," I interrupt with a frown. My face feels warm. "I feel like that's not allowed."

"What's not allowed?"

"Talking about other people being hot."

"Counterpoint." Mateo's mouth curves after they say it, and it makes me finally relax a little, this echo of all the times we threw that word at each other in class over the past year. How fun Mateo is clearly finding it, being able to say it now with playfulness. *Competitive and Smug Smile* (affection level uncertain but maybe good). "The expectation of jealousy over a partner being attracted to other people is a product of heteronormativity and we don't have to play into it at all. In fact, being close with another person should be an *opportunity* to gossip together about all the people you find hot."

I chew this over.

"Well," I say, "I do find it very hot when you say 'heteronormativity.' So I suppose I can go along with this premise."

"Good. So, as I was saying, Kevin is obviously superhot. But—" Mateo interrupts themself with another laugh. "Penny! Your face."

"*What?*"

And—oh. It is possible Mateo pointing out Kevin's hotness—*again*—has made me scowl. Again.

I kick Mateo's foot under the table. I don't know what else to do.

"Ow!" Mateo laughs even harder. "What was that for?"

"I don't know!"

"You're the one who asked about this!" They kick my shoe back.

"I know!" I shove their sneaker once more. "I want to know!"

And despite myself, hearing how angry I just sounded about my own request makes me burst into a giggle along with Mateo.

"I am not at all surprised," they say, "that our first date is starting with violence."

And then they pick up a packet of Smucker's grape jelly.

And they *flick* it at me like a paper football.

I gasp as it hits my shoulder.

This is, like, seriously dumb.

But I pick up some orange marmalade and flick it right back at them.

It hits them square in the forehead and I shout, "Ten points!" before I can stop myself. The man in the booth behind us turns to squint at me over Mateo's shoulder. "Sorry!" I whisper, although I'm not sure the word actually comes out because I'm laughing so hard.

The half-second distraction is apparently enough for Mateo; they reach across the table and shove a creamer down my shirt, so quick I can't even bat their hand away. They slam back into their side of the booth, a smirk of victory on their face, and my mouth drops open in shock.

"Thirty points," they say. "At least."

The clatter of plates hitting the table makes us both jump.

The stony stare our waitress delivers with them sobers us up almost completely.

Almost. Considering I still have a nondairy creamer stuck in my bra.

I am very consciously not thinking about how close

Mateo's hands just were to my bra.

We bite our lips until she walks away.

"Truce?" Mateo asks. Part of me wants to argue about our scoring system, but—

"I'm hungry." I dig out the creamer and grab my plate of fries. "So yes."

Our food snuffs out the last of our laughter. Mateo scoops a dollop of whipped cream from the top of their pie with a finger. I shift my fries around until there's a hole in the exact center of the plate, the perfect place for the lake of ketchup I squeeze into it.

Mateo freezes with a fry halfway to their mouth.

"Do you always do that with your ketchup? Just like that?"

"When there's enough room on the plate, absolutely."

"Fascinating."

"There's nothing worse than watching someone pile ketchup right at the edge of their plate. I'm always staring at it the whole time, stressing out about when it's going to drip onto the table. And—wait."

I pause, staring at them chomping their fry.

"Do you not use ketchup at *all*?"

"When the fries are good enough," Mateo says around a bite, "you don't need it."

"Oh my God." I drop my hands onto the table in despair. "I don't even know where to start with that. Condiments are one of the greatest joys in life. It's food snobbery to pretend otherwise. You have to know, in your heart, that these are going to taste better with ketchup."

Mateo just grins at me. And bites into another fry. "Sure."

They must know that is the most infuriating answer.

It hits me then. Mateo wasn't lying. They actually *do* enjoy arguing with me.

I breathe through my nose and refocus.

"Okay. So why didn't it work out with superhot Kevin Swanson?"

Mateo's grin falls. I immediately hate myself for making it disappear.

Even if I do still want to know.

They drop their gaze, pick up a fork, and dig into the pie.

"He's not a bad guy or anything, but he was . . . never great about me and, you know"—they wave a forkful of pie through the air. "Gender stuff. He kind of misgendered me a lot—"

"*What?*"

"Which"—Mateo breathes out through their nose, stabs their fork into their pie—"I don't think he ever did intentionally. Or, like, to be intentionally hurtful, anyway. But he'd also, like . . . sigh and roll his eyes sometimes when he apologized, and . . . I don't know, it started making me feel bad, like I was this annoying burden to him, and . . . yeah. It wasn't great."

"Wow. So, Kevin Swanson sucks."

But when Mateo only continues to stab their slice of pie, avoiding eye contact, I force down everything else I want to say.

"I'm sorry, Mateo," I say instead. "It shouldn't be hard to treat you the way you deserve."

They glance at me, forcing the barest upturn of their lips. *Sad Ghost Smile.* Bottom three.

"Thanks. But it's okay." They shrug. "Honestly, I think he was just excited to find another kid who was comfortable enough to be openly gay with him in Verity, you know? Which I get. I just . . . wasn't what he actually wanted."

I process all this while they take a sip of water.

"But, look, Penny," they go on before I can say anything, "dating me . . . I don't want you to be my pronoun police, okay? That's not, like, your job."

"Okay," I reply softly. "Sure."

"Because"—they shift uncomfortably—"then I *am* being a burden on you. You know? And I'd always rather just keep on with my day when it happens than, like, make a big speech every ten minutes about how I feel really weird about gender, because I don't even know what I'd say exactly in that speech, and it wouldn't change their minds half the time anyway, and . . ." They breathe in and out. "It means a lot to me that you get it. Okay? That's all that matters to me."

"Okay," I say, forcing myself to sound stronger this time, to show I do get it. "But, Mateo . . . you are never, ever a burden."

Man, do I want to kick Kevin Swanson in the shins and *really* make it hurt.

Mateo only brings another sad, dry fry to their mouth.

"Back to my rule, though," they say. "In fairness, now you can tell me about someone *you* think is hot. If you want."

I think for only a second.

"Your sister."

A half-chewed fry flies across the booth.

"Ew!" I laugh at the same time Mateo shouts, "Penny!"

Their ears go dark pink, probably in embarrassment about the projectile spit. I want to tell them I'm still attracted to them, but I don't get a chance before Mateo sputters on.

"You cannot say my *sister*!"

"Why not? Her boobs are *incredible*."

"Penny!" Mateo shouts so loudly that this time half the restaurant turns to stare at us. Mateo covers their face with their hands.

"Okay, okay! Um. Let me think." I worry my lip before I say, tentatively, "Is it equally weird to say Elen?"

Mateo's hands lower enough for me to see their eyes. A funny expression rests there.

"Literally any answer is better than my sister," they drop their hands and say. "So, yeah, I guess it's cool you're into MILFs. Unless"—they freeze, eyes going wide—"you tell me you think my *mom* is hot too."

I shrug. "I don't know. I haven't met your mom yet."

"*Penny.*"

"Okay, okay!" I laugh. "I promise not to be attracted to your mom."

"*Good.*"

After a minute, their face turns pensive. They fiddle with their fork and glance up at me.

"You can say *him*, you know."

"What?" I furrow my brow. "Who's *him*?"

Mateo continues to look at me like they're sure I'm going to get clued in any second now. When I don't, they sigh.

"Roman Petroski," they say. "And maybe... Julian Portillo?"

"Oh!" My face warms even though I tell it not to. "What? Um."

Mateo's expression turns even more grave when I take too long figuring out what to say.

"Well," I eventually get out. "I mean, you've seen Roman, right?"

Mateo drops their gaze, fiddles more with their fork.

"Yeah. I have."

"And Julian and I are just friends because we're both nerds on the Knowledge Bowl team."

They lift their eyes back to me. "That's it?"

"*Yes*." I roll my eyes. Mateo seems to be struggling to walk the walk on their own idea here, and part of me wants to give them a hard time about it. But another part of me is singing. Because Mateo is ... *jealous*?

"Okay," Mateo says, but they're still a little grumpy about it.

I clear my throat around a smile.

"Anyway. You have to promise never to tell Elen that I might possibly be semi-attracted to her. Sometimes."

"Promise." They straighten and take an actual bite of their pie. "Tell me what I missed at the shop while I was gone."

So I give all the little details, all the tiny things only Mateo and Candace would think were funny too: the horrible customers and the sweet ones, the random things DJ said out of nowhere about signs he'd received from the universe this week.

"Tell me about Cascadia," I say.

"Boring as shit," they reply immediately. "You would've liked it."

I laugh. "Is that a compliment?"

A smile. "Yes." And then: "I missed you."

I swallow. "I missed you too."

"I also missed the shop." They tilt their head, an amused look on their face. "Which I didn't expect. And my Xbox. But that I did."

I think about what else they've told me they miss. And it suddenly, actually, sinks in then, opening up around me, expansive and wonderful: I can ask Mateo anything. I can *know* them.

And maybe I'll know them only until they leave. But Hannah's always telling me to focus on the present. And I feel it now, safe inside our booth. Nothing else exists. A summer night, endless and free.

"Mateo," I say. "Tell me about California."

Their eyes search mine. I stare back.

Tell me everything. I want to know it all.

"Your old neighborhood," I say. "Your old friends. Your tenth birthday. Why you want to go back."

After a long beat, they settle back in the booth.

They smile.

And they tell me about California.

EIGHTEEN

Longest-Ever Duolingo Streak:
62 Days (Last Summer)

When I walk into the house later that night, a quiet figure waits for me on the couch.

"Hey, kid," Mama D says. She's illuminated only by the lamp in the corner of the living room; it highlights the lines around her eyes, her short-cropped gray hair. "Twelve oh five. Not bad."

I put a hand on my chest, soothing my panicked heart. It's just Mama D. Not a murderer. I repeat it to myself, blinking at her to be sure: *Just Mama D. Not a murderer.*

Her navy scrubs are still on. She probably hasn't been back from the hospital very long. Still, something warms in my chest at the knowledge that she didn't drop into bed when she got home. That she's here. Waiting for me.

"Come 'ere," she says.

And like that, I am floating from the foyer into the living room, sinking onto the couch and into her waiting arms. I press my face against her chest and she squeezes, tight, around my shoulders.

"I've missed you, kid," she whispers. "You know that, right?"

Tears prick behind my eyes.

"Yeah," I say into her scrubs. My voice comes out hoarse. "I know."

I have seen her this summer, of course. We live in the same house. It's just so sporadic, unpredictable. I last saw her two days ago, at breakfast. Sometimes I wish she were, like, a banker working nine to five. That she'd always be home for dinner.

Her hug relaxes; she runs a gentle hand up and down my back.

"So how was the hot date?" she asks, voice lighter, more like regular Mama D.

"It was just Grumpy Toad's," I answer, cheeks heating. I hope I progress out of the blushing-at-all-times phase of dating soon. I fear my skin might eventually implode.

Mama D snorts. "I know. Mom told me. If Grumpy Toad's isn't a date, dating in Verity has seriously changed since I last checked."

Another minute passes, Mama D's strong hand at my back still soothing every nerve in my body.

"I like them," I whisper.

Mama D's hand stops.

"I know," she says.

And on another day, I'd probably protest. Feel defensive about how Mama D could know this when I've hardly seen her this summer.

But right now, all I think is *Of course she knows*. Mom and Mama D always know.

There's a pause before Mama D resumes her back rub and asks, "They/them pronouns?" to confirm. I nod, the top of my head hitting her chin.

"Well," she says, "they know if they hurt you, me and Mom'll kick their ass, right?"

I laugh, a tired, wheezy echo in the dark living room. "Yeah."

After a moment, I add, "I taught them how to drive a stick shift."

Mama D's hand stills again. "No kiddin'." I hear the smile, the pride in her voice, and I bite my lip on a grin.

"Well, their dad taught them the basics, but I helped. I think."

"That's my girl." She ruffles my hair. "The only way to drive." I close my eyes, already half asleep. Maybe this act will finally get her to forgive me for accepting an automatic.

Like clockwork, she follows up with "Dolly still working all right?"

"Yeah, Mama D. Dolly's fine."

She grunts. "She better be. I told Dave if she breaks down before you graduate, he owes me a thousand bucks."

I laugh. "Seriously?"

"Yeah. I won't hold him to it, though. I'll just make him do something humiliating instead. All right, kid." She nudges my shoulder. "Let's hit the hay."

Before we split in the upstairs hallway, I whisper, so as to not wake the triplets: "Mama D? Thanks for waiting up for me."

She ruffles my hair again, aggressive like always, so it falls over my eyes.

"Thanks for coming home in one piece, kid."

In the end, I'm simultaneously too exhausted and keyed up, again, to fall asleep. I get two restless hours, maybe, before my alarm goes off.

And today, I'm opening the store with DJ.

Per usual on a DJ shift, I have to pull most of the weight. He's on his phone constantly. He spills coffee grounds on my shoes. He sneezes on an entire tray of chocolate frosted. Every single thing makes me laugh.

By the time Candace and Mateo show up at noon, I feel half delirious and can't explain why everything is so funny. I can't explain anything. I string together a bunch of non-sensical sentences at their arrival, and Mateo asks, "Are you all right?"

"I am extremely exhausted." I smile.

"Dude." Candace leans an elbow on Mateo's shoulder. "You look out of your mind. Know what this would be a good time for? A Penny AMA."

"Okay!" I agree.

"Penny." Mateo frowns. "Are you going to be able to drive home?"

I take my time contemplating this question because Mateo looked really serious as they asked it. But a few seconds in, I forget what the question was.

"Dunno," I eventually respond. And then I boop their nose with my finger. It's the obvious thing to do. Their nose is right there.

"All right." Mateo is untying their apron.

"That's funny," I say. "You just put that on."

"I'm driving you home. Candace, can you cover for me until I get back?"

"Aye, aye, Captain." She salutes.

I gasp somewhat dramatically. "Mateo, you'll get in *trouble*."

"I won't get in trouble, Penny. I'm positive Elen would be on my side here."

"I do love Elen," I mumble contemplatively. Mateo's hand is warm at my back, gently shoving me away from the counter.

Next thing I know, I'm in Mateo's truck. I watch them walk around the hood, and I think they just shut my door for me, like a real gentleman. Except they're not a gentleman. Maybe being a gentleman should just be called, like, being a nice human. Mateo is a very nice human.

"You are a very nice human," I say when they get in.

"Thanks, Penny. So are you."

"Yeah?"

"Yes, a very nice human who probably did both your own and DJ's work this morning after getting home late from Grumpy Toad's and who needs approximately twelve hours of sleep."

"Wait. Did you drive here? Are you driving to work now?"

"Yeah. My dad finally trusts me enough. Would've been

helpful last week during the heat wave when riding my bike almost killed me, but—"

"Your dad should always trust you." I frown.

"Yeah," they say, pulling out of the lot. "Well."

"Oh!" I remember, suddenly, what we'd said last night we'd do next. "Dates! Let's discuss our next date. Dates, dates, dates."

"Maybe we should discuss this when you're more . . . sane."

"Let's do something cliché. Like dinner and a movie or something. Or a picnic. Do you have a picnic basket? Or we could, like, wander around the mall and get a Jamba Juice and hold hands. I feel like that's what dating people do, even though it seems kind of boring, and the mall always makes me nervous because I just think about shootings. Oh, we could go to the movies! Did I already say that? Movie theaters *also* make me think about shootings. But I don't know, maybe, like, twenty-five percent less than malls do. What's your favorite movie candy?"

"Penny."

Mateo reaches over and grabs my hand. Squeezes, then releases it to shift into another gear. They're quiet, and before I can think about it, my eyelids are drifting closed. Their hands are so soft. I would like to hold them forever.

I think they say, "Junior Mints," before the comforting rumble of their truck makes the world disappear.

I wake up at six p.m., groggy and confused, and reach for my phone.

I'm greeted by a row of laughing-crying faces from Mateo. Followed by:

Mateo: text me when you're awake

I snuggle farther under my comforter to hide my smile, even though I know no one else is here. I like making Mateo laugh, even in text form.

I send a proof-of-life text. And then, after a moment, I open a different message chain.

Penny: fine.
Penny: you were right.
Swapna: ooh yay!!
Swapna: I love being right!
Swapna: remind me what I was right about this specific time
Penny: me & Mateo
Penny: we're dating now
Penny: fyi
Swapna: OH
Swapna: MY
Swapna: GODDDDDDDDDDS
Swapna: YES!!!
Swapna: I WAS SO RIGHT!!!!!!
Penny: you were :)
Swapna: AHHHHHHHHHHHHHHHHHHHH
Penny: AHHHHHHHHHHHHHHHHHHHHH

Swapna: im crying

Penny: no you're not

Swapna: i am in my heart

Penny: me too
Penny: it's gross

Swapna sends strings of emojis and memes. I know what I want to ask next; it's why I texted her in the first place.
Still, I hesitate.
Why is this so hard?
But if I can kiss Mateo, if I can stay out until midnight on a hot July night, I can do this too.

Penny: hey swapna? can we hang out again sometime this summer?
Swapna: like just you and me? Or the team?
Penny: both, i think
Swapna: yeah! that'd be awesome
Penny: cool :) i'll text you more later
Swapna: cool :)
Swapna: AHHHHHHHHHHHHHHHHHHHH
Swapna: sorry just had to get that out one more time

I force myself to get up then, even if it's just for a few hours, because I know it'll be worse if I don't. Between early-morning shifts and staying out with Mateo, my body barely knows up from down. I realize as I shuffle toward the stairs that I genuinely don't know what the date is. It's Monday,

I think. But the actual date? Who knows.

"Penny!" Bruno shouts, jumping into the foyer as if he'd been awaiting my descent. "Join us for the cinema!"

"The cinema?" I ask around a yawn. It seems late to go to the movies. It's almost the triplets' bedtime. I think.

"Bruno's word of the week," Mom shouts from the kitchen. And when I'm closer, in her regular volume, hands sudsy as she rinses out snack containers in the sink, she adds, "They're actually just watching *Bluey* in the living room."

I smile and slide my socked feet in that direction.

"The cinema," I say with a horrifying accent as I join Bruno and Nikki on the couch.

"The cinema!" they shout in return.

"*Cinéma* is French, you know," I tell Bruno. "You're leveling up."

"Okay," he says, eyes glued to the screen.

I cuddle in behind Nikki. She hugs my arm with both of hers.

Bluey makes me cry. I text Mateo about it.

The next thing I know, I'm waking up in my bed again. I can't fully remember how I got there.

But whether it was the triplets or my moms who dragged me, unconscious, up the stairs, when I picture it, it makes me laugh into my pillow, my heart full and warm inside my chest.

"Knock-knock." I keep my voice light and casual. Elen's office doesn't actually have a door; it's really only the back wall of the kitchen, demarcated by metal shelves filled with boxes of supplies. I rap my knuckles against the cardboard closest to me.

"Penny." Elen turns, pushing her purple glasses up the bridge of her nose. She's wearing one of our new T-shirts, the one with Mateo's pink donut walking on stick legs and holding an umbrella. "What new ideas do you have for me today?"

"Well." I stand straighter, clutching my phone, holder of my *Save Delicious Donuts!* Google Drive folder. I've achieved enough consecutive hours of sleep that my brain feels clearer today, ready to move on to the next phase of the campaign. "Can I sit?"

She gestures to the folding chair next to her.

"I know a food truck might not be in the financial picture right now," I start. When I researched the licensing that goes into operating a food truck, I'd realized Elen was right. It isn't feasible for Delicious Donuts right now. Not until we're on a stronger track. I mean, I don't have access to Elen's financials or anything, but even I know there are still too many dead spots throughout the day.

But there's always next summer.

If I can stop Elen from selling the shop, I could have at least another summer of working here and adding to my college fund. Maybe *two* summers, maybe more, depending on how life after graduation goes. Thinking about how I still have time to save both my future and Delicious Donuts' is the one thing that makes me feel most centered these days.

"I still want to keep that option on the table because of how it could open up the business to special events. But maybe we don't *need* a food truck for that. We can still attend events as a vendor, and we could even host events here."

"Penny, I'm already stretched pretty thin staffing-wise as it is. I don't know—"

"Verity Days." Interrupting Elen, especially when her voice sounds like that, is a bold move, I know. But I'm feeling bold about this. "Delicious Donuts is already at the end of the parade route, which is clutch. But maybe we can have a table in the park too."

Elen raises her eyebrows. I keep on before she can shut me down.

"A lot of people just visit the park during Verity Days, to see all the different vendors and let their kids play. We still keep the shop open, but maybe we have a table in the park and offer some special Verity Days–only pastries and drinks. Sell the new merch. Remind anyone who passes by that we're open here seven days a week." I scroll down my document, needing to tell her my other ideas before she kicks me out of this chair. "And then things like National Donut Day. I know we already missed it; it was back in June, but—"

"Penny. Slow down a second. Let's go back to Verity Days."

"Okay." I straighten my spine again. "Let's."

Elen taps her fingernails on the arm of her chair before she sighs. "It used to be one of our biggest days of the year."

My stomach sinks. "Used to?"

She lifts a shoulder, lets it fall. "Attendance at Verity Days has been decreasing for years. And being at the end of the parade route *used* to be a boon, but more recently, I look out the windows and I see only frazzled parents on their phones trying to find their kids before they move on to the next thing or people heading straight into the park. It's still busy, still a good sales day, there just seem to be fewer people open to casually wandering in for a donut amid everything else."

"Because they have to *see* us." I scoot to the edge of my chair. "Mateo's sign out front will help with that; they can make it bright and bold for Verity Days, and maybe we get some extra signage too. And for everyone who wanders into the park"—I burst open my fingers—"we'll be there too. No escaping us."

I smile when Elen laughs.

"Have you looked up the table fee?" she asks.

"It's not bad. Fifty bucks. We'll just have to reserve it soon. Vendor registration closes at the end of the week."

She nods, rubbing her jaw with her pointer finger. This is her tell. She's considering it. She's going to say yes.

"You know," she says slowly, "I always wanted to sell more Armenian treats. We have some delicious treats, you know." She shoots me a look as if I was about to say they didn't. "My dad, when he started this shop fifty years ago, chose to make donuts because he missed his mother's baking so much. And of course"—the corner of her mouth tilts—"donuts were cheap."

Elen looks into the distance. Something complicated passes behind her eyes, something not for me.

"I still wonder if he ever wanted to add more to the menu. But Verity was even smaller then, more insular and homogenous than it is now, and I imagine the majority of his clientele wouldn't have gravitated toward anything with a name they didn't recognize even if it was delicious. By the time I took over, our product—standard American donuts—was well established. I've thought about mixing it up, at least adding some ponchik or gata, but . . ." Another unreadable look. "Alex is really good at making the standard product. My hands . . ." She stretches out her fingers in her lap, looks down, rotates her wedding ring. It is perhaps the most vulnerable I've ever seen Elen Arshakyan look. "They increasingly don't work so well. I'm not suited to making large batches of pretty much anything. Thank God for our Alex."

A fond smile replaces the gloom as she shakes out a hand.

"Anyway, sorry for boring you with all this. Send me a link for how to reserve a table in the park. Maybe just once, Delicious Donuts can honor my tatik."

She turns back to the computer, scooches her chair into the desk. I'm clearly dismissed, and I'll be leaving with a win.

But I glance back down at my document. "Elen? Can I suggest one other thing before I go?"

"Make it quick, Penny."

Right. I stand, a promise to get out of her hair.

"I think another way to draw in the community is to have local art on the walls. And maybe each time we put up a new artist, we open for extended hours for a night, maybe offer a few more specialty items, invite the public to come in and browse. Like an art-gallery opening, but low-key."

Elen gives a slow tilt of her head. She's considering this too, but she's not as sold.

"Maybe. We can talk about it later, okay? Let's get through Verity Days first."

"Of course. I was just thinking, maybe the first artist we feature... could be Mateo."

At this, she pauses her mouse-clicking finger. Turns her head my way.

"Is this art-gallery idea yours? Or Mateo's?"

"Mine. I actually haven't told them about it yet. I just thought, um, it could be cool. Especially when we showcase the work of our employees."

Another small smile.

"We'll talk about it after Verity Days, Penny."

This time, I actually accept her dismissal and head back out onto the floor.

But I can't hide my grin.

I know I just won that one too.

NINETEEN

College Fund: $2,813
College Application Fees: $400 ☑
Enrollment Deposit: $200 ☑
First Year Textbooks and Lab Fees: $1,400 ☑

July slides into August in a blur of Delicious Donuts shifts, babysitting, and kissing Mateo della Penna. Trips to Grumpy Toad's when we can. Texting each other every night until we fall asleep. I know, distantly, that there are things to worry about, but I simply don't seem to have the time. I cancel an appointment with Hannah to take one of Candace's shifts, which upsets my moms, but I need the money, and I'm doing okay anyway. *More* than okay. More okay than I've ever felt.

Even if my Duolingo streak is irrevocably broken.

And then it's Verity Days.

"I'll take a blueberry bagel with extra cream cheese, please," Adrian the postal carrier says with a wink, sunlight dappling his cheek through the tree our table is stationed under.

"Oh, um," I sputter, feeling a little weird that Adrian just winked at me. "We actually don't have bagels available today. Just donuts. But we do have some special pastries Elen and Alex have prepared, along with—"

"Penny." Adrian smiles, holding up a hand. "I was just joking about how I always order the same thing. I'll take one of those matzoon cookies and an Arnold Palmer."

"Oh!" I say, recovering. "Great! That'll be five dollars even."

"And you know what?" Adrian pulls out his wallet. "I'll take one of those stickers too."

I process Adrian's card while Mateo picks up the matzoon, a fluffy, nutty cookie I have already eaten three of (Elen gave me express permission) and pops it into a paper bag. Adrian chomps into it immediately while Mateo works on pouring half iced tea and half lemonade into a plastic cup from the two big glass containers on the edge of our table.

"Thanks, guys," Adrian says with a nod. "See you on Monday."

"Thanks!" I wave, perhaps a tad overenthusiastically, as Adrian walks away. My Verity Days adrenaline has yet to wear off, even four hours into personing the booth (Mateo and I couldn't decide whether *manning the booth* was a sexist phrase), even with the increasing heat of the day making sweat run down my back and between my boobs.

"Do we think it's weird that Adrian knows me by name?" I ask, leaning back in my folding chair.

"I would say yes," Mateo replies, bringing their phone out of their pocket, "but I think we've learned today that everyone knows you by name. Although," they add after a pause, "I could do without the winking. You're sixteen. He's old."

"Yeah." I grimace.

"I'm gonna text Elen that we need more lemonade, pronto."

"Can you tell her we could use some more plain glazed too?"

Candace, DJ, and Elen's husband are running the store today while Mateo and I person our table in the park. Elen's been running between both all day.

Mateo finishes typing and shoves their phone away.

"This is going great, right? It's going great," I answer myself before Mateo can open their mouth.

"Yes, Penny." Mateo slides me their *Slightly Exasperated but Affectionate* smile. "It's going great. As I have assured you approximately every twenty minutes for the past four hours."

"Good." I nod. "Thanks for continuing to reassure me instead of strangling me every twenty minutes. Truly top-tier people-who-are-dating behavior."

"I do what I can."

I glance around the park, at the array of booths lining the perimeter. Other local restaurants are selling small dishes and snacks; the Lions Club is giving out snow cones. Small-town entrepreneurs are selling homemade candles and soaps. Lawn games are strewn across the grass. People throw beanbags for cornhole; kids run around all of it in pure chaos. Nikki, Bruno, and Emma had been an enthusiastic part of that chaos earlier until the signs of overexcited overtiredness kicked in and Mom took them home. A group of friends who look to be in their twenties have been hogging the giant Connect Four for, like, forty-five minutes.

Nora, of Nora's Dance School, is giving free waltz lessons in the gazebo, its white railing decorated with blue and silver streamers. I took ballet classes with Nora when I was a kid until I realized it hurt my feet and I was almost absurdly horrible at it.

My eyes keep straying back to the gazebo, though, anytime there's a break in customers, to the old folks and the young couples alike, who are waltzing around the worn floorboards, knocking into each other and laughing in the small space while Nora's instructions and the tinny music she has pumping out of a portable speaker ring through the park. The music weaves between the distant din of the band playing at the other end of Main Street. The entire road is shut to cars; the sidewalks in front of the businesses spill more booths with items for sale.

I'm proud of how things are going in our tiny piece of it all. Our cash box is full; Mateo and I are now both experts at using the handheld card reader.

Elen and I had an official-feeling meeting a few days ago to go over the final game plan, double-checking our list of everything we needed. We checked in with each other again last night just to make sure the details were set. I appreciate the way she's been talking to me—like I'm a real partner in running this.

Not just a kid.

Like she trusts me.

And I lost only one to two hours of sleep max last night imagining everything that could go wrong. A marked improvement for me compared to previous nights-before-big-events. I can't wait to tell Hannah.

"Okay." I force my eyes away from the gazebo and back to Mateo. "Seems like we might have a bit of a break here. Show me the stuff."

Mateo bounces their knee, glancing around the park to make sure no one's approaching the booth before they lean down and take a tablet out of their bag.

"I feel like I've hyped you up too much for this," they say as they swipe open the screen. I've tried at least five times to get them to show me what they've been feverishly working on the past few weeks, but we keep getting interrupted by customers. And while customers are great, Mateo gets cagier and cagier each time they bring out their iPad. If someone comes looking for a donut in the next five minutes, I might have an inadvertent band-practice-room moment.

"And *I* feel that you are misusing the word *hype* here. Being as, for the past three days, you've been like, 'Eh, I don't know, they're kinda all right, but maybe it's cool, or actually they're probably bad, or I don't know, whatever.'"

Mateo laughs. "I do not talk like that."

"You so do!" At least when they're talking about their art, they do. It drives me up the wall.

"Listen." Mateo angles the iPad away from me. "Do you want to see them or not?"

"Yes!" I cry. "Please."

Mateo bounces their knee again as they hand over the iPad. They scoot their chair closer, leaning their elbows on their knees so they can point at the screen.

"I messed around with a few more logos just for practice."

In addition to the umbrella-holding donut design, our new stickers and T-shirts feature a logo Mateo and Candace crafted together: The words *Delicious* and *Donuts* are drawn in a font that looks like it's made of donuts, slightly puffy with pink frosting dripping off the edges of the *D*s and *S*s, the two words curving over a steaming mug of coffee. I adore it.

"I thought it'd be good to experiment with some more lettering. And—" They reach over, swiping so fast I can barely see each design.

"Mateo!" I bat their hand away, holding the tablet out of reach. "Let me look at them!"

I soften, though, when Mateo bites their lip and bounces their knee harder.

"I want to look at them," I say more gently. "Okay?"

Mateo breathes out. Doesn't reach for the tablet again. "Yeah. Okay."

They speak again after a few seconds: "I've actually . . . I've actually been really enjoying it. Messing around with the program, figuring it out more. It was nice of Candace to show me the basics. I don't know why I've never wanted to do stuff digitally before; I think it just felt like everyone else is already so good at it, you know? Like there are a million illustrators with incredible portfolios online and I'm already so far behind. So I thought if I just stubbornly stuck to my pencils, it'd make me, like, unique or something."

"Mateo." I look up from the screen. "You *are* unique. And you're not behind on anything."

"I am." They mess self-consciously with their hair. "You

should see these portfolios of, like, twelve-year-olds."

"It's also not your fault," I add, "that Verity doesn't offer digital illustration classes."

Mateo huffs out a long breath. "Yeah. Yeah, that pretty much sucks."

The Verity High art department consists of exactly two teachers: Ms. Fuentes, who does drawing and painting, and Mr. Delfino, who does ceramics.

"But Candace said there are continuing-ed classes at Benton I could sign up for, and there's lots of online stuff. I should probably get on it soon if I want any chance at catching up."

"Mateo." I reach out a hand and wrap it around their wrist. They are sounding how *my* brain sounds, and it is disturbing. "Sign up for classes if you want, but I promise that you're okay. You're already so good. And I'm positive there are lots of high schools around the country with depressing art departments but kids who still go on to be super-successful. Okay?"

Mateo nods but doesn't say anything. I go back to the tablet.

Some of the designs don't actually make sense for Delicious Donuts—flowery lettering, fancy curlicues, and doodles around the corners—but they're all great.

"I love how different they are," I say. "Shows you have a wide range, you know?"

"Yeah. I've been messing around with other stuff too, not just lettering. Like . . ." They grab the tablet, tap the screen a few times. They glance at me, hesitate a moment before handing it back. "Like this."

My brain short-circuits.

The screen is . . .

It's me.

But it's also . . . not me at all.

The drawing is a straight-on portrait of my face, except my hair is floating around me, filling the screen; it glows brighter than it does in real life. The background is a rich, royal blue; in the corner, there's a crescent moon.

And the freckles on my face—they're stars. Silver and gold, shimmering against my skin.

Like I'm part of the night.

"I normally like drawing things as they are, real-life portraits, you know?" Mateo's words rush together. "Playing with perspective but still showing the world like it is if you look at it the right way. But I thought it'd be good to try something more . . . dreamy or whatever, to show I can do different styles."

I nod. My hand is covering my mouth.

"Do you like it?" they eventually ask, and I realize I'm inadvertently torturing them.

"Mateo." I force words out of my throat. "It's beautiful. I can't believe . . ." *That you can imagine me this way.*

Even though I know it's not about me.

It's about Mateo. The way their brain works. How they can sit in front of an empty screen and create something like this.

I tear my eyes away from it to look at them.

"It's amazing. Also, I really, really want to make out with you right now."

Mateo laughs, looking away with a blush, the tension visibly easing from their shoulders.

"Maybe after this we could drive somewhere in my truck and . . . find a place to do that."

"Yes," I answer immediately. "Yes, please."

They run a hand through their hair, their knee resuming its bouncing.

"I would just ask you to come over," they say, still staring out at the park, "but my parents want to meet you first. I was actually wondering if you'd want to come to dinner sometime? At my house?"

A hint of nerves kick up in my chest.

"Meeting the parents. So official."

"Yeah, they're kind of old-school." Mateo looks down and kicks the leg of my chair. "It's okay if you don't want to. They just asked the other day, so I thought . . ."

"Of course," I say. "I'd love to."

Mateo has been talking to his parents about *me*.

"And then maybe you can come have dinner at my house sometime too?" I add.

"Yeah," they reply. "I'd love that."

"Cool." I look at the drawing on the tablet one more time.

It occurs to me then, what all the work they've just shown me must mean.

"So you are going to apply to art school?" I tilt my head, make them meet my eyes. "That's why you're trying out different styles? So you can have a portfolio to submit to schools?"

They stare at me, face briefly unreadable. Their eyes drop to the tablet in my lap.

"Maybe. I don't know."

"Where would you like to go?" I ask. "If you could go anywhere?"

This time they don't hesitate.

"Cal Arts in Santa Clarita is supposed to be good." They scratch at the back of their head. "And Otis is supposed to be cool, but I'm not sure if I want to be in LA. Maybe CCA, which is in San Francisco. We've never lived there, but I think I might like it. But . . ." They trail off. "They're all pretty expensive. Maybe I could just start at a Cal State school, tell my dad I'm undecided on my major, then figure out a plan when I'm there."

I swallow, staring steadfastly down at Starry Night Penny.

"That all sounds great, Mateo," I force out over the lump in my throat. "Anyplace would be lucky to have you."

Don't make it about you. Don't make it about you.

But I do.

"Can I ask you something?"

Out of the corner of my eye, I see Mateo look at me.

"I know you love California. I know all the history you have there. But can I ask . . . what's so bad about Oregon?"

And then a customer walks up.

By the time we've served them their donuts, I want to take back my petulant question.

"Sorry. You don't—"

"There's nothing *wrong* with Oregon, Penny. Well—no, the winters are the worst, like, objectively. But you have to realize . . ." Mateo takes a slow breath that only makes me hate myself more. "Sorry, I'm trying to figure out the best way to say it. In San Bernardino . . . like, white people are the minority, you know? And I know I can be pretty white-passing, but I'm *not*. So moving here was like—"

"I know," I whisper. "I mean I don't. I'm sorry."

I'm sorry I asked, sorry I didn't think more about the obvious answers before I did. I'm sorry I've never been to San Bernardino. I'm sorry Oregon has felt hostile to them when it's the only place I've ever known. I'm sorry that they don't love all the things I do: the forests and the mountains and the coast that raised me. I'm sorry that even if they did, it wouldn't make up for the rest of it, all the things I've never had to experience, the frustration in the way they said *not*.

"Penny." Mateo's voice is soft as they run a finger along my wrist. I shiver. "I know you're excited about Oregon State. But have you ever contemplated going somewhere else? There are so many good schools in the Golden State, not just Stanford. Like, *so* many. And so much nature too! Thousands of cool trees for you! Have you seen any of it?"

Pressure builds behind my eyes. I can only shake my head.

Because I haven't. I haven't seen any of it. There's a whole world of things I haven't seen.

"We wouldn't—" Mateo hesitates before pushing on in a rush. "I'm not saying you have to go to California, Penny—obviously you should go wherever you want to go. I'm just saying there are good options there. It could work, you know, even if we're not in the same town. I just think you'd love it so much. I'd even let you drag me camping in the mountains if you wanted to."

Mateo squeezes my wrist, throws me a smile. Their shy one. Their hopeful one. Their first-day-I-met-them smile.

And then it collapses.

"Penny?" They frown and reach up to push my hair out of my face. "Are you okay?"

"Yeah." I swipe furiously at my cheeks. "Sorry. Sorry. I'm fine."

"*I'm* sorry. Did I—"

"No. No." Mateo didn't do anything wrong. They are daydreaming of a future in California two years from now with *me*. It is the nicest thing that has ever happened to me. I don't even know how it's possible to care about them like this—this much, this fast. I want exactly what they want. It feels like my lungs are going to collapse anytime they smile at me like that. Anytime I walk into a room and see them. Anytime they touch me. Anytime I think about them at all.

It's not their fault that California is significantly more expensive than Oregon.

"Hey, bitches!" Candace swings an arm between us, plopping a box of fresh donuts and pastries onto the table, and we abruptly break apart. "Sorry to disrupt whatever was just happening here, but we brought a shit-ton more lemonade, as requested, and it weighs a million pounds. Mateo, come help me lug it over here."

As soon as Mateo stands, a line forms at our booth again. Elen steps seamlessly into Mateo's place and wraps an arm around my shoulder.

"How it's been going?"

"Good!" I take a deep breath, try to clear the remaining emotion from my throat. Focus on Verity Days again. "Really good."

We serve six customers in a row; Candace and Mateo replenish the lemonade and iced tea. Mateo goes to retrieve more plastic cups and paper bags from the shop; Candace arranges the pastries on the table under glass tops to keep the flies away.

Elen turns to me.

"Thanks for suggesting this, Penny."

She's wearing a wide-brimmed straw hat and boxy, cool sunglasses. She looks more relaxed than I've ever seen her.

Pride swells in my chest when she says, "This was a fantastic idea," and gives my arm a squeeze.

A second later, a couple approaches the booth. Elen's hand drops from my arm as she gasps. "Shelly!"

In a beat, Elen is around the table and resting her hands on the woman's shoulders. Taking her in. The white woman is small and smiling, wearing a brightly colored silk wrap twisted around her head.

"Oh, Shelly. It's so good to see you."

"It's good to see *you*," Shelly says, hugging Elen.

"How are you feeling?"

The women pull apart and Shelly shrugs.

"Been better, but you know what? I've been worse. So I'm holding on to that for now."

Alfredo, standing next to Shelly, places a hand on the small of her back.

"We're all holding on to that for now."

Shelly. Alfredo. From my first day at the shop. Shelly's sick, and Alfredo loves her.

And I know this only because they both love Elen.

"Here." Elen reaches over and lifts one of the glass tops. "Try one of my vozni."

Shelly bites into the round pastry, laughs as the crumbs it's covered in sprinkle down her shirt. Her eyes go wide with an enthusiastic "Mmm!" as she hits the custard inside.

Hannah's voice whispers in my head, a voice that, more and more these days, sounds simply like my own. *Stay present, Penny. Just stay here awhile.*

I try my very hardest.

Elen, of course, refuses to let Shelly and Alfredo pay for their pastries; she walks away from the booth with the two of them once Mateo returns. I watch her wander around the other tables after Shelly and Alfredo go, watch how she stops every five minutes to say hello to someone else, to chat and give hugs and laugh. The warm feeling in my chest grows as I watch her, as I watch everything, absorbing it all, trying to let myself feel just *this*, the here and now, an afternoon when the world is filled with only kindness.

"Mateo." I've been waiting to bring this up because I haven't known how they would react. I decide to ask now because if they say no, I know I'll be able to let it go. "I had an idea."

Mateo turns to me with the most affectionate curve of their mouth.

"No shit."

I roll my eyes, but I'm smiling.

"Yeah. About your art." I turn my chair toward theirs. "What if we hung some of it up on the walls of Delicious Donuts?"

They stare at me before their shoulders sag.

"Penny, I have to admit something to you. I am *really* tired of drawing donuts."

"No, no." I laugh. "Not donut pictures. *Your* art." I tap their chest. "What you just showed me on your tablet. Pieces from your sketchbook. Whatever you want to display." *Here*, I think. *While I can still be part of it.* "I suggested to Elen the other day that we should highlight local artists like a lot of coffee shops do, you know? Like an art gallery. Another way to connect to the community. I said we should start with you."

Their eyes search mine. And then they look away and stare out at the park.

"You absolutely don't have to if you don't want to," I continue. "I promise. I still think it's a good idea, but I'm sure there are other artists we can connect with if you're not interested. I just thought . . . well, your work deserves to be seen. And I thought it'd be a nice way to finish off the summer at the shop, you know? I was thinking we'd have a casual little art-gallery opening, keep the store open late so you could invite anyone you wanted to come see."

Mateo finally looks back at me. "Like who?"

I shrug as if I haven't already started planning it in my head.

"I chatted with Jack the other day, because the library likes to highlight artists from around here too, and he knows some local arts groups that would love to show their support. And I was thinking you could invite Ms. Fuentes if you want? I'm not sure if she checks her school email during the summer but we could try. And if that feels like too much, we could just invite your friends. Your family . . . if you want. Maybe some of the regulars would stop by."

Mateo's face has remained completely neutral this whole time.

But finally, they reach for my hand. They bring it to their face.

And they kiss my wrist, letting their lips rest there while my face heats.

Until they peck another line of kisses up my arm toward my elbow, and I laugh and tug my arm away. "Stop," I say, because it tickles, and we're in public.

"Okay," they say, and I know they're not talking just about the kisses.

"Yeah?" I look in their eyes, and they sparkle back at me.

"Yeah."

I smile.

And then Keena walks up with her three girls and wipes out the last of our old-fashioned glazed.

Customers dwindle as the day wears on, as the lazy heat increases. I eat two more matzoons. I've drunk so much lemonade, my teeth hurt.

Candace leans against my chair after her last run from the shop. What's here is all we have left.

"Hey," she says. "You two. Go take a fucking break. We're

almost out of here anyway." She motions to the gazebo. "Go have a waltz."

My heart stutters.

"I've seen you looking over there all day, Penny," Candace adds when neither of us moves. I blush again. It's embarrassing, realizing you're apparently obvious about everything.

Mateo stands first.

They offer me their hand.

My hive of bees hums to life.

"That's right," Candace says with approval. She collapses into my chair as Mateo and I walk away.

We cross the summer-dry brown grass hand in hand. Walk up the steps into the gazebo. It feels so nice, so couple-y, strolling through the park, holding hands with Mateo after a successful day, that I don't even know what to do with myself. Other than pretend I can keep this. That it can always be just like this.

"Hello." Nora greets us with a tired smile. "We were just about to start our last lesson."

The only other people in the gazebo are a man and a woman who look to be in their seventies. They're already in each other's arms, ready and in position.

Nora helps Mateo and me mirror them, moving our arms and nudging our feet into place. It occurs to me only when she's almost done that she's likely putting us in the typical gendered positions.

"I'll lead," I blurt out to Nora. "If that's okay?" I ask Mateo, worried they'll think I'm assuming something. It's not that

I don't think Mateo should lead; they've talked to me, a bit, about how they shift between embracing their masculine and feminine sides. Maybe they feel like leading too. It's just that it's been a nice day, all things considered, and . . . I want to.

But they only grin at me. My bees crescendo.

"Please."

To Nora's credit, she doesn't miss a beat; she switches our hands without comment.

"Have you ever done this before?" Mateo asks when she walks away.

I shake my head. "You?"

"No. I'm crew, remember?"

The music starts. Nora leads us through the steps.

I am not much more successful at this than I was at ballet. I step on Mateo's toes approximately thirty times. Neither of us can stop giggling, although we try to stifle it, which only makes us laugh harder. At one point, Mateo's elbow hits the back of the older woman next to us, and they burst out, "Oh my God, I am *so sorry*."

To which the woman does not reply at all.

She and her partner have not looked at anyone but each other since we stepped into the gazebo.

They already know the dance by heart.

I have to bite my lip so hard to keep from laughing that it hurts.

"Shut up," Mateo says, and steps on my foot on purpose.

We get the basic box steps down—kind of. I attempt to

twirl Mateo under my arm once. I'm pretty sure we actually do it all wrong, but Nora only smiles at us.

I'm not thinking about college, or climate change, or the state of my bank account, or California.

I'm at Verity Days with Mateo.

And we're waltzing.

TWENTY

College Fund: $2,900

"Jessica! My girl! *Say no!*" Swapna shouts at the TV.

Jessica says yes. She even cries as she does it, fanning her face in joy.

Swapna groans and collapses back onto the couch.

"Imagine crying over that cardboard box of a human. I bet these two won't even make it to the altar."

We're in Swapna's basement watching some reality-TV dating show Swapna has been obsessed with all summer. I disclosed halfway through the first episode that it's actually the first reality-TV dating show I've ever watched. Swapna paused Netflix to have a rather dramatic crisis over (1) what is wrong with me, and (2) whether she should have started me on another show to "fill in" my education.

I assured her I was fine starting with these skinny, sparkly people crying on a beach in Fiji. Privately, I was skeptical that I'd be interested in any of it. I was still game—because it was my first time ever seeing Swapna's basement and it's really comfy down here, and it's a different kind of Penny summer—but skeptical.

That was four hours ago.

I am now oddly invested in Jessica and Brandon, even though they are both the *worst*.

Swapna throws popcorn in her mouth. "I'm now rooting for Tad and Maddy *exclusively*," she declares, a statement she has made regarding at least three other couples since we embarked on this journey. It's somewhere near midnight now; her parents fell asleep an hour ago. At which point she immediately unearthed a bottle of cheap candy-flavored wine she'd stolen from her older sister earlier in the week when we made these plans.

I'm honored Swapna stole for me, so even though I've never drunk much, I'm obviously sharing it with her, for friendship. Also because it tastes like candy.

It's probably 40 percent responsible for my investment in Jessica and Brandon.

"Have they ever had any trans people on any of these shows?" I ask as I take another sip.

"Please. They haven't even given us a gay Bachelor yet. The world is full of cowards, Penny."

"God." Nothing has ever felt so true in my life. I want to scream out a window about it. "Seriously."

I watch some woman yell at some dude about the tiniest miscommunication I have ever witnessed. Something about a suitcase. I am concerned about the women on this show. Dating men seems to have really fucked them up.

"But they have to know," I sputter a minute later. "There are, like, so many queer people who would absolutely be up for crying on TV."

"To be fair, some shows have had queer people," Swapna says. "Although they almost always just look and act like the straight people."

"This is what I'm saying!" I shout. I know, of course, that I look like the straight people too. Somewhere in the back of my mind, I know that's okay, that there's not a certain way I or anyone has to look. Somewhere even further back in my mind, I realize that something has just happened there, inside my head. That I know *straight people* are not me. I mean, it's probably always been there in my head; I just never—

Whatever. The point is, at the moment, I only want to know "Where are the freaks?"

Swapna cups her hands around her mouth and bellows, "We want the freaks!"

"Freaks," I whisper. "Freaks, freaks—oh my God, Jessica. Do you even *like* him?"

Jessica and Brandon break up twenty minutes later.

By the time we reach the season finale, I'm so disgusted, my attention finally starts to waver.

I am also very, very sleepy.

"Hey, Swapna," I say around a yawn. "How was Massachusetts? I meant to ask earlier."

I know from Instagram that Swapna spent the last week of July outside of Boston visiting family and touring college campuses.

"Oh, you know." Swapna shrugs. "Full of aunties. We visit every summer. Also, *so* humid and gross. I know my family wants me to go to school out there, but I might agree only if I can come back here every summer. I was not built for East Coast humidity."

"Better than forest-fire smoke maybe."

Swapna squints.

"*Maybe*," she says. "But, Penny, have you been there? It's like you can't *breathe*."

I make a noncommittal hum, suddenly regretting asking about this. I don't want to admit I've never been to the East Coast. I don't want to hear about the campus of MIT. I don't want to be selfishly mad at Swapna that any of it's a possibility for her.

I don't want to admit that I'm increasingly jealous, the more I think about it, of even Mateo's visit to Cascadia. Everyone has gone somewhere this summer except for me. Even if I know, rationally, that camping with the triplets would be a nightmare.

I don't think the candy wine is mixing well with any of these thoughts. I get out my phone and scroll aimlessly on Instagram while Maddy gets fitted for her wedding dress on the TV. My first stop, as always, is seeing how many followers @verity.deliciousdonuts has now.

"Swapna." My brain veers itself to safer ground. "Did you know the donut is the second most profitable food in the country, after potato products?"

"Hey, now. *That* is a good useless piece of trivia to know."

"It's not useless, though." I tap my way to Northwest Donuts' account. "Because it's proof that *they*"—I shove my screen in Swapna's face—"overcharge for their products! Their donuts are *twice* the price of Delicious. Their specialty ones are almost thrice as much!"

"Thrice." Swapna squints at my phone, then yanks it out of my hand. "Nice."

"Yeah. I think it's my word of the summer."

"Remind me why you're yelling at me about Northwest Donuts? We don't even have one here."

"And we *won't*, Swapna. Have I not told you? They are my *enemy*."

This is when Swapna starts to laugh.

I fill her in on my summer mission. By the end, she's laughing so hard she snorts.

"*What?*"

"Oh, I just think donut-business enthusiast Penny is my favorite Penny yet." And after another giggle: "Your boss probably had no idea what she was signing up for when she hired you."

"Swapna." I grab hold of her arm. "She *really* didn't."

And then we both laugh, and for the first time in a long time, I don't feel like I'm being too much.

I just feel loved for being me.

"You have to help me," I say once we've calmed down. Because it suddenly seems obvious—how have I not enlisted the brain trust of the Knowledge Bowl team? I turn to face Swapna on the couch, pretzeling my legs. "I need dirt on

Northwest. I think that's the only way to *really* convince Elen she shouldn't sell to them. The CEO looks squeaky clean, but he's a CEO. You know he's probably donated to like"—I throw up a hand in frustration—"the Heritage Foundation or something."

"I dunno." Swapna already has Greg McCafferty up on her phone screen in all his North Face–clad glory, was googling him the second I started talking about it, and this is why I love her. "He doesn't strike me as a Heritage Foundation guy, but I guess you never really know."

"You *never* know," I say with feeling. The room is a little topsy-turvy.

"We should get Carmello on this," she says, and I gasp in affirmation. She immediately FaceTimes him.

"Dude." His sleepy voice enters the room. "You know what time it is? I thought we finally decided everything about whatever."

The first thing Swapna and I had done in this basement, before reality-TV dating shows made me concerned for America's entire adult population, was organize another Knowledge Bowl get-together this summer. We'd landed on a board-game night, but there had been a *lot* of arguing in the group chat about which board games should be in play. Since, shockingly, every nerd in the chat had a different one they were passionate about, each of which takes a minimum of approximately twenty-five hours to truly play.

I had suggested we have some basic crowd-pleasers as backup, like Apples to Apples. To which Blake had replied,

Please, Penny, we're not plebes.

"This is a new thing," Swapna tells Carmello. "Penny needs to know how to find the financial donations of CEOs."

"Ah." An audible yawn. "Well, there's the Federal Election Commission database, if you want to look up political contributions."

"I do!" I shout. "I do want that."

A few minutes later, Carmello is fully awake and on his laptop, helping us navigate the database. I yell in surprise when we actually find Gregory McGreggerson's name. And then I gasp.

"Wait," I say. "He donated to that dude, that dude who ran for Senate last year—"

"Oh, that dude is a *bad dude*," Carmello confirms.

"Yeah, *fuck* that dude," Swapna says.

"If he donated to *that* guy . . ." I trail off, both elated and sick to my stomach that I found what I wanted.

"Jackpot," Carmello finishes for me. "I'm sure you can find more dirt. I'll text you a few apps and portals you can look through. Northwest Donuts might not be big enough to show up in some of them, but you can try. I'm going the fuck to sleep after that, though."

"Fair. Thanks, Carmello."

He salutes and hangs up.

"So we're taking down CEOs," Swapna summarizes, before clicking off the TV. The next season started playing while we were talking to Carmello. I think Maddy and Tad got married. Maybe they're truly in love. Maybe they'll have five kids and move to California together. "I'm assuming you've also strategized about how you're going to secure your presidency of iTuna?"

"Oh." My phone pings with a series of texts from Carmello. "Um. Not... really."

"I mean, I'm sure you have it in the bag anyway."

"Maybe." I literally haven't thought about iTuna since June; since the first time Roman came into the shop, maybe. I'd kind of forgotten I even had an angle for my relationship with him, that he could help me become president of the conservation club. Every time he's come in since, I'm always just jealous that he's part of theater and knows Mateo in a way I don't.

I click on Carmello's first link.

"I think I'm going to focus on first-chair flute for band instead," I say, just to have something to say.

"Really?" A note of surprise enters Swapna's voice. "I thought you wanted both."

"Yeah." Of course I want both. I just—"Um. I don't know."

"Sorry if you're not ready to talk about extracurriculars yet." Swapna yawns and sinks farther down onto the couch, wiggling her feet under my thighs. "I know we still have a few weeks for all that. Have you done any of the summer work for AP Chem yet, though? Gods, it's going to be *brutal*."

I download an app and search another database while it loads.

"Yeah," I say, distracted. I'm sure it will be brutal. But like Swapna just said, I still have a few weeks before I have to think about that. "Did you know almost every culture has their own version of a donut?" I did some research after tasting Elen's Armenian treats at Verity Days. "Yeast, flour, sugar. It's like . . . a basic building block of humanity."

Swapna forces a half laugh into the pillow under her cheek, but I can tell she's mostly out.

"Sure, Penny," she slurs.

Within a half hour, I have four more awful far-right candidates that Northwest Donuts' CEO has donated to; I've also found two articles from last year about how they shut down an effort by their employees to unionize. Swapna snores softly next to me.

This is it. This is everything I needed.

I slide carefully away from the couch, find some blankets and extra pillows, and make myself a bed on the floor. Figure out how to dim the lights.

Except I'm not sleepy anymore.

I snuggle into the blankets as best I can and press my nails into my cuticles, my fingers into my wrist, counting the beats of my pulse as I stare into the dark, the quiet of Swapna's basement buzzing in my head.

TWENTY-ONE

College Fund: $3,300ish (I think)

I'm standing in front of Mateo's green house, and my nerves are somehow even worse this time.

Even if I know they shouldn't be. It feels like years since I drove here for our first driving lesson.

Mateo opens the door, and I breathe out.

"Hey."

"Hey."

They're wearing a *Hadestown* T-shirt and jeans. I tug at the bottom of my dress. I wasn't sure if a meeting-the-parents dinner required a fancy outfit. I told myself that even if it didn't, this sundress-plus-light-cardigan combo was casual enough not to be dorky, but—

"You look nice."

Mateo smiles as they say it, reaching for my hand. My skin heats, but my heart somehow calms.

These conflicting sensations of someone you like liking you back—desire and comfort all at once—are truly wild to experience at the same time. Especially wild that you experience them, like, constantly—every time they touch you, or look at you, or exist in the same sphere.

"Come on." Mateo tugs me into the house. "Dinner's almost ready. Dad's gone, like, full-out Italian supper for you. And Mom made sure everything's vegetarian."

I can smell it as I slip off my sandals. Garlic and tomato sauce and cheesy warmth.

It smells like . . . *home*. Like family.

The kind of smells that haven't permeated the Dexter-Laroche household in a long time.

Guilt tugs at my brain as soon as I think it. Just because my moms are busy, just because we've been surviving on box mac 'n' cheese and frozen pizza for years and have no real discernible connection to whatever random mixture of Northern European countries we descend from, it doesn't make us any less of a family.

Even if Mateo's house smells *really* good.

I stop short next to a recess in the foyer wall that holds a porcelain statue of a woman clad in blue and white. It is . . . large.

"This is Mary," Mateo says.

"Right." I nod. "The Virgin."

"So they say." Mateo shrugs with a small, self-conscious smile. "Being half Italian and half Mexican makes us . . . five hundred percent Catholic, approximately."

"Oh." I don't know exactly what to say to this. "I'm . . . agnostic, I think?"

"Is this Penny?"

I turn to find a short woman with dark hair swept back in a thick ponytail, a red apron over her white tank top.

"Hey, Mamí," Mateo says, and oh my God.

I have just met Mateo's mom. And it's possible the first words she heard out of my mouth were that I was super-indifferent about Jesus.

Thankfully, her dark eyes sparkle as she cups my cheeks in her palms. "Look at these freckles. I could just eat you up."

"Um," I say with eloquence. "Hi, Mrs. della Penna."

Her smile widens. "Please, call me Regina."

"Thanks for having me, Regina."

"Is that Penny I hear?"

A large man I assume is Mateo's dad barrels into the room. He throws an arm around Regina's shoulder and beams at me. He's wearing an apron that says *I'm not yelling, I'm Italian* and has a dishrag draped over his shoulder.

"H-Hi, Mr. della—"

"Call me Ed."

Ed shakes my hand vigorously, and then both Ed and Regina step back to continue smiling at me. Regina clutches her hands to her chest. I'm not sure either of my moms has ever worn an apron to cook in their entire lives. And for a moment, I feel like I've stepped inside an old family sitcom.

It is entirely wholesome.

And not at all what I expected.

"Dinner smells delicious," I hear myself say.

"Oh, I like you," Regina says.

"Mateo. Son." Ed claps a meaty hand on Mateo's shoulder. "Can you round up Lía? Dinner will be on the table in ten."

And that brief moment of tension that flits across Mateo's face when their dad says *son* . . .

Yeah. That was more what I'd expected.

Words pile up in my throat. *That felt a little unnecessary, Ed. You'd already said Mateo's name. Did it feel aggressive to you too, adding on a gendered term?*

But Mateo only nods, drops my hand, and walks away to shout the message up the stairs to Lía. I follow along behind them, not knowing what else to do. When they turn and say, "Want a tour?" with one of their genuine smiles, my shoulders relax, and I nod. But I can still feel the residual tension radiating from their body, present in the corners of their eyes.

We walk from the living room to the kitchen, from the bathroom to laundry room. I search for their cat, Luna, at every step, although Mateo assures me she hides whenever a new person enters the house and will be impossible to find for the next six hours. Which, of course, only makes me search harder. They hold my hand with their left and constantly run the other through their hair. All normal unconscious Mateo stuff.

But the whole time, I just want to yank them behind a closed door and kiss them. Hug that *son* away.

The atmosphere at dinner is better, or at least it starts off better, because Lía's there. I can somehow feel Mateo's tense edges softening the moment she sits next to them.

"Mateo tells me you have three six-year-old siblings, Penny?"

Regina asks as she passes me the garlic bread. She's sitting to my right while Ed sits at the head of the table like . . . like a real patriarchal family unit, I suppose. It continues to feel a little odd for me, like I'm still stuck in the sitcom. Maybe because I've never lived in a patriarchal family. And dinners at our house are normally so chaotic that no one's really the head of anything.

"I do," I confirm. "Bruno, Nikki, and Emma. Although they'll all be turning seven in a few months."

"Ay, dios mio. Tus pobres madres!" Regina throws her fingers up and across her face in the sign of the cross. It makes me laugh a little, even if I don't know if it's wrong to laugh at the sign of the cross. Just like I didn't quite know what to do when we held hands before the meal and said grace.

Mama D was raised Catholic too, and Verity is, like, 90 percent Christian and pretty loud about it, so I know some things. But the only times I've ever been inside an actual church were for Girl Scout meetings.

"Mateo tells us you excel in school too," Ed says once everyone's plates are full, and, okay, I should have expected this to be the Penny Hour, but I have to mentally adjust a little. Put on my Impressing Adults cap that I'm used to wearing during the school year but that I only now realize I haven't had to throw on in a while. Talking to Elen and customers at the shop feels different, less weighted with my college-app-worthy accomplishments. "Do you have plans for college?" he asks.

I straighten my spine and rattle off my environmental

science aspirations, the benefits of the program at Oregon State. Possibly getting my initial coursework done at BCC. Regina clucks her tongue and smiles even more warmly at me.

"How nice that you'll be close to home too! Bet your family loves that."

I smile politely at her, twirling my fork in my fingers. In actuality, me and my moms haven't talked about college in a while. Maybe because I've avoided talking about college ever since I heard the conversation about Nikki's medical bills through the vent.

"Yeah," I force out. "Although"—I glance briefly at Lía—"I was curious how you like USC, Lía."

Because . . . like I said. Just curious.

Lía talks about the campus, the dining-hall food. Being excited about taking the classes she actually wants to next year, now that she's past the freshman reqs. When I ask for specifics, she really takes off, face lighting up in a way I haven't seen before as she tells me the courses on her wish list: Archaeology of the Americas; Culture Change and the Mexican People; classes about magic and healing, sex and gender, culture and film. She talks about minoring in Spanish to become fully fluent. She and Mateo grew up hearing Regina's occasional casual use of it around the house and at the homes of relatives back in California, but mostly, they've been raised English-speakers in their mixed-heritage household, a fact that feels more incidental than purposeful based on the looks Regina and Lía exchange as Lía talks.

"I want to minor in Spanish too," I say. "I mean—I obviously don't have the cultural background, but especially if I ever travel for environmental work, I just . . . feel like we should all know it."

Regina turns her fond smile, which had been laser-focused on Lía, on me. She pats my hand.

"Ah, my dear," she says, the tilt of her mouth turning wry. "Ten cuidado a quién le dices eso."

"You know"—Ed lifts his beer pointedly—"many consider Italian to be the most beautiful language of all."

Both Lía and Regina roll their eyes in a way that I can tell is well practiced.

"*Dad.*" Like that, Lía switches from anthropology student to annoyed teenager. "We've talked about this. Italian courses are on my list too, but the significance of standing with Spanish-speakers in this country right now . . ."

The argument is barely heated; Ed smiles with his eyes at her the whole time, even when Lía starts talking about how she wants to add Regina's lineage, Dominguez, to her name.

"Yeah," Mateo pipes up, the first thing they've said in a while. "Me too."

My brain starts to wander as the conversation meanders.

I know I used to dream of a school like USC as a possibility for me. But right now, all I picture is Mateo. Mateo della Penna Dominguez. Meeting their sister for coffee. Walking across a college campus filled with palm trees. The California sun shining on their hair. A warm, ocean-scented breeze lifting it off their forehead. An oversize sketchbook stuck under their arm.

I don't realize how lost I am in this daydream until Ed reaches over and cuffs Mateo on the back of their head. I jump, startled.

"I'm glad Mateo finally has another good influence in his life," he says. "Maybe you and Lía can team up to get his head in the right place."

More words pile up in my throat: *Mateo's really smart, Ed. Have you ever debated American history with them? Isn't it obvious, in any case, how special they are? Their head's already in the right place.* But my brain's too thrown by the misgendering to get any of the words out.

Mateo doesn't look up from their plate when they say, woodenly, like they've said it a hundred times before: "College isn't for everybody, Dad."

My lower lip sticks out in a frown before I catch myself and school my face.

They're right, of course; college is by no means necessary for a ton of people, but... Mateo had that whole list of schools ready to go when I asked them about it during Verity Days. Mateo *wants* this.

They must just be hiding it from their parents because they think they'll disapprove of what Mateo wants to go to school *for*. But has Mateo even tried to tell them?

No, they must have, because of the way they said that *Real men don't go to art school* thing once, but maybe they should try again. Mateo's parents had to have seen their artwork, seen how talented—

"Do you want some more salad, Penny?"

I blink at Regina's question. Shake my head and dig into my ziti as the conversation moves on.

The food is great, and Lía even makes Mateo laugh a couple times, which I'm grateful for. Because otherwise, there is definitely something going on with Mateo.

They threw me a few smiles across the table when we first sat down. But as the dinner stretches on, they increasingly avoid eye contact, leaving me feeling somewhat stranded over here between their mom and dad, lost every time Ed misgenders them and I don't know what to do. *I don't want you to be my pronoun police.* But it's hard not to flinch every time it happens.

Lía, at least, always uses the right pronoun. Regina does too, once, albeit with such an obvious hesitancy that it almost feels worse.

It's not a hostile environment, exactly; Ed in particular laughs throughout the dinner. Other than the dig at Mateo about college, he looks at both of his children with fondness and is especially friendly to me. I'm stuck somewhere in the confusing in-between of enjoying this delicious dinner and hating every second of it. All I want Mateo to do is look at me so I know they're okay, but they won't.

Until our plates are almost clean and they stand abruptly.

"Me and Penny are going to go hang out in my room."

I stare up at them, my last bite of garlic bread still in my hand. Their voice sounds . . . off. Something is definitely not right here. Of course something's not right; their dad hasn't used the right words for them all night. But—

They turn from the table before I can get a good read on their face.

"Door open, young man," Ed says, voice stern. But the corner of his mouth tilts as he says it, like he's secretly pleased about . . . something? That we're going to hang out in Mateo's room? Does Mateo's dad, like, *want* us to go make out in his house?

My stomach squirms.

"Door open," Regina repeats, an eyebrow arched. Her mouth is flat for the first time all evening; she's clearly less enthusiastic about the situation.

Mateo is already on the move. I abandon my garlic bread, throwing everyone a "Thank you for dinner" and a smile I hope looks normal before rushing after them.

I quick-walk in their wake up the stairs and down a carpeted hallway to the last room on the left.

They wait for me to step inside.

And then Mateo definitively closes the door.

They stare at the back of it for a long minute—there's a poster there for a band I don't recognize—as if needing to dwell in this moment of defiance. Even though the rest of their family is still downstairs, unaware they've even done it.

I stand in the middle of the room, pushing my fingernails into my cuticles. I was so looking forward to thoroughly inspecting Mateo's room, but now all I can look at is them—the back of their neck, the tightness of their shoulders, the closed door in front of them.

Finally, they sigh. The tension drops out of their body as

they throw themself onto the bed in the corner of the room. They flop on their back, holding their hands over their face.

Cautiously, I lie down next to them. They lower their hands as soon as they feel my weight dip the mattress, and hold out an arm. I gratefully snuggle into their side, resting a palm on their chest. Like that, I can breathe again. Whatever mask I'd tried to put on for Mateo's parents is lifted, and I'm just so, so glad to be next to them again. I force all the words in my throat to hold, waiting for Mateo to speak first.

"I have a confession," they say.

"Yeah?"

Mateo sighs once more, staring at the ceiling.

"When I told my parents we were dating, when they invited you over here . . ." Mateo shakes their head once, twice, their hair shifting against the pillow. "They both got this look on their faces, my dad especially. Like . . . like I'd finally turned straight. Or cis. Or something. Like I'd finally done something right."

I bite my lip, waiting for them to continue. My pulse beats in my fingertips.

"I should've said something right then. Assured them there's still nothing straight about me. About"—they motion with their free hand to me, to them—"any of this. But for some reason, I almost started . . ." They swallow. "Looking forward to it. To them actually being excited to meet someone I care about, you know? Me not being . . . a problem."

"Mateo."

"So fucking dumb." They blow out a long breath. "Anyway.

As it turns out, it actually felt way fucking worse somehow."

I shift my hand from their chest and snake it around their side. I don't know what to say, so I just hug them.

"Sorry," they add after a minute. "I know it's kind of fucked up. That I was . . . using you, in a way."

"It's okay." Because this isn't about me. It's about Mateo and their parents and what the world forces on us. "I get it. You can use my girlness anytime if it's useful to you."

I feel the huff of a half laugh ruffle my hair.

"I can't believe you have to live with that every day," I say after a minute, my voice soft. "Them misgendering you all the time. That must be so hard."

Mateo remains quiet. I worry I've messed up until suddenly they shift, sliding their arm out from under me. They turn until they're on their side too. Until we're facing each other.

"You know." Our faces are so close, our noses almost touch. I'm so happy to have their eyes back. "You're the only person who has never once misgendered me from the moment we met. I had been thinking about it back then, during the move. What I was going to do when I started at my new school. I was still pissed about leaving California, but part of me thought, *Well, maybe this is my chance. To start fresh, use new pronouns where nobody knows me, so people can get to know me for who I am from the beginning.*

"But then my dad dropped me off at school that first day. And as soon as I walked in, I was like, *What the fuck was I thinking?* Middle school here was clearly just as shitty as middle school there. Of course I couldn't stroll in and be like,

Hey, I'm the new genderqueer brown kid. I mean, I could've if I were braver, but . . . anyway. Then you were so . . . you."

Mateo smiles, a small, serious thing.

"And I just knew. That I could trust you, that it wouldn't be a big deal. And you didn't make it a big deal. You never have."

My breath catches in my throat. Not from what Mateo's saying; being a courteous human being shouldn't be a big deal.

Mostly, I'm having trouble breathing because of the way Mateo's looking at me.

"Do you think I'm a coward?" Their eyes search mine. "Because I don't call my parents out on it?"

I start to shake my head, but Mateo keeps talking as if they weren't truly looking for my answer.

"I know it's not perfect, going along with it. It felt more embarrassing with you here. But most of the time it's just . . . easier. And honestly, it doesn't always bother me when they use the wrong pronoun. Especially my mom. Every now and then, she'll try to use *they*, like she did tonight. Which is almost more painful, seeing how awkward she is about it."

I laugh even though it's not funny. "Yeah," I agree. "It's bad."

"Right?" They laugh with me. "Like she's saying something she's sure she's pronouncing wrong, not one of the simplest words in the English language. But . . . I feel like she still sees me, you know? As much as she can. She knows I'm different and she's mostly okay with it. The pronouns don't matter as much when I know she's not disappointed in who I am. It's just when my dad goes all . . ." Mateo takes a breath and then speaks in a lower voice: "'Well, *son*, *real* men study engineering and chop down trees with their dicks.' It's like, what the hell is he even trying to do here? He *knows*." Their voice softens in defeat. "He knows."

I reach up to tuck their beautiful hair behind their ears.

"I don't think you're a coward, Mateo," I whisper. "Not one little bit."

Mateo stares at me. Lets me keep messing with their hair, over and over. Until they lean forward and kiss me.

And they kiss me and kiss me and kiss me.

Somewhere, in the back of my mind, my anxiety can't quite forget that we are in Mateo's room. That Mateo's mom or dad or sister could open the door at any moment. But my body's pretty sure that the advantages of being with Mateo like this—comfortably, horizontally, perfectly soft and close and aligned—are so superior to making out in their truck like we've mostly been doing that the risk is worth it. Our legs intertwine; their mouth wanders down my neck while my hand ventures under their shirt. I've lost my cardigan; the hem of my dress has drifted up to a place I should probably be concerned about but can't quite muster up the energy to fix. One of their hands follows it, tingling up my thigh; I make a noise I didn't expect.

And immediately stiffen in embarrassment.

"Penny," Mateo says into my collarbone. Their voice sounds strained.

I close my eyes, working to steady my breath.

Mutually, our bodies grow still.

"Yeah," I say.

It's getting harder and harder each time I make out with Mateo to stop making out with Mateo.

Last week after Verity Days. Every day for the past month that we've had a closing shift together, in the shadows behind the shop once we've locked up.

The truth is, I had barely even let myself dream about these kinds of things—this kind of physical closeness, this *want*—in my lonely late-night fantasies about my future college self. It was all deep conversations and science lectures and long walks and maybe some, like, really good hugs whenever I let myself get carried away with the imaginary future person who would Get Me.

Which, listen. I know. I know.

I just could never quite imagine physical desire as a realm I'd actually feel truly comfortable in. Let alone be . . . ravenous for.

"Mateo," I say, not really wanting to talk about this but also *needing* to. "I don't . . . I don't know if I'm ready yet for . . ."

"Sex." Mateo finishes my sentence. Their forehead is still pressed against my neck. Their hair tickles my chin.

"Yeah." I swallow. "But I also kind of . . . want to."

My face heats almost painfully. Like a sugared circle of dough dropped into burning oil.

Mateo lets out a very long breath before finally lifting their head. They rest it back on their pillow, looking at me.

"Yeah."

"But we're too young, right?"

I'm infinitely irritated at myself, cheeks somehow heating

even further as soon as the question leaves my mouth. I know exactly how childish it sounded. When everything that runs through my veins when Mateo touches me is . . . the opposite of childish.

Mateo smiles at me, lazy and intimate.

"Pen, I'm pretty sure there are people in our class who have been having sex since, like, seventh grade."

"I know." I wrinkle my nose. "Gross."

Mateo laughs.

"But like . . ." I press on, trying to articulate what I'm feeling. "All those people are way cooler than me."

Mateo's smile fades as they lift an eyebrow. "I feel the opposite, actually."

I blow out a breath, frustrated.

"You know what I mean, though."

"I really don't."

Annoyed, I drop my eyes to their chest, away from the intensity of their stare. I'm embarrassed and confused, but now that my brain has opened this can of worms, as always, it can't stop. Mateo runs a hand up and down my arm. "Have you . . . " I ask.

Mateo doesn't answer right away, silence hanging between us. I immediately regret asking. Their hand pauses on my arm.

But then they sigh.

"Not with Kevin Swanson. He wasn't ready either."

And for a second, I hate Kevin Swanson a bit less.

Just a little bit, though.

"But a couple summers ago, before freshman year . . . there

was this guy. He doesn't go to Verity; I met him online. We met up in Salem, and . . . anyway, it was bad. Like, I try not to even think about it."

I frown.

"Did he hurt you?"

Mateo shakes their head vigorously, covering their face with a palm again.

"No, nothing like that; it was just . . ." They laugh a little, dropping their hand. Their cheeks are flushed. "*Bad*, Penny. It was bad."

Their laughter makes me smile, though I'm sure whatever happened that summer isn't something to smile about; it's something I don't want to think about either. But I am glad they told me. That they continue to trust me.

"I'm sorry, Mateo."

"It's okay. I'm just saying that everything we've done, every time I've gotten to kiss you and touch you, has been so much better than that. Which means I know it would be different with you."

"Yeah." I swallow again, wishing I had something more eloquent to say.

"I think, sometimes," they say slowly, eyes turning pensive, "the *idea* of sex is larger than life, bigger than actually *having* sex. You know? Like there's so much pressure and expectation around it, around having it or not having it. But in reality, like, actually doing it isn't that big of a deal, in the end, when you both want to do it and you trust each other and no one else knows but you."

I let Mateo's words sink in. They are very mature and reasonable. Honestly, they make me want to have sex with them even more. Like, right now.

But then I think about the mechanics of it.

I lift my head from the pillow, propping myself on an elbow.

"But, like—" I gesture at nothing. "Mateo. We would *be naked*. You would be—"

I *am* glad we're talking about this, I am, but I still cannot process *out loud* exactly which body parts would—and—oh my God.

"We don't *have* to be naked," Mateo says. "Technically. Even though, to be clear"—their eyes travel to my exposed collarbone—"I would prefer it."

Oh my *God*.

"I think it's definitely a big deal!" I splutter, my voice sounding way too loud for such a delicate conversation.

And the part of me that wants this so bad feels... ashamed, like I'm ashamed of my body, or theirs, when I'm not. I *want* to be sex-positive. It's just... I don't know. I need *all* of me to be ready, not just the extra-horny part. Discovering I even have an extra-horny part has been a lot to process.

But Mateo only laughs again. And then they wrap both arms around me and pull me against their chest.

"Okay," they say softly into my hair. "Okay."

And I feel so safe and cared for I could cry.

Even when Mateo speaks again a minute later.

"Last thing, though. If you ever do feel comfortable doing more, it doesn't have to be, like..." They pull back to make a lewd, middle-school gesture with their fingers that I want to roll my eyes at. But incredibly, it only makes me more turned on. Good God, how is this not mortifying for people? "Pee-in-vee, you know?" Mateo finishes, as if the gesture weren't enough. "There's other stuff we can do."

"Yeah," I say. "I know."

Like, I'm pretty sure I know.

"Seriously, though." Mateo kisses the top of my head. "No matter what, I'm good, okay? Just . . . keep letting me know how you're feeling."

I turn that over in my mind a few times. What *No matter what, I'm good* implies. That Mateo would likely be down to have sex with me, like, right now, if we could. But that they also don't mind if we don't.

I turn my face farther into their chest, rubbing my nose against their T-shirt.

"How are you so good?" I mumble into the cotton. "I can't believe I was such a jerk to you for so long."

"What was that? I only heard *warugoobeevoolong*."

I laugh, and before I can answer them, Mateo's door swings open.

Their hand tightens against my arm but relaxes when we see it's just Lía. She waves her hand through the door and is gone again.

"That doesn't look like there's room for Jesus!" she shouts as she walks back down the hall.

Mateo breathes out and says, quietly, "Lía's a good sister."

"Yeah," I agree, smoothing my dress back over my legs,

something I very much wish I had done before Lía opened the door and probably saw my underwear. "She is."

Mateo traces patterns down my arms again.

"I bet you're a good sister too. We haven't talked about it much, but it must be a lot, helping take care of three little kids."

I shrug. It is, but my mind's wandering somewhere else. Someplace far away from the triplets.

"Hey." I tap a finger against Mateo's chest and stare at the navy-painted wall next to the bed. "What you said before, about . . . nothing about any of this being straight."

"Mm-hmm."

"I've been thinking more about that lately."

Even though Mateo is already still, I somehow feel them go . . . stiller.

"Yeah?"

"I guess I've never thought too much about, like, myself and . . . or, like, I have, because probably everyone has, but since I've never actually dated anyone before, it didn't seem like something I had to, like, decide, but so . . . I guess I'm not? Straight, I mean."

Wow. Even more eloquent than I thought that would come out.

"Well . . . yeah," Mateo says after a long silence. And somehow I feel relieved when I hear the not-so-hidden laughter in their voice.

I prop myself up on an elbow again to look at them.

"Because I'm dating you, right?"

"Because you're dating me, but, Penny..." Mateo grins up at me. "When I asked you at Grumpy Toad's who you think is hot, your first two answers were women."

"Oh." I flop back down on the mattress and stare up at Mateo's ceiling. "Okay, yeah, but ... everyone thinks women are hot. Because, like, they are."

Mateo turns to muffle their laughter into my shoulder.

"Oh." I blink some more at the ceiling. It's like an *actual* light bulb, like high beams, flicking on in my brain. "Oh no, Mateo. That's a super-gay thing to think, isn't it?"

They laugh even harder into my skin, squeeze me so tight my ribs hurt.

I start to laugh with them, but something is bubbling up in me so big and light that I know I'm on the edge of some kind of precipice, that if I truly start laughing I won't be able to stop. And I need to grasp the edges of this conversation before it's gone.

"Okay, okay, but wait. So am I, like ... bi? Because there's still ... you know, like, Roman Petroski—"

The glee in Mateo's eyes fades, but only a little. I can't finish my sentence, but I can feel Mateo gets it. I'm not attracted to everyone, but I'm also attracted to ... *everyone*.

"It's not something I can answer for you, Penny."

"Are *you* bi? Or—"

"I prefer queer." Mateo lifts a shoulder. "There's nothing wrong with bi, or pan, or ... I mean, I know people get real specific about their labels sometimes, but queer's always felt more fluid to me. And if there's anything I'm most closely aligned with, it's being . . . not exactly one thing."

I look back at the ceiling.

Take a few deep breaths.

Mateo waits for me. So patient and good and hot.

Finally, after a minute—

"So I'm queer."

Mateo leans in and kisses my neck, just below my ear. They don't say anything, but their touch is a confirmation. A reassurance.

You would think, with queer parents, I would have figured this all out before. But whenever I did think about it, I never felt like . . . I don't know. Like I was the kind of person who had the right to claim that for myself.

I've always been so *boring*.

But now that I've said it out loud, something clicks into place in my chest, and I feel . . . special. Powerful, almost. Stronger inside my skin than I did before.

After a moment, I turn to Mateo. I touch their ear, where their pierced hole is almost completely closed up.

"What would you do?" I whisper. "If you didn't live with your dad." I think, again, about their art schools in California. And this time, right here, inside this conversation, I'm 98 percent not sad about them. "If you didn't live in Verity."

Mateo studies me a moment and then flops onto their back, a small curve in the corner of their mouth as they stare at the ceiling. *Dreaming Mateo Smile.*

"Well, I'd get these repierced." They touch their ears. "I think on at least one side I'd get a whole bunch, actually, so I can have shiny stuff all up and down, you know? And I want to pierce my nose too."

They rest their hand on their stomach.

"And I think . . . I don't necessarily feel a need to wear, like, dresses and pearls and stuff, but I think I could really get into caftans. Kimonos. Open, flowy shit with, like, booty shorts underneath." They laugh. "You know? A real queer Stevie Nicks kind of vibe, but with, like, Celia Cruz flair."

Their smile grows.

"And then the next day I could switch into, like, punk."

"Like fishnets and stuff?"

Mateo's nose wrinkles.

"I don't know. I think just . . . a lot of ripped shit and sharp things that could hurt you."

I picture it, and it feels like seeing a whole new dimension of Mateo. Like they're peeling their skin back and showing me different layers. Ones where they can be queerer than they can be now. Ones where they can be free.

I rest my forehead on their shoulder and smile into their T-shirt.

"Anyway. That's all kind of superficial stuff, but I think if I could do whatever I wanted, I'd only go to art school for, like, a year, or two, max. Just so I can learn the stuff I need to know that I couldn't get at Verity High. And then I'd peace out, and . . . I don't know. Find a wealthy benefactor or something. I'd spend my days walking around whatever city I'm in and making art."

A pause.

I wonder, idly, if Mateo owns booty shorts.

"I know that's not really how it works. But if we're fantasizing here . . . yeah."

Another moment passes before Mateo shifts their shoulder against my face.

"What about you? If you could do anything you wanted to do."

I'd get to be with you forever.

The thought comes to my brain so fast, so simple and easy and true, that I almost say it out loud.

Except.

Except none of Mateo's dreams had anything to do with me.

I swallow. Try to steady my pulse before I answer.

"I'd plant enough trees," I say slowly, "to keep the whole world cool. And then I'd invent something. Something we could put in the oceans or the forests or all the big empty spaces of the world like we've put windmills and solar panels, except . . . it would trap carbon dioxide and break it down. Balance the atmosphere, you know? So all the storms stop being so scary, so everything stops drying out, so we can save more water. And then . . . then we could focus on saving everything else."

A confused lump forms in my throat. Why was that so hard for me to pull out of my brain when it used to be so close to the surface? I feel envious or embarrassed or *something* that I didn't have something closer to Mateo's dreams to share. They're able to picture themself moving through the world, strong and beautiful and full of color in this concrete way, and I . . .

I have never truly pictured myself beyond how I am right now.

"But." My voice comes out scratchy. "I know that's not really how it works either."

If there were an easy way to magically solve climate change, someone would have done it by now.

I want to give a better answer. Something more personal, something about *me*, not just my anxieties about environmental destruction. Maybe Mateo wants me to talk about Stanford. But I'm tired of thinking about those dreams.

I've spent almost every waking hour since I was in sixth grade thinking about college. I don't want to think about any of it anymore. Right now, I don't want to think about anything outside of this room.

Mateo turns back onto their side. Scooches down until we're face to face.

And even though Mateo's door is still open, they kiss me again. And I kiss them back until we're even more entangled than we were before, until I'm dizzy. Mateo slips the spaghetti strap of my dress down, does something with their mouth that hurts but that I think I like anyway. We kiss until I think, *I have become a reckless person*, and it doesn't even scare me. Reckless is better than boring.

We kiss until, with another pained "Penny," Mateo makes us stop.

Until I have the presence of mind to look at the time, to accept I have to go.

We take a few minutes to cool off before Mateo walks me

down the stairs to their front door. Ed and Regina wave at me from the living-room couch, distracted by an episode of *Chicago Fire*.

I'm about to open the door when Mateo says, "Hey. Look who showed up to say goodbye."

They lean down and pick up a white cat with a patch of gray covering one ear. They wrap Luna in their arms, kiss her head, and grin. They wave one of her paws at me.

And for a second, time seems to freeze. It's like I'm taking a picture of this moment, storing it inside every nucleus in every cell in my body. Like if I opened Mateo's front door and discovered the apocalypse, maybe it would be okay. Because this would have been enough.

When I get home, Mom's sitting in the living room frowning at her phone. Emma's asleep next to her, her tiny face smooshed onto Mom's leg. It's late, far past the triplets' bedtime; I wonder if Emma was having trouble sleeping again.

I almost ask about it, but then Mom looks up at me, and her mouth drops open.

"Penny," she says, voice soft. Her hand holding the phone slowly falls to the couch.

"Hi." I clutch my bag in my hands, self-conscious. Can she tell, somehow, all the feelings swirling inside of me? Is she . . . is she disappointed in me? "Did I come home too late?"

Mom shakes her head and clears her throat as if she's snapping out of a trance. She smiles at me, but it doesn't feel like a regular Mom smile, the one she normally tosses out so easily every day.

"No, Penny Bear. You're just fine."

"Emma's okay?"

Mom runs a hand over Emma's back. "She's fine too. Just needed some extra one-on-one time. And they're all too big for me to carry up the stairs. I haven't had it in me to wake her up."

"Do you need help?" I'm already walking closer, ready to help get Emma to bed, but Mom holds up a hand. Shakes her head.

"We're good, Penny Bear." She gives me another wobbly smile. "You just get yourself to sleep, all right?"

I bite my lip.

"Okay. Good night, Mom."

"Good night, love."

When I flip on the light in the bathroom upstairs five minutes later, Mom's funny looks suddenly become clear.

Oh my God.

Little purple bruises from the base of my neck down to my collarbone. I slap my hand over them with a small gasp. I'll be able to cover them up, I think, with a T-shirt that has a thick enough collar, but in the exposure of my sundress, they are all too visible for the world to see.

I stare at myself in the mirror, at my wide eyes and wrinkled dress.

And feel my heart, beating like a songbird underneath my palm.

TWENTY-TWO

Amount Spent on Gas for Dolly
This Summer: Too Much

What was it I said to Mateo earlier this summer about August?
Once you hit August, it's all over.

I've been avoiding my coup de grâce of Save Delicious Donuts!: Telling Elen that the CEO of Northwest Donuts is a man who doesn't deserve to own any of Verity's Main Street. Who probably hates everything me and Mateo and Candace are. Who probably thinks the Arshakyans themselves aren't American enough.

But while Elen has been supportive of all my efforts thus far, I know this conversation will be hard. I know it'd be easier to just let it go. Mateo has implied that maybe I should just let it go.

And I know I can't.

The day of Roman Petroski's end-of-summer party, I break.

"I have to tell her today." Mateo and I are on the floor of my room, their artwork spread all around us. They're trying to decide what pieces to include in their Delicious Donuts gallery, which will debut in just two days.

They look up at me, the bridge of their nose wrinkling.

"Today? But . . . we were just there." We both opened the shop this morning, an unfortunate scheduling, being that we'll be up late tonight at the party, and my brain normally blinks out around dinnertime on days that I open. We spent most of the shift laughing at ourselves for not having the foresight to request at least a mid shift. The only thing keeping us going is knowing we both have tomorrow off. At least, until we go in in the afternoon to set up Mateo's art.

"I know, but as I was leaving, Elen mentioned that she'll be at the shop late tonight finishing up some paperwork and making sure the lobby walls are all clean and ready for us."

"Cool."

"Yeah, sounds like we'll just have to bring the pieces tomorrow, and everything will be pretty much ready to go. So I was thinking I'll stop there on the way to the party. It feels like the perfect time, just me and her, so I can say everything I want to say." My stomach roils even as I force my voice to sound confident about the plan. "You can head to the party on your own and I'll meet you there."

Mateo's been staring down at the floor again, but they pick up my hand, kiss me on the wrist. Their act of reassurance that makes my heart flutter every time.

"Okay. Just remember that no matter what she says, you've done so much for her this summer. She should be thankful, and you should be proud."

I swallow. "Thank you."

"Now, please tell me again that this bike one isn't fucking dumb."

I slide closer to their side and rest my head on their shoulder. "It's not. Someone will definitely buy that one."

In reality, Mateo already has the pieces they're going to show picked out, knows which ones will be for sale and which ones won't; they likely already knew what they wanted the moment I suggested the gallery to them at Verity Days two weeks ago. But they insisted they needed to look through everything here, where their brain is clearer than in their own house.

Even with all the self-deprecating jokes they've made over the past two weeks about their donut-shop gallery, the closer it comes, the more nerves they show. It's different, displaying their work in public versus a high-school hallway.

I've never felt so honored in my life, being witness to those nerves. Being surrounded by Mateo's talent, cocooned inside the beautiful mess of it, here on my bedroom floor.

I know it's possible that Mateo's brain is simply clearer *anywhere* other than their own house, that perhaps my house is only convenient for this task. But they've spent so much time here lately, carving their own little spot inside our realm of chaos, that I like believing it's more than that.

First my moms had their turn: after my dinner at Mateo's house, they made their own nice meal here for Mateo. Which, don't tell them, wasn't as good as Edward della Penna's cooking but was still a *big deal* for the Dexter-Laroches. All of us home sitting around the table with nice plates and everything.

Mateo drew everyone's portraits after dinner, sitting by the bay window, sketching them one by one. Those portraits have become prized possessions—for the triplets but I could tell for Mom and Mama D too.

And then we made s'mores in the backyard.

They've come over a few times since then to help me babysit, and they're this painfully wonderful combination of awkward and kind with all three of my siblings that makes my heart feel like it's going to explode out of my chest.

I can't quite remember the last time I had anyone slip into my world like this. I'm not sure if I've had anyone here, seeing all of my life, since the triplets were born.

"Did Ms. Fuentes ever get back to you?"

Mateo nods, their hair brushing against my cheek. They move to examine another drawing.

"Yeah. She's coming."

"Mateo! That's great."

Mateo smiles, shakes their head.

"What?"

They only lean over and kiss my temple. "Nothing."

The light is perfect and golden when I pull into the parking lot of Delicious Donuts a few hours later. Elen's standing on one of the orange booths hammering a nail into the wall when I unlock the door and walk in.

"Penny," she says, "you have to apologize to Mateo for me about this."

She rests the hammer against one hip and gestures toward

the wall with her other hand. Specifically, toward the rectangles of paint on which the posters that have always been here were hanging. They're currently propped against the front counter in a dusty stack.

"I can't remember the last time I took those frames down. Can you believe the paint used to look like this?" She laughs.

It is a little funny, seeing how much the sun that streams through the windows every day has affected the shop, the sporadic blocks of brighter yellow where the posters used to be.

If anything, it gives more credibility to my feelings: Look at how long this little shop has been here. Look at how comfortingly consistent it's been.

"Mateo won't mind," I assure her. "It'll probably make them laugh."

"Gosh, I hope so. Now." She maneuvers herself down from the booth, brushes her hands together. "What are you doing here on a Saturday night when you should be out there being young?"

I smile even as my nerves tumble in my stomach. Because little does she know that, for once, I actually do have plans to do that.

I just have to do this first.

"I was hoping to talk to you about something."

"Naturally." She gestures toward the booth she was just standing in; I slide into one side while she sits in the other. I place the folder I've brought with me between us and take a deep breath.

"I want to start by thanking you for how much you've let me run with my ideas this summer. It's been a really meaningful experience for me, and I hope it's helped your business." Elen nods, tilts her head. Waits for me to continue. I lick my lips. "We haven't actually talked about Northwest Donuts since June, though."

It's almost imperceptible, but I still see it. The way every muscle in Elen's face freezes.

I push forward in a rush, flipping open the folder.

"I know it's your decision, and I may be overstepping boundaries in bringing this up at all, and it's possible you've already turned down the deal anyway, but I've been doing some research on them this summer, and the CEO, Greg McCafferty, he—"

"Penny." Elen's voice is so quiet and serious, I actually shiver, but I have to keep going. I've worked too hard not to get this out.

"He's donated to a lot of awful causes, a lot of horrible politicians. He may have started his business in Seattle, but he lives on a ranch in Texas now, so he's not even loyal to the Northwest."

"Penny—"

"And he's actively worked against his employees unionizing. Last year, their health insurance—"

"Penny!"

She says it so loud this time that I flinch, dropping the paper in my hand. It is the first time Elen has ever yelled at me. Her hands are curled into fists, hovering just over the edge of the table, as if she just held herself back from slapping it. Her eyes are clenched closed, her chest rising on a deep breath.

"Penny," she says more quietly, forcing her eyes back open. "Please. Stop. I don't want to know."

I swallow, heart hammering. "I'm sorry. Like I said, I don't want to overstep. I thought I could just leave my research here with you, and—"

"Penny."

She turns to the side, stares through the windows at the twilight painting Main Street. Eventually, she turns back to me. Her face is different this time. It's vulnerable, open, like she's not my boss at all.

Her face looks so, so apologetic.

And in the split second before she says it, I feel myself trying to memorize this, the perfect curve of her eyebrows, the gray streaks in her thick dark hair, the light from the windows painting the side of her cheek, the way you try to capture a memory as it's happening when you know something's ending.

"I don't want to know because I've already said yes, Penny. I'm selling the shop to Northwest Donuts."

What hits my chest is such a funny combination of horror and a complete lack of surprise. Like as soon as she says it, my brain says: *Of course. Of course. Did you really think you could save this place with some Instagram posts and stickers?*

And I feel so ashamed, so young and small, that I don't even know what to say. Don't know how long I'll be able to sit here. How long I can keep my face composed.

"Oh, Penny. I'm so sorry. I've been so selfish. I should have said something to you earlier, when I knew for sure I'd be taking the deal. You've just . . . you made this summer so *fun*. This shop has been my entire life. But sometimes, when you've done the same thing for so long . . . it starts to lose its color, like these walls here. You start to forget why any of it matters."

Briefly, Elen covers her mouth with an elegant hand. She drops it just as quickly, blinking and shaking her head. When she meets my eyes again, they glimmer.

Cool, composed Elen Arshakyan is actually choking up.

And all I feel is numb.

"You brought back the color this summer, Penny. Everything you've done—Verity Days, documenting it all online, the stickers and the T-shirts . . . these are all things I can now take with me for the rest of my life. You made me feel like my little donut shop was *important*. It's . . . it's been such a gift, Penny. Like the proper goodbye I didn't know I needed."

"But . . ." I know this is exactly what Mateo told me: *Just remember that no matter what she says, you've done so much for her this summer*. I know that Elen is saying nice things. But all I can feel is *Bullshit*.

"But I still didn't save it."

"Penny, you're sixteen. You're an *incredible* sixteen-year-old, but even you can't change the circumstances of my life. But . . . you *tried* to save something you cared about." Elen leans forward, clasps her hands together on top of my folder, as if what she's saying now is important, like she wants me to listen. But everything has gone a little blurry. I can't quite focus on any one spot. "You stepped into this place and you made it better from day one. The only person who has anything to be sorry about here is me, for taking advantage of your kindness, and I may not ever forgive myself for that. But, Penny, sometimes trying is the entire point."

These are the same exact things I always tell myself, the things I have honed in my brain with Hannah's help. It's always important to try.

Bullshit, bullshit, bullshit.

My breathing picks up, my throat tightens. I cannot have a panic attack here, in front of Elen. I can*not*.

I make myself ask the last few questions I need to know, telling my body that we're going to leave soon. That this is all almost over.

"But . . . why? Why not pass it on to Alex, at least?"

Elen's face calms into the Elen I know. Steady. Confident.

"I want to retire, Penny. Running a small business is hard, especially one as small as this. For three decades now, I've barely been able to take a vacation. I want to do all the things I haven't been able to do with my life for too long. As for Alex . . . Alex is autistic, Penny. My son is skilled at many, many things, especially making donuts." She smiles, still sad, but true. My brain processes this new fact, reliving every short interaction I've had with Alex this summer. Wishing I had understood him better earlier. "Running a business is something many people on the spectrum can do, of course, but it is not something *Alex* will ever be able to do. My deal with Northwest is contingent on them keeping him, so he can keep his routines. It's a way to make sure my child is secure while finally letting myself step back. As scary as that is for me, it's . . . time. For *me* to try."

I nod. Absently push my nails into my cuticles under the table.

"You deserve that," I make myself say. "Alex does too. I'm glad that . . . that everything's working out. When will the sale be final?"

"This fall sometime. I've been letting the bank and my lawyer do their thing for a few weeks now. But it sounds like the transition should be relatively seamless. The shop might be closed for a week or two. Their management will likely do some new training, bring on some new hires, obviously redesign the place. I have to truly let go at some point, but I am hoping that this will still be an important stop on Main Street. Just one with a new logo on the door."

I nod again, staring blankly into the empty space behind Elen's shoulder.

For a few weeks now.

The words fall out of my mouth clumsily: "I have to quit, Elen."

Elen's shoulders droop; her mouth pulls into a thin line.

"Well. I can't say I'm surprised. I know school is starting up again soon anyway, but . . ." She shakes her head, sits up straight again, as if her mind is already recalculating what this will mean for the schedule. "I only ask that you finish out your shifts this week. And then I'll wish you a very wonderful junior year as long as you promise to stop by and eat Alex's donuts sometimes."

"Okay." I'm already getting out of the booth. I need to go. *Need to go, need to go.*

"Penny." Elen stands, clasps her hands in front of her. "I hope . . ." She stops herself, shakes her head again. "I'll miss you, Penny, just like I still miss having your mother down the street. I hope we can all keep in touch somehow."

"Okay," I say again. *Need to go, need to go.* I shuffle to the door. "Bye, Elen."

She lifts her hand in a silent wave.

I stare down the road before I get inside Dolly. The lampposts have turned on. I've spent a lot of time with this view these past two months, often after stealing kisses with Mateo behind the shop. I've wondered if a street had a memory, how many other kisses this one has seen. How many secrets and tears and inside jokes, how many sunsets and dripping ice cream cones.

When I look down it now, all I see is an empty storefront at the end of the block, a dark space where my mom's dream used to be. To my left, I see a small business started by immigrants that's being taken over by a corporate chain. I see all the spaces between that will be empty one day.

All I see are the things I'll never be able to save.

TWENTY-THREE

Days Until Junior Year: 6

Thank God for Google Maps.

I follow the voice of its navigation to the Petroskis' upscale community in the deepening dark. I am barely hanging on, but I can turn here. Turn left at the light. Look for my destination on my right.

The numbness that was sitting blankly in my gut turns into unease at the number of cars on Roman's street. I finally find a spot. Clutch the strap of my bag as I walk toward the house. I probably shouldn't have brought my bag; maybe it's dorky to show up to a party with a bag, but I feel naked without something to hang on to. I tug at my jean shorts, which are sticking to my thighs; it's still far too hot out, even at night. My phone buzzes in my pocket.

Mateo: Just got here, let me know when you're around <3

I press a palm to my chest when I'm outside Roman's door. Try to regulate my breathing. Stare at Mateo's text. Mateo. I'll get to see Mateo soon. Everything's fine. I can breathe.

And then I open the door.

There are clusters of people absolutely everywhere, all drinking from plastic cups. The house is just as nice as I'd always imagined: sand-colored stones surrounding the fireplace; high ceilings; lush carpet in the living room and shiny hardwood everywhere else. Everything is loud—the people, the music blaring over everything. It feels like I've walked into an actual teen movie.

I don't know what I'm doing here.

I shuffle among the clusters, searching for Mateo. I see only people I know but don't *know*. No one I've ever been bowling with, no one I've sat with in the cafeteria or bonded with on bus rides to competitions. I see only people who have rolled their eyes at me when I've argued about something too passionately in class, people with shinier hair and curvier hips and cooler clothes. People who belong at parties like this.

I start going through the periodic table in my head. Move on to listing tree species. I hold two fingers against my wrist, count my heartbeats.

And then I pass a door that's slightly ajar.

A door to a room full of books.

I step inside just to catch my breath.

I'm going to have to tell Mateo I failed, and they'll probably look at me just like Elen did. Full of sympathy. Poor naive Penny.

I walk around the room, still clutching my wrist, for five solid heartbeats until it dawns on me where I am.

Dr. Petroski's office.

I realize it when I come to a series of plaques and framed memorabilia on the wall.

My eyes snag on a silver award from *Hatfield Marine Science Center, National Oceanic and Atmospheric Administration, Oregon State University.*

It sits below a degree from Stanford.

Hatfield. I stare at the name for a while, repeat it to myself in time to my heartbeats.

Hatfield. I gave up my dream of an internship at Hatfield for a summer of donuts.

And somehow, even that turned out all wrong.

Swapna's voice echoes abruptly in my head: *Have you done any of the summer work for AP Chem yet? Gods, it's going to be* brutal.

I lose track of my pulse. My hands hang limp at my sides.

I haven't done any of the summer work for AP Chem. I haven't done anything.

I can't remember the last time I opened my college fund spreadsheet. I think I've marked off three financial goals. Out of a million.

I've just been waking up each day thinking about kissing Mateo, pretending the summer was never going to end. I let August sneak up on me with barely even a thought.

Junior year is the one that counts. The AP courses, the SATs, the application essays.

I don't know why I'm standing in Roman Petroski's house. I have no idea who I am.

But I'm pretty sure my throat is closing up.

I push out of Dr. Petroski's office, barrel past classmates down a hallway. I just need to find Mateo. I just need to get out of here. I just need to go home.

I stumble into a huge kitchen at the back of the house. Roman turns and smiles, lifting his cup in the air when he yells, "Penster! Come here, get yourself a drink!"

There's a bowl of Hawaiian Punch–colored liquid on the kitchen island; I watch Nola King accidentally dip her elbow into it a second before Caiden Mitchell ladles some into his Solo cup. My stomach turns. I grab a Bud Light Lime-a-Rita from a cooler just to have something in my hand.

"I'm glad you came, Penny. I've actually been wanting to talk to you about something."

I crack open the can and take a sip. It's so hot in here. Roman's wearing another one of those barely-a-shirt tank tops that expose half his body.

Where is Mateo?

Roman rests his forearm on my shoulder.

"You and della Penna have gotten close this summer, right?" He takes a sip from his cup, looks into the distance. I follow his gaze, and finally, I see them. Through a doorway in the next room, chatting with Talanoa and a bunch of theater kids.

Mateo looks over when they feel us looking at them. Catches my eye and smiles.

The smile falters when they look from me to Roman. And then Rachel O'Connor says something, and they turn their head away.

My body sways to move toward them, but Roman's arm is still on my shoulder.

"Do you think—" he says. I turn my head, impatient when Roman doesn't finish his sentence. He finally drops his arm, runs his hand through his golden curls. Licks his lips. He seems oddly nervous, has a tense set to his jaw I've never seen before. He looks me in the eye and finally asks, "Do you think they'd be into it if I asked them out?"

It takes a few seconds for my brain to catch up. But when it does, part of my stomach drops all the way out of my body.

Roman keeps talking about how he's been trying to work up the nerve to ask Mateo out all summer, and I keep staring at his pretty, earnest green eyes, but my mind has officially left the party. My mind is outside this kitchen, outside Verity, somewhere far away.

I didn't know Roman was queer, but why wouldn't someone as beautiful as him want someone as beautiful as Mateo? It makes sense, really. I've never heard Roman misgender them either. He would be good to them, I bet.

Obviously, this scenario makes more sense to Roman—more sense to the entire world, probably—than the possibility that Mateo could actually be attracted to *me*.

Even though I know Roman follows Mateo on Instagram.

He always likes all their posts. And all those times he's dropped into the shop . . . maybe some part of me knew this whole summer that Roman had a crush on Mateo too. But . . . Roman has also seen me and Mateo together, at Delicious Donuts, in all the photos Mateo's posted of me, of us, this past month.

Maybe photographic evidence isn't enough, though. Maybe the posts exude *Look at my cute straight best friend* energy. Maybe everyone thinks I'm Mateo's beard.

I realize, quite suddenly, that I actually can't breathe.

"I have to go."

I think I say this, anyway. I hope I do, hope I haven't just left Roman midsentence, but either way, I am moving, away from Roman Petroski, away from all the clusters of people who are not my people, until I am outside, where the air is still too warm. I am three houses away when I realize I'm still clutching the Lime-a-Rita.

I dip under a camellia bush and drop the can out of my shaking hands. It spills over my flip-flops, trickles between my toes. I can't breathe. How will Mateo and I navigate the school year? Will we hold hands in the halls, make out at our lockers? I hate the people who make out at their lockers. It always feels so braggy, makes me so uncomfortable. My lungs are closing up. Will Mateo even want to be seen with me like that? Will anyone believe it if they do? I'm pretty sure I have entire books I was supposed to have read for AP Lit. I haven't finished a book all summer. School starts *next week*. I can't breathe.

I reach for my bag, tear a cuticle getting to my phone. There are texts from Mateo, and guilt rips through me, but I need—I can't breathe. I'm dying. I think I'm going to die.

"Penny?" Mom's voice should anchor me, but I really can't breathe. I've been through this before—I should know, I should understand—but all I can feel is that I don't want to die. "Is everything okay?"

"Can you come get me?" I manage to choke out.

"Of course." Rustling in the background, then she's back with me. "We're on our way. You're at the Petroskis'? Penny, I need you to stay with me on the phone, okay?"

"Yeah." I know from the tone of her voice, from how fast she's reacting, that she knows, that I must sound like I'm dying. I can hear, distantly, my own ragged gasps for breath, and I'm so embarrassed but so glad to hear her voice, so glad that she's coming, that she and Mama D will help me not die. "I'm"—*gasp*—"a few houses down." *Gasp.* "I don't know."

"Okay. We're getting in the car. Uncle Dave was already over, so me and Mama D are both coming, all right? He'll watch the kids. We'll be there soon. Penny, I need you to tell me if something happened, if someone hurt you."

"No. No, nothing ha-happened."

Because, God, nothing did. Roman said one little thing, and I don't know why I'm dying now.

"Okay. Okay, I believe you. Can you hold on to something for me, Penny Bear? A tree or the grass? Feel it under your fingers and take a breath for me."

I hold on to the trunk of the camellia bush. Feel its bark dig into my fingers.

"Okay," I whisper.

"Good. Good. Can you hear anything?"

No. I cannot hear *anything*, not even my own breathing anymore. My head is an empty echo chamber. My heart rate spikes. My throat's closing.

"Okay, that's okay, Penny Bear. Can you tell me what you're looking at? Keep your eyes open, honey."

I lick my lips. "Camellia bush."

"Okay. Good, that's good. I love a camellia bush!"

Somewhere, part of me smiles. I know she does.

"We'll look out for one. We're on our way. We'll be there soon, okay? Can you smell anything right now?"

I try. I really try.

"Hot," I say. Which I know, even as I say it, isn't a scent, but it's the only thing I can grasp. The bark of the camellia underneath my hand and the way it smells hot. Everything is too hot. The planet is dying. I can't breathe.

"Tell me about it," Mom says, like we're just casually complaining about the weather, and I think I want to laugh, except I think I might be crying. I really hope whoever lives here does not call the police on the crying girl hugging their camellia bush.

"Can you think about a favorite song? Can you sing it to yourself, love?"

I shake my head. I'm pretty sure I've never heard a song in my life.

When I don't answer, Mom does it for me. She starts singing the song she's always sung to me since I was a little girl, since it was just me and her, way back when.

And I think I cry harder when she reaches the *oooh-ooh-ooohs* of "Diamonds on the Soles of Her Shoes," because her voice breaks a little too. But when she makes the funny sound she always does to imitate the saxophones, I laugh. And then I realize I can breathe enough to laugh, and she laughs back. And she says, "Okay, Penny, we're almost there. We're going down the street . . ." I hear Mama D in the background, and then: "We got you. We'll be there in one second. We got you, Penny."

And then Mama D's pulling me up, away from the camellia bush. She and Mom give me quick, tight hugs and then step back, making sure I can breathe. Which I can. I can breathe now, and I feel the shadow of exhaustion that always hits after a panic attack leaning in.

Mom holds my hand as she leads me to the car. Gets in the back seat with me while Mama D turns the ignition, puts the radio on low.

"I'm sorry," I say. "Nothing happened. I'm sorry."

Mom takes my hand again. "We got you." She gives it a squeeze. "We got you."

We're quiet the rest of the way home. Mom never lets go of my hand. The familiar feeling of shame is starting to wash over me, but I try to concentrate on Mom's hand. On the silhouette of Mama D in front of us, steady and strong.

When we get inside, I slide off my sticky flip-flops, and

Mom smooths my hair, cups my face.

"All right?" she whispers.

"All right," I answer.

And then she lets me go.

I take a quick shower, hot as I can stand it, to rinse off the sweat and Lime-a-Rita. I throw my clothes in the hamper.

And only then, when I get into bed, do I get out my phone. My eyelids are heavy as I take in Mateo's texts.

> Mateo: where'd you go? can't find you
> Mateo: r u still here?
> Mateo: penny? this sucks
> Mateo: ok penny wtf i just left to drive to your house to find you but then i saw dolly on the street?
> Mateo: penny please text me back

Fuck.

I'm okay, I text back as fast as I can.

Add I promise, so they won't come over.

And I'm sorry.

I know they deserve more of an explanation. But I'm so tired. I couldn't explain what just happened to them, to my moms, to myself right now if I tried.

Mateo starts typing. Stops. Starts. Stops.

"I love you," I whisper just before I fall asleep.

TWENTY-FOUR

College Fund: I Don't Know.

When I wake in the morning, my body aches from my teeth to my chest.

My mind is clear, though. Like a spring sky after a thunderstorm, except without any of the optimism.

I find myself focusing on that can of Lime-a-Rita. Did my moms think I'd been drinking? That I had a panic attack because I got too drunk? Did they pick up the can for me or was it left there? Did I *litter* on a stranger's yard?

I stare out my window.

I check my phone. No messages. My heart plummets a bit further, but my eyes blink at the time. It's just after noon. I never sleep this late.

Yet even as I force myself out of bed, my body protests. It's like all my nights of poor sleep over the past two months have caught up to me, and my muscles are refusing to function.

But I have to get up. I know I do. My moms have enough

going on. I can't make them more worried about me. I have to be okay.

"Penny." Mom puts down her magazine when I walk into the kitchen. Smiles big and gentle. "It's good to see you. How are you feeling?"

"Tired." Like a zombie, I open up cabinets and the fridge without landing on anything I actually want to eat, even as my stomach grumbles. "I'm sorry. Again."

"It's okay, Penny Bear. I'm just glad you're okay." Mom leans against the counter next to me as I investigate the cheese drawer. "We don't have to talk now if you're not ready, but... I called Hannah's office this morning. We moved up your appointment from next week to tomorrow."

I squeeze my eyes closed and shut the fridge.

"I don't want to," I whisper.

I can't handle someone else examining my life right now. I have to get a grasp on it myself before I can put anything into words for Hannah.

Mom sighs.

"I know you're sixteen, Penny, and we try to let you make your own decisions. But we're still your moms. And sometimes, we still get to call the shots. We shouldn't have let you cancel last time." She squeezes my shoulder. "I haven't seen you that way for a while, Penny. You need to talk to someone."

I know she's right.

But I still don't want to.

I glance at the clock on the wall behind her. And like that, it hits me. I don't know why it didn't as soon as I woke up.

Maybe my mind isn't so clear after all.

"Oh, *shit.*"

Mom's entire body startles. "*Penny.*"

It's possible I've never cursed in front of her before. *A different kind of Penny summer*, I think, and I almost want to laugh, except that dread is taking over all my senses.

"Mom, I'm sorry, but I—I gotta go."

I race up the stairs before I can hear what she calls after me. Shit, shit, *shit.*

Today's the day after Roman's party.

The day Mateo and I are getting Delicious Donuts ready for their art gallery.

Elen was going to close up shop after noon and then leave it up to us to get everything ready for the gallery-opening party tomorrow night.

And I was too busy being mentally ill to remember.

I throw on fresh clothes, barely comprehending what they are. I have the presence of mind to brush my teeth only because of the sudden realization that my mouth feels rank.

I was supposed to meet Mateo at the shop over an *hour* ago. Fuck.

"Penny." Mom stands in front of the door as I frantically throw on my shoes. "I'm worried about you."

"I know, Mom, but—I promised Mateo I'd help set up their art gallery at the shop, and then I slept in and totally spaced, and—it's important. I'll be back tonight. And—oh, *shit*, my car."

Dolly's still in Roman fucking Petroski's rich neighborhood.

I'm more comfortable driving Mama D's Subaru than Mom's van, but Mama D's at work. Like she always freaking is.

"Can I borrow the van? Do you need to go anywhere today? Please. I'll bring it back as soon as I can. I promise."

Mom sighs again, like I have made her weary, and it makes me want to curl up into a ball and cry. But my eyes are already swollen from crying so much last night. So I bite my tongue and force a smile when she says yes. I kiss her on the cheek, and then I'm out the door. And it's possible that once I'm inside the van, once I'm racing toward Main Street, I do cry, a little, because I *hate* messing up, and I'm in the middle of a day where I am messing up so many things and there's nothing I can do except live through it and sometimes I don't want to be here. In Verity. Sometimes I don't want to do anything I'm supposed to do. Sometimes I want to stop caring so much about my grades and the future and being a good person who does important things. Sometimes I want to join a band and travel the country in their tour bus. I have no musical talent other than the flute, so I wouldn't be *in* the band, but I could learn how to run lighting or something. I could be useful, and no one would ever even have to know who I was. I could just float around in the background like a mote of dust.

Except I would miss Emma and Bruno and Nikki so bad.

I turn into the Delicious Donuts parking lot so fast that I almost crash through the front windows. The van squeals when I slam on the brakes, and I say a silent apology to Mom.

But there's a more pressing apology I need to make now.

Their back is turned when I burst in. They're standing in

front of a booth, holding a framed drawing. It's one of the first ones they showed me this summer, after Grumpy Toad's, when we started dating and they finally let me look. It's their front yard from the perspective of the grass, their dad's truck in the background; the flowers of Regina's garden look otherworldly. It's one of my favorites. It shows how different and wonderful and *special* their perspective can be.

"Mateo. I am so, so sorry I'm late."

They don't turn. Don't move.

The only sign that they've heard me barge in is the way their shoulders bunch toward their ears. And, as I walk toward their side, the way their jaw locks and pops in their cheek.

"It's fine," they say. "You disappear at the party we were supposed to go to together without even saying hi first. Makes sense you wouldn't show at the weird donut-shop gallery you made me agree to either."

A cold, invisible fist grabs me by the chest.

I *know* it makes sense that they're mad, and they have every right to be, but it feels so horrible, so much worse than any time we've ever argued before, that it's hard for me to imagine speaking or doing anything else ever again.

But somehow, after a minute, my lips move.

"I'm sorry," I whisper, "if you didn't actually want to do the gallery. I can explain to Elen—"

"It's too late, Penny. The event's tomorrow."

A beat. Mateo's shoulders drop. And finally, they put down the picture and turn toward me.

"I'm sorry," they say. "I'm just . . ." They wipe a hand over their face before hugging their elbows. They meet my eyes as they lean against the booth. The anger drains away, and they look so much like *my* Mateo again, I want to throw myself at them. "Are you okay?"

I tear my gaze away from their face at the question. Scuff the toe of my shoe along the floor. I should have prepared what I wanted to say. My head feels full of gauze.

"I'm sorry about last night, Mateo." That's a good start. "I . . . had a panic attack, and I just had to get out of there."

I hear them suck in a long breath.

"I thought . . . maybe something like that had happened. But I don't know why you didn't find me or text me about what was going on. I was so freaked out that something awful had happened, and then I was hurt that you wouldn't tell me anything, and . . ." I look back up to see Mateo shaking their head. "And then I just kept thinking about how the last time I saw you, you were all cozy with Roman in the kitchen, and . . ." Oh *God*. "I don't know. The whole night felt weird."

"It *was* weird," I agree. "But for the record, nothing happened with me and Roman."

"I know."

"He actually likes *you*."

I don't know why I say this. Roman is the least important part of everything Mateo just said, the least important part of anything right now.

And I know I don't owe Roman anything—Roman made me feel epically embarrassed last night—but as soon as the words are out of my mouth, I feel like I've betrayed him.

Shared a secret I shouldn't have shared.

Mateo's nose scrunches in confusion.

"Roman likes *me*?"

"Yeah. He . . ." I clear my throat. "He was telling me that he wanted to ask you out."

"Huh." Their head jerks back an inch before a measure of clarity reaches their eyes. "Oh. I guess that's why he's been randomly sending me TikToks all summer."

They try to smile at me, and I try to smile back. An awkward second passes. Their smile fades.

"Saying that to you was a weird thing for him to do," they say slowly. "But it feels like I'm still missing something here."

I swallow, my eyes returning to my feet. I dig my thumbnail into my cuticles.

"Elen's selling Delicious Donuts," I say, voice small.

"Oh." I sense Mateo take a step toward me; I take a small step back. "Penny—"

"And I'm never going to be able to go to California."

When Mateo doesn't say anything, I look up to see them frown.

"What?" they eventually say.

"I mean, I hope to go there *someday*, like to visit, at least, but I don't have enough money to go out of state for college, but you deserve to go to art school there, and be happy, and—"

"Penny. Hey, Penny. Slow down. I don't care—"

"I've just been thinking about the school year and where we go from here. I'm so busy, you know? During the school year, and I don't know how to make time for . . . this, and

I don't . . ." All of a sudden, my word vomit cuts off. I can't make myself look at Mateo, but they're just as silent as me. The shop is *silent*, and it's killing me.

"I just don't know if we . . . fit. You know?"

"You don't know if we . . . fit," Mateo repeats. I force myself to look at them when I hear the tone of their voice.

Bury me in the ground.

Mateo was still open to me a mere minute ago, and I should have let them hug me, should have appreciated it more, because now they're gone. Now they are so, so far away, from their voice to the set of their jaw to the look in their eyes, and I know, I just know, that I'm never going to get them back.

But I can't be mad, because I just made it happen.

They look away from me and shake their head. "You know, part of me always worried this would be the case in the end."

"What would be the case?" The question comes out of my mouth automatically, a defensive reaction to the anger emanating from them. Even though as soon as I ask it, I realize I don't actually want to know the answer.

Mateo shrugs.

"That I'd only ever be a summer experiment for you."

I suck in a breath, blinking fast and furious to keep the tears away.

"Mateo," I whisper. "No, I just—"

"But you know what?" They lift their hands and take a step back as if they're wiping their hands clean of this whole thing. Of me. "Glad I helped you work out some shit. I hope you get to marry Roman Petroski one day, or Julian Portillo, or who the fuck ever, and I hope you have a great life planting a million trees together, but right now, I think I need you to leave."

The floor tilts beneath me. My stomach clenches, and I realize I never did eat breakfast. That I haven't eaten anything in a long time.

"*Please*, Penny. Please just go."

"But the gallery—"

"I texted Candace when you didn't show to help me. And she'll be here in . . . hey, look at that. Now."

The bell jingles behind me, and as if Mateo had conjured her from thin air, Candace breezes in, a cup of iced coffee from the Dutch Bros on Route 72 in her hand.

"Hey, my dudes." She takes a sip from the pink straw as her eyes dart back and forth between us. "Whoa. You okay, Pen?"

"Yeah." I attempt to clear my throat. Mateo turns away and picks up a frame. "I, um—" I clutch my mom's keys in my hand so tight it hurts, backing away from Candace, from Mateo, from Delicious Donuts. "Let me know if you need anything."

And I'm gone, driving Mom's van away from Main Street, even though all I *really* want is to be back inside hanging Mateo's artwork next to them, listening to Candace's music, laughing at her jokes.

But the summer's almost over.

Along with the different kind of Penny I got to be, for a little while.

TWENTY-FIVE

Days Until Junior Year: 5

I find myself at Treehuggers.

"Hey, Penny." James smiles when he sees me. Which, under normal circumstances, would have made me feel pretty good. James hardly ever smiles. "We've missed you around here."

"Yeah. Hi. Um. Can I plant some trees?"

James's smile fades as he looks at my face. After a beat, he stands from where he'd been staring at the front desk's computer screen. He scratches at his beard and motions with his head.

"Yeah, Penny. Come on back."

I follow him through the office to the warehouse. They're clearly gearing up for the big planting season this fall; it's packed. The lack of green things outside—the brown grass, the wildfire smoke that's covering most of the West Coast—has made me itchy. Being surrounded by green things in this warehouse fills my lungs with comfort.

We stop in the middle of a row. James scratches at his chin again.

"Ideal planting conditions won't start for a good few weeks, not until we get some more rain. The ground most places is pretty rock hard—"

"I know," I interrupt. "I know it's the worst conditions and timing ever, but . . . if I could just try. One or two small ones, that's all."

"Yeah. Yeah, you can, Penny. Here." We walk to a big map attached to a whiteboard. "Up in Buzzards Hill. We've been working with the county on diversifying some of the forest in the transition zone here. Making the plant life hardier, more disease-resistant." He knocks a blunt finger against the map. I nod. Transition zones. Disease resistance. Some part of me feels better already. "Since it already has significant tree cover, the soil might be more amenable than a regular urban planting. You can do your best, and we'll go out and check on them later this week. If you can't make it work, just bring 'em back."

I nod again. "Sounds perfect. Just tell me what to do."

An hour later, I'm sweating on Buzzards Hill.

My knees are covered with dirt, my arms sore from how hard I've had to stick my shovel in the ground over and over again.

It feels good to have something to concentrate on.

I've already got one oak planted, an oak that will take generations to fully grow, but I hope it does. I hope a few generations from now, this grove of trees is still here, outside of Verity, the peaks of the Coast Ranges in the distance.

I'm working on digging a hole farther into the tree line

now, this one for a western red cedar. Once you get through the dry upper layers, there is rich soil to be found if you work hard enough for it. My arms are starting to scream, but it's worth it, in the end, when I tear off my work gloves and sink my hands in.

The weight of past Augusts returns to my bloodstream. The heaviness of my own brain, the restlessness. As familiar as a headache.

Things will make sense again when I get back to school.

There will be new things to learn again when I'm in the safety of a classroom.

I think I'll keep my head down this year, though. Focus on my science classes and on doing what I need to get the grades in the rest of them. I'll back down from the arguments. I'm tired of arguing over things I'll never win.

I rest my fingers in the soil until the heat of the day and the lingering smoke in the air get to be too much. I repack the soil, haul out the watering bags from the van, and arrange them around the trunk flares. Take photos and note their location for James.

I feel dizzy when I step back inside the van. It occurs to me I might be dehydrated.

I wonder what Mateo's doing. What the shop looks like now, with their art covering the walls. All my productive feelings of the past two hours are whisked away and I feel empty again, not knowing. Not being there.

I take a deep breath and drive home.

* * *

I think I'm good—that I might somehow survive this day—until I walk into the house, dirt still stuck under my fingernails, and see Mom.

Sitting quietly on the couch. No one else around. Like she's been waiting for me.

And, well. What else can I do?

She runs a hand through my hair. Kisses the top of my head. "What's going on, Penny Bear?"

I say it into her chest. It feels so awful to say out loud. But I feel like I need to say it to someone. Might as well be Mom.

"I think we broke up."

At least, I'm pretty sure we did. That I was the one who did it.

I wish . . .

I don't know. I just always thought these things would be more clear-cut.

"Oh, honey."

Mom sighs; my head rises and falls along with her chest. She rocks me back and forth a bit like she used to, like I'm still the size of the triplets. "I'm so sorry. It seemed like you really cared about each other." She pauses, runs a hand through my hair again. "Even if . . . well, I can't deny it's all freaked me out a little, seeing you grow up so fast. But then again . . ." I'm still buried in her shirt, but I can hear the sad smile in her voice. "Sometimes it feels like my whole life has been watching you grow up too fast, Penny."

I don't know what to say. Don't know if I'm supposed to have anything to say to that.

What comes out of my mouth instead is "I quit Delicious Donuts."

Maybe next summer I can find a job that pays more. Somewhere I can get even more hours. I don't know. My limbs feel heavy when I think about it.

"Well, wasn't that the plan anyway, for you to quit at the end of the summer? You're so busy during the school year. Working is important, but we don't want you to burn yourself out."

"You don't—" I sigh, pushing away from her. Frustration fizzles through my exhaustion. She doesn't understand.

And suddenly, I need to say it. Need to tell Mom everything until I'm empty, until I can go to sleep and not think about anything ever again.

"I know about my college fund, Mom."

Mom's face transforms from concern to confusion.

"What do you mean, you know about your college fund?" She lifts my chin with a finger and makes me look at her.

"I know that it doesn't exist. That you had to use it for Nikki's medical bills."

Mom's eyes cloud, her frown deepening. "And why do you think that?"

"I can hear you guys when you're talking down here at night. Through the vent in my room. I heard you saying something about it last winter."

Mom's face changes once more. Her eyes morph into something soft, something that makes me want to start crying. *Again.*

"But it's okay," I continue swiftly to reassure her, to distract my tear ducts. "I don't want you to worry about it. I'm going to work as much as I can over the next couple of years and maybe start at BCC after I graduate, and—"

"Honey. Penny. Stop." Mom squeezes her eyes shut for a second like I'm hurting her. "Whatever you heard, it was never meant for your ears. No matter what, we'll work it out, okay? *We're* working on it." She runs a hand down my cheek. "You're sixteen, Penny. We don't want you to be worrying about how to pay for college."

I frown. "What else do you think sixteen-year-olds worry about?"

Maybe other sixteen-year-olds worry about different stuff. But Mom knows me.

And—

Something she said clicks in my head. We're *working on it*.

"Wait." My eyes widen in horror. "Is that why Mama D's been taking so many shifts at the hospital? To replenish my college fund?"

Mom shakes her head, emphatic.

"No. I mean—" She sighs again. Some of the fire dims in her eyes and she gives me a tired smile. "Look. Can we always use more money? Of course. That will always be true. We might be in a particularly tight spot right now with some of Nikki's medical stuff. All of which, by the way, is none of your concern. But the thing about your Mama D is . . ."

Mom looks away. Opens and shuts her mouth, as if contemplating what she wants to say. Finally, she looks back.

"Mama D's a workaholic. Especially since the triplets

arrived, and everything with Nikki . . ." She tilts her head. "Mama D didn't have a lot, growing up." I nod. I knew that. "And now, earning money for us, providing for us . . . it's her love language."

She gives me that same tired smile, runs a hand over my hair again. Her eyes are warm, as if Mama D's workaholic tendencies make her love her even more while simultaneously frustrating her. It's a look she's given me over the years.

"Except what *I* want," Mom continues, "is for us to spend time together. To hold on to what we have now before you do run off to college. I mean, heck, if she works any more, we won't even qualify for financial aid for you!"

She gives a small chuckle but quickly walks it back once she looks at me, her face turning serious again.

"Which we will, Penny. We'll get financial aid for you. We can get loans." She cups my cheek in her warm palm. "If you want honesty? A lot of people these days can barely afford anything. Most people can't truly afford college for their kids anymore. But something I promised myself after that first astronomical bill from the NICU six years ago: We can't let it hold us back from *living*." Her hand squeezes my cheek tighter. "All I want for you, my beautiful, thoughtful, bighearted little girl, is to be able to go wherever you want to go." The curve of her mouth is bittersweet when she whispers: "I know you want to get out of here, Penny Bear."

I swallow around a lump in my throat. "But—"

"Penny." Her voice turns firm. "I saw you researching NYU on my computer when you were in the sixth grade.

Follow your dreams, baby."

I look down. Stare at my hands.

"But I love Verity too," I whisper. Because I do. I know Mom's right. I've always wanted to see the world. To get out. But fighting for Delicious Donuts this summer, getting to know Main Street again . . .

I know I still have two years of high school left. That I don't have to decide anything right now. But the future still looms closer than it ever has before.

And suddenly, the idea of leaving Verity seems huge and scary.

"I know you do, Penny. You can love a place and still want to leave it." Mom squeezes my knee. "Life is all about feeling too many different things at the same time. But you don't have to figure it out right now. All I want you to know is that me and Mama D will support you no matter what. You understand?"

I nod. My throat is still thick. "I understand."

"And I want you to know that we've been talking about it, me and your Mama D, and she's going to start taking fewer shifts. I know she wants to be around more too. It's just . . . hard for her to trust, sometimes, that everything's going to be okay."

She lifts my chin with a finger again.

"A little like someone else I know."

I try to smile back.

"Elen is selling the store."

Mom's eyes widen in surprise.

"That's actually why I'm quitting. I thought maybe I could

still work on weekends here and there, but she's selling it to Northwest Donuts. I've been trying so hard to convince her not to all summer, but . . ." And now the tears do come. I break away from Mom, covering my face. "I couldn't save your store, and I couldn't save Elen's."

"Penny. Penny, my goodness, you were, like, ten years old when I closed Rosemary and Time."

"I know." I cry harder. "Part of me thought . . ." I shake my head at myself. What *did* I think? That somehow I could bring Mom's store back if I got enough people to return to Main Street. Even *I* know how unrealistic it sounds. I just shake my head again, unable to say it out loud.

I'm going to miss Jack, and Bao, and Keena.

"I think," Mom says after a long silence, the words careful and slow, "when we see Hannah tomorrow, we ask if we can see her more often. At least for a little while."

I nod, staring at my lowered hands. My tears slow. "Yeah. Yeah, that might be good." And then: "I think I need to sleep now."

Mom pulls me into another hug.

"You know how proud of you I am, right?" she whispers. "I wish you would stop thinking you need to solve the world's problems, but"—and God help me, if Mom says she's proud of me for trying, I'm going to lose it—"I love you more than anything."

She kisses my forehead.

And although it feels wrong, not texting Mateo first, I get in bed and let myself sleep.

* * *

On the day of Mateo's art-gallery opening, I sit in Hannah's office. She smiles, warm and gentle.

"Penny," she says. "How have you been?"

I take a deep breath.

And I tell her about my donut summer.

TWENTY-SIX

@Verity.Deliciousdonuts Follower Count: 472

I watch Mateo's gallery opening via Instagram.

Specifically, via Lía's Stories.

The first image punches me in the gut: Mateo standing in their front yard, looking beautiful and shy, hands stuck in the pockets of their black jeans. *SO PROUD OF THIS CHIQUE*, Lía shouts in all caps across the bottom. I hold my thumb over the screen, keeping them there, for a long time.

But eventually, I let go. And then, in a heartbeat, we're at Delicious Donuts. Someone—Elen? Candace?—has strung twinkle lights from the ceiling, making the tiny donut shop actually look cozy and perfect for an art gallery. My heart squeezes that I didn't have that idea first. My heart breaks that I'm not there.

Next is a photo of Regina and Ed all dressed up and standing in front of one of Mateo's newest pieces, done with their favorite pencils. It's a close-up of the back of their dad's truck that looks deceptively simple at first, just a corner of the license plate, the empty space of the bumper around it. But Mateo has drawn every detail, the shading of every brush of dirt along the metal. It's breathtaking. The work of someone leveling up. The work of someone trying.

These fools are proud too, Lía types. And then, in smaller print near the bottom: "That's my truck!" 😂

I stare at this one for a while too. Mateo's parents *do* look proud. They look happy.

Why is their dad standing there like that? It's not like he's ever supported anything Mateo has truly wanted. I don't understand it.

I click to the next one. Lía is showcasing the individual pieces of artwork now, just a close-up of the frame with no commentary, and a small, delusional piece of me almost wonders if she did this for me. If she knew that I would want to see.

I contemplated attending. I know it's probably hurting Mateo's feelings that I'm not, but maybe I'm being self-important with that. It just . . . didn't feel right. Like it would be worse to show up a day after I broke up with them without any warning. They deserve the space to shine on their own.

There's the corner-store drawing. The flowers in their yard. Starry Night Penny.

I didn't know if she'd be there. If Mateo might want to erase me from this entirely. I wouldn't have blamed them if they had, but something suffuses my chest, spreads throughout my entire body, when I see her there on the wall.

I let that Story fade to the next—a print of another digital piece, one they've been working on, a tribute to Venice Beach, to California. Full of all the vibrant colors of their family's home state, the colors they can access on their tablet that they had never experimented with before with their pencils and charcoals. I love both sides of Mateo's creativity: the grayscale and the vivid rainbow.

My finger shoots out to pause the next Story as soon as it loads.

My breath is shallow, trapped in my lungs.

I haven't seen this one before.

I'm behind North Falls. The waterfall cascades off the side of the page. Even in Mateo's simple pencil, it somehow shines silver on the paper. The portrait shows my profile, my face turned up toward the water, a small smile on my lips. Even with all my freckles, which Mateo has portrayed with shocking accuracy, I look . . . so, so pretty. Luminescent.

It's different from the dreamy experiment of Starry Night Penny, where Mateo could play with imagery, make me into something I'm not.

This is Mateo's original signature style. The way they see the world.

The way they saw me, that night.

My tears blur through the last of the Stories: Mateo posing with Ms. Fuentes. Candace and Talanoa. I'm so glad they're all there. I hope Mateo's able to enjoy themself, to feel proud.

I hope they're able to forgive me someday.

I wake up the next morning and get out of bed. I take a hot shower and brush my teeth.

And then I focus on the list I made with Hannah.

My body is still a little sore from the panic attack and from the tree planting, which, my muscles admit, maybe wasn't the *best* idea. My heart still feels incomplete every minute that goes by with a quiet phone. I open a blank screen in my Notes app, type all the texts I want to send. *How was the gallery opening? How are you feeling? You were never an experiment to me. I miss you.*

But there are only a few days left of summer.

I can still be present. I can ask for what I need. I can start now.

When I descend to the first floor and find both Mom *and* Mama D at the kitchen table, it feels like a sign from the universe.

"Mom," I start, clutching my scribbled notes from my session with Hannah for strength. "You said the other day that all you want is for us to spend time together. Well—" I swallow. "I need you—need you both—to actually *show* that. To try harder at it. I know life is always busy, especially with the triplets, but all my other friends have *done* things with their families this summer. Gone on vacations, gone camping. That night Mateo came over for dinner and we made s'mores felt like the first time in forever that we'd . . ." I look down at my notes as if they could help me, though I know they're just a jumble of words. "That we'd done something like that."

I look up again, force myself to glance at my moms. Mama D has reached over to grab Mom's hand, and Mom's lower lip is trembling, but they're both looking back at me with serious eyes. They're listening.

"I know there's only a few days left of summer. But I want to go camping. I know all the campsites have probably been booked for months, but . . ." I sigh. "I want to go on a hike, at least. I want to leave Verity. All of us, together. I know your work schedule is intense, Mama D, but I think you can make it happen. For me."

Mama D stands. Wraps me in her arms.

"Yeah, kid." Her voice is gruff. "Damn straight we can make it happen. How does Detroit Lake sound?"

The tension leaves my body. Mama D loves the outdoors as much as I do. The three of us went camping together a lot when she and my mom first started dating; I think that was another reason why I was able to love her so easily, so fast. We learned to love each other at Cascadia. On Mount Jefferson. At the coast; next to waterfalls. All the places we feel most alive.

Of course she would know just where to go. Detroit Lake sounds perfect.

"Or"—Mom touches my arm—"I could get Dave or Grandma Jean to come watch the kids, and we could go—just the three of us?"

I shake my head, but I appreciate the sentiment.

"No," I say. "That's okay. I want us all there. Even if—" I let out a weak laugh. Being honest is draining. "It might be a nightmare." Bruno is a whiner on hikes; Nikki is terrified of bugs. Emma is impatient and marches ahead without waiting for her siblings.

Mom and Mama D look at each other.

"Today's my day off," Mama D says, and she turns back to me. "Want to go now?"

I laugh again, surprised. I'm supposed to work later and was hoping to just rest until then. Maybe start some of my reading for AP Lit. My stomach twists in guilt at the idea of canceling on one of my last shifts, but . . . I remember what I talked about with Hannah, about considering my own returns on investment.

I'll get DJ to cover, maybe. I'll make it work.

"Yeah," I say. "Let's go now."

TWENTY-SEVEN

Number of Weirdos on the Knowledge Bowl Team: 6

Two days before school starts, I stand in Carmello's living room and stare at my fellow members of Knowledge Bowl, all gathered here for board-game night. It's time for the next item on my list.

I don't necessarily plan to ask this before I've even said hello, but that's what happens.

"Have any of you ever been in love?"

As one, the Knowledge Bowl team freezes. Then they all turn to stare at me.

"I am only qualified to discuss Catan," Lani says after a beat.

"Also geography and international politics," Carmello adds on Lani's behalf. Lani is our ringer on the team for any geography question, plus she knows almost a freakish amount about what's happening in the world. I'm extremely jealous of her brain. And time management. She's somehow able to fit in so much NPR.

"That's true," Lani agrees. "But mostly, in this moment, Catan."

"Actually, what I meant to ask," I say, amending my question, "is if any of you have ever been in love and then royally screwed it all up."

"Oh, Penny." Swapna sighs and drops into an armchair in front of me. "What did you do?"

I frown a bit. "Why are you so unsurprised that I did something?"

"Well, there's the fact that you literally just implied you royally screwed it all up."

"Oh. Right. My brain isn't working well these days."

But even as I say it, I don't know if it's necessarily true. I need the support and the creative brainpower of my friends. But my head has actually felt clearer with each day that I've been working on my new affirmations, my new intentions. I even survived my final Delicious Donuts shift today. I'd made Candace jigsaw around with me this week so I wouldn't have to work with Mateo.

But I'm done avoiding them now. I'm ready to be brave.

"There's also the fact," Swapna says, "that when I roomed with you for the Knowledge Bowl tournament in Portland last year, I watched you debate with yourself for fifteen minutes about whether you should set your alarm for five fifty or six o'clock."

"There are a lot of factors that go into the right alarm time. Five fifty and six o'clock are very different—wait. What does that have to do with anything?"

"I'm saying, with affection, that you overthink things. And I can theorize how that would lead to . . . complications in relationships."

I'm quiet a minute. Wondering if I should feel offended.

Except Swapna is pretty much spot-on. So.

I look her in the eye.

"Help me."

"On it." She heaves herself off Carmello's family's armchair, takes my hand, and leads me into the hall.

"We're not going to wait to start shit, just so you know," Blake says. He is sitting at the dining-room table, extremely focused on arranging some wizard-y looking game pieces on a circular board.

"I wouldn't expect anything less!" Swapna calls.

At the last minute, Julian steps into the hallway with us, hands in his pockets.

"Is it cool if I come too?"

"Yes," I say. "Please."

I've never been great at asking for help. Which Hannah and I have talked about. But in the confines of Carmello's house, even though I've never been here before, surrounded by Julian and Swapna, I feel safe.

We end up in the laundry room.

"Spill the tea, Dexter," Swapna says as soon as she closes the door.

I lick my lips. Tuck my hair behind my ears. And then I give a brief summary of how I broke up with Mateo because I wasn't sure how we'd work during the school year, and because

I was sad about Delicious Donuts, and because Mateo's going back to California in two years and I don't know where I'm going to end up. Because I haven't been able to quite trust what my mom said about being able to afford anything other than here.

Both Swapna and Julian listen with pensive, nonjudgmental faces, arms folded across their chests.

"You *are* busy during the school year," Swapna says slowly. "But there's gotta be some way to make it work."

"Agreed," Julian says. "If taking AP classes means you can't date, then, frankly, we're all screwed. The California thing holds more weight, but still, two years is a long time to figure things out."

"Yeah." I bite my lip. "It sounds dumb when I say it out loud."

"No," Swapna says sincerely. "I get it."

"Me too," Julian says.

But I know taking a lot of AP classes isn't the *real* reason I told Mateo we didn't fit.

"There's another thing." I take a deep breath. "Before I messed things up . . . okay, question: If you guys only knew me and Mateo casually, if you only followed us on Insta, would you know we were together? That we were dating?"

"Um, *yeah*." Swapna gives me a look like I've lost my mind. I turn to Julian for confirmation. He nods, face still serious.

I wipe my hands on my shorts.

"Even though we're so different?"

Swapna snorts.

"Please. You are not. You two are both total weirdos."

Reflexively, I give an affronted huff. "I am not a weirdo."

Swapna gestures with gusto toward Carmello's living room. "Penny. Have you forgotten who we are or something? We are all weird. That's what makes us us."

"I know, but, like—" I dig my nails into my palms, frustrated. "We're, like, nerdy weird. Mateo is *cool* weird. There's a difference."

Swapna leans back. Both she and Julian study me.

"I disagree," Swapna says after a minute, and her voice sounds the tiniest bit hurt. "I think there's something at the heart of all freaks that brings us together. And if a *cool* weirdo wouldn't want to associate with a Knowledge Bowl weirdo, then they're not a weirdo or cool at all. They're just an asshole."

I mess with the hem of my T-shirt.

I know in the equation of Mateo and me, they are definitely not the asshole.

I take another deep breath.

"We went to Roman Petroski's party. And Roman had no idea we were together. We were in the kitchen, Roman and me, and he talked to me about how *he* wants to date Mateo, like Mateo dating *me* wasn't even a possibility that had ever entered his mind, and I think . . ." I shred my already shredded cuticles a bit more. "I think it sort of blew up all my worst insecurities."

Both Swapna and Julian sigh.

And look totally sympathetic.

I expect to feel pathetic, but something about their faces makes me feel . . . relieved.

"Well," Swapna says eventually, voice soft, "it's like I said. Roman isn't a freak. He doesn't see it because he's an idiot."

"And," Julian adds, "if he's crushing on Mateo . . ." His shoulders lift and fall. "Sometimes you see only what you want to see."

"An excellent point," Swapna quickly agrees.

"But." I bite my lip. "I mean, you've seen Mateo, right? And you've seen me."

Swapna frowns again. "What do you mean?"

"I—" My bravery starts to leave me. My words curl up in my throat.

"Penny. Are you saying . . . do you think"—Swapna's voice turns reprimanding—"that Mateo is cooler than you because they dye their hair?"

My mouth opens and closes. "No?" I manage to squeak, hating that it comes out as a question.

"Penny. My gods. Have *you* seen Mateo's Insta?" Swapna's phone is already in hand; her fingers scroll with purpose, then she shoves it at me. "*Look.* This is the face of a person who is extremely attracted to you no matter what color your hair is."

"I know," I whisper, only able to glance at the photos through half-squinted eyes. I know Swapna's right without having to look at them again. I've seen their drawings of me. I know the way they touched me, the way they kissed me. I know all of these things; it's just . . . still hard, even now. To truly *believe* them.

If there's one thing being with Mateo has taught me this summer, it's that I still have so, so much to learn about myself. To *trust* about myself.

"Part of me feels like"—the words come out of my mouth before I realize I'm saying them—"maybe I can't be good with Mateo until I figure out so much more about *me*."

Swapna lowers her phone.

"Damn," she says. "You're really getting deep with this."

"I've been talking with my therapist a lot," I manage with a weak smile.

"We're all figuring out stuff about ourselves all the time," Julian says. "That doesn't mean we can't fall in love while we're doing it. I mean—" He lifts his shoulders. "Maybe it does mean that sometimes. Depends on how well you think you can balance it all. I just have a feeling, knowing you . . . you can balance it if you really want to."

I stare at him. Try to infuse some of his confidence in me into my own brain.

"But the California thing," I eventually say. "You agreed it holds weight."

"Sure. But what matters," Julian says, voice firm, "is if you care about each other *now*."

"Yeah." I look down again. "I know."

"Are they good with your siblings?" Julian asks after a minute.

"Oh my God," I cry, pained, as I look back up. As I think about Mateo's after-dinner portraits, their bewildered but kind reactions to the chaos. "So good."

Julian grins.

"You gotta get them back," Swapna says. Julian nods.

"I know. I *know*. But what if it's too late?" That's mostly what I've been hearing in the back of my mind every day that goes by without any communication between us: *Too late, too late, too late.* "I was pretty shitty, you guys. I broke up with them, like, out of nowhere. It's very possible they actually hate me now."

"No," Julian says quickly. "I highly doubt it."

Swapna's been quiet—for Swapna—over the past few minutes, but a light starts to shine in her eyes.

She leans away from the dryer.

"Dexter, I know we came together tonight to strategize, like, bards and clerics and world domination and stuff—at least some of those nerds back there did—but you and me? We have a new mission now." She glances at Julian. "You too, if you want."

Julian nods again. Swapna looks back at me.

"Project Win Mateo Back."

I look at each of them. My chest had already started to feel lighter yesterday, at Detroit Lake.

It feels even lighter now.

Maybe Swapna and Julian would pick up their phones if I texted them in the middle of the night.

Maybe I have had my people all along.

"You think it's possible?"

Swapna says, "Oh, yeah. Anything's possible, baby."

But Julian chooses a slightly different tactic when he says,

"Do *you* think it's possible? You're the one who knows Mateo, knows what happened between you two."

I take another shaky breath.

"I really, really want it to be."

Julian smiles.

"Then all right. Project Win Mateo Back."

I glance at each of them once more before I nod.

"Project Win Mateo Back."

TWENTY-EIGHT

Days Left of Junior Year: 180

On the first day of school, I stand in front of Mateo della Penna's locker and try to breathe.

I think through the affirmations I crafted with Hannah that I've been trying to repeat each day.

I am more than a babysitter.
I am more than my GPA.
I am more than the college I do or do not attend.
I am more than my bank account.
I am more than my parents' bank accounts too.
I am more than my fears of the things I cannot control.
I am beautiful.
And I can do this.

Or, more accurately: I can try. Trying is what I'm good at, after all.

Project Win Mateo Back turned out to be pretty simple in the end. Swapna, Julian, and I quickly realized we didn't have the time or resources for anything extravagant. I didn't want to go too hard anyway, freak Mateo out too much.

I just have to get them to talk to me.

And then it'll be up to them to decide.

I stare at the periodic table on Ms. Kellogg's door across the hall while I wait. Focus on the sound of the other over-anxious, arriving-at-school-too-early students shuffling by. Feel the corners of the pink box balanced in my right hand, the cellophane surrounding the flowers clutched in my left.

And I think about the first day of school a year ago when I thought I heard Mateo tell Talanoa that I was the worst.

And who knows: maybe today Mateo will *actually* think that.

But at least this time, I won't walk away. Won't let my anxiety fill in the empty spaces before I can discover the truth. This year, I'll be brave.

I stand in front of their locker as the hallways start to fill and the time ticks closer and closer to first bell. Kids stare at me when they pass, at my box and my flowers and my pulse pumping away in my neck. Some of them give me puppy eyes, say *Aww*. Most of them snicker.

None of them are Mateo, so I don't say anything to any of them.

Elen's eyes had lit up when I walked through the door of Delicious Donuts forty-five minutes ago. "Miss us already, huh?" Her smile had gotten even wider when she heard my order: A half dozen Boston creams. A half dozen apple fritters.

So she remembered our first day too.

Candace knew immediately that she was out of the loop.

"What's going on here?" she demanded as she started to ring me up. Elen walked over and canceled the order.

"This one's on me."

"Why are you smiling like that, Elen? You know something."

Elen neatly folded the lid of the box into the sides and nudged it across the counter to me.

"Penny's going to get them back," she said.

"Oh, thank God," Candace replied.

I realized then what I'd subconsciously known all summer: No employee of Delicious Donuts had ever misgendered Mateo. Not DJ, not Elen, not Alex.

It shouldn't have felt like such a miracle. But it did, especially in a place like Verity. A small miracle, maybe, but an important one. As comforting as the smell of Earl Grey, as the soft sweetness inside a stretch of fried dough.

Elen had grabbed my hands and held on tight. "Thank you for coming in, Penny," she said, voice quiet, just for me, eyes sincere.

And I almost cried all over again then, at the loss of Delicious Donuts, at the grief of summer turning into fall. But I'd put on mascara and everything today, and I had to keep up my strength.

Strength that ebbs out of me, bit by bit, as the first bell rings, and Mateo is still nowhere in sight. This had been one of my biggest worries about the plan, that I wouldn't see them at all, and the flowers are already starting to wilt, and my palms are sweating up the box, and—

And there they are. Coming down the hall with Talanoa.

They stop short as soon as they see me. And then they stay there, in the middle of the hall, too far away, Talanoa glancing with big eyes from them to my gifts and back, his mouth forming, *Oh, shit*, while Mateo only stares.

They have new hair.

The fuchsia and rich purple are gone. Replaced by a pastel pink as light and gentle as a cherry blossom.

It might be *too* pretty, actually. I wonder in that moment if it's going to kill me. Something is going to kill me if Mateo doesn't come closer. If they only walk on by.

But then I remember that today is about me taking action. Being honest. Not letting them walk on by. At least not yet.

I stride toward them and thrust the presents into their chest.

"These are for you," I say. "Obviously."

After a beat during which I almost lose consciousness, Mateo lifts their hands and takes the flowers and the donuts. I step back immediately, before our hands can brush, before I reach up and touch their face.

"I was hoping you could meet me at lunch. In the practice room in the band wing, where you saw me having a panic attack freshman year."

Talanoa makes a small noise. Mateo is staring at the flowers.

"I just have some stuff to say, and it's okay if you don't want to hear it. But I was hoping you would. So. You can take the morning to think about it."

The second bell rings.

Talanoa says, "Dude." Ms. Kellogg steps out of her classroom and hollers, "Time to get to class, kids!"

Mateo still doesn't look at me.

I turn and run, literally, down the hall and around the corner to Señor Hernandez's Spanish 3 classroom, where I am officially late on my first day. Señor's eyebrows lift in surprise as I slam into my seat. It's possible my classmates are staring too.

I get out my Chromebook and look at the whiteboard, trying to calm my heart.

Junior-Year Penny is going to be a little different too.

Unlike in sophomore year, Mateo and I do not share every class.

But we are in the same second period, World History with Ms. Bednarik. The social studies hall is on the opposite side of the school from Señor's room, so I get there just before the second bell and drop into an open seat in the front.

Bednarik is old-school, one of the teachers who's been teaching at VHS for over twenty years. All of her tests are pen and paper; she uses an old set of textbooks at the back of the room, despite the fact that all of our history textbooks have been online since we were in middle school.

But even though old textbooks are hugely problematic, I could kiss her. Because in the first minutes of class, Bednarik has us rearrange ourselves into alphabetical rows.

Mateo has their donut box and their flowers on their desk. They do not look up when I pass by to take my place behind them. But other kids jostle their shoulder and point at the box as they walk to their new seats.

"Are those donuts?" Jackson Bustamante asks. "Can I have one?"

Mateo only shakes their head. And with their right arm, they sweep the pink box closer to themself. Protecting it, head down.

Something like hope flares in my chest.

I stare at their hair. At the curve of their shoulders.

I have been in love with them for so long.

Once everyone's seated and Bednarik starts going over the syllabus, Mateo quietly shifts the box under their desk. Places the flowers on top.

They get out their sketchbook.

And as their back hunches forward over a blank page, a pencil in their hand, something settles inside of me.

Something that feels like coming home.

I stand outside the practice room and close my eyes.

Yesterday, after I bought Mateo flowers at a shop in Corvallis—peonies and purple asters, dahlias and cornflowers, blooms that somehow reminded me of them—I sat alone for a while in the living room. I put the National Geographic Channel's *Earth Moods* on the TV and opened up a journal. (Bruno said, *"Nooooo,"* when he came in and saw I was watching *Earth Moods* yet again, but Mama D—who is working only fifty hours this week—silently yanked him back out by the collar of his T-shirt.)

I made a crooked chart on a blank page and wrote across the top:

Next Summer.

I could apply to Hatfield this time. Or I could get a new job. I made another chart on the next page.

Oregon State Versus Everywhere Else.

Everything has shifted now in ways I'm still trying to translate onto the paper. There are more factors than I considered before. For next summer, for college, for the whole wide-open future. More things that matter to me, things that hit different.

My path forward feels more complicated than ever.

But somehow, it also feels better.

I take another deep breath in front of the practice-room door.

This is the part of today I'm most nervous about. Whether Mateo will show or not. If they don't, I'll take some time to make a new chart. Shift things until I feel okay.

Because I'm more than a babysitter and my GPA.

And I'm more than a girlfriend too.

Julian was right. I can balance it, if Mateo's willing, everything

I am and everything I'm still figuring out alongside being in love. But if it doesn't work with Mateo, I can rebalance again. I can choose the things that work for me, can hold their weight differently at different times of my life. We are always more than just one thing.

When I open the door, my first thought is that the practice room smells exactly the same, even after a summer free of band geeks with questionable hygiene.

My second thought is *Oh, thank God.*

Because Mateo is here.

They're sitting on a chair in the corner, staring at their wilting flowers, but they stand when I walk in.

"Hi," they say.

"Hi."

I breathe out and close the door behind me.

"Thanks for coming."

They nod. They're looking at me, and even if I can't quite read their expression—or perhaps I'm too scared to actually look that hard—I take the eye contact as a good sign.

"I'm so sorry, Mateo." I step toward them until we're only a few feet apart, say it all fast before I lose my nerve and because they deserve to hear it right now, right away. "I know I messed up. A lot of things happened at once, and I kind of freaked out. But I didn't mean it when I said we don't fit. I didn't mean it at *all*. It was all just my own insecurities bubbling up—it had nothing to do with you. You were never, ever an experiment for me, Mateo. I think"—I take a breath—"I think we fit so hard, and I'm working some stuff out in therapy, and you have every right to say no, but . . . I miss you so much. I was hoping you'd give me another chance. I *am* busy during the school year, but I'll do whatever I can to make time for you. I'll give us all the time in the world."

"Oh, thank God." Mateo's shoulders slump as they say it. And then a surprised look takes over their face, like they hadn't meant to say the words out loud.

Relief fills my veins so quickly that a sharp giggle exits my mouth.

They said it just like Candace had this morning. Like I said it in my head three minutes ago. Like the whole world is simply ready for things to be put back to rights. Like all my worst imagined scenarios are popping like soap bubbles in front of my eyes.

Mateo immediately tries to school their features. "I mean—" They clear their throat as they roll a hand. "Continue."

But the moment's already broken. It takes every ounce of restraint I have not to fling my arms around their neck.

Still, I bite my lip in an attempt to hold back my smile.

"I'm so sorry I didn't attend your art gallery, it just didn't feel right, but I'm so proud of you for showing your work. I will *always* be proud to know you exactly as you are or as you ever will be. I promise to be there in the future. I mean . . . there might be times I screw up. I still have anxiety; I will likely always have anxiety, and I'll likely always be doing just a *little* too much, but I'm working on saying no. On scaling back, prioritizing the things that give me as much as I give them. My own ROIs. Like, there will probably be lots of nights where I have to work on AP stuff, but I've decided I'm going to give up on iTuna—"

I jump when Mateo cups their hands around my face. I've been so busy rambling I didn't even notice them stepping toward me.

"Penny," they whisper, and I stop breathing. "Whatever you want to do for yourself works for me, but please know I never want you to scale yourself back for my benefit. And what the hell is iTuna?"

I laugh, as much as I can without oxygen. "Never mind," I wheeze. "I'll explain later."

And then they're kissing me. I still don't know if I'm breathing or not, but I'm kissing them back anyway, and my nerves collapse all at once into the comfort of it, the *feeling* of Mateo's mouth on mine, and—

And they're stepping away from me, and I'm so unsteady, so taken aback by all of it, that I actually gasp. I clap my hand over my mouth in embarrassment at the sound, staring at Mateo as they push their fingers into their new hair, exposing the tips of their ears, gone deep pink.

"Sorry. I—" They cover their face with their hands for a second, then lower them and look me in the eye. "Okay. I have to say some stuff."

I nod furiously, hand still over my mouth. "Of course," I say to my palm.

They take a deep breath of their own as they place their hands on their hips.

"I accept your apology. But I *was* really hurt by you cutting me off, by you saying we don't fit. Because that's what I've been afraid of since the beginning. I mean—" They swallow. "I've always kind of worried that I wouldn't really fit with *anyone*, but then when I thought I *did*, somehow, with you . . ."

They close their eyes on a small huff.

My heart hummingbirds in my throat.

"I'm so sorry," I whisper. They shake their head.

"No, it's okay. I guess I'm just saying I'm still working out some shit too. But I do feel horrible that I wasn't there for you more during the panic attack, and I've hated just . . . not being able to *talk* to you. How did you even get home that night?"

"My moms," I croak out, finally dropping my hand from my face. They nod, staring at me for a moment.

"I know you're a busy person, Penny," they say again, voice softer. "I will be too, especially when theater starts up and with work, because . . . I'm going to keep working at the shop, on the weekends and after school and stuff, even after the switchover, if Northwest keeps me on. I mean, assuming it doesn't suck too much after Northwest takes over. Will you . . . be mad at me for that?"

"No." I shake my head. "Not at all. Promise." If anything, I'm jealous. I still don't think I can work there, but I can't be mad at that at all.

"Okay. Good." They blow out a breath, as if they'd been really worried about that, which, I know, it's my fault for being such a weirdo about the shop, but it's also so *cute* that they were worried. I love them so *much*.

"Anyway, I know things won't be exactly like they were in the summer, and we can work that out. But will you let me help you more? Will you loop me in next time you have a panic attack?"

I blink, eyes hot.

"To be completely honest," I make myself say, because I told myself I'd be honest with Mateo today, "I don't know if I can promise that. My brain sort of stops working when I get that bad, but . . . I'll try. I'll really, really try."

Mateo nods gently, lips pinched.

"Okay. One last thing. I said some pretty harsh shit that day too, at the shop. I know I wasn't . . . an experiment for you. I was feeling insecure, which isn't an excuse, but . . . I'm sorry. I know I hurt you too."

"Thank you," I whisper. "And, Mateo . . . you know I'd never, in any universe, leave you for Roman Petroski, right? Or, like, *anyone*."

Their shoulders slump. A faint, sheepish grin tilts their mouth. "Maybe."

"Oh my God." I can't help it, I throw myself at them, arms around their back, my face against their neck. "Mateo. I only want someone *exactly* like you. You are *everything*."

Mateo wraps their arms around my shoulders. Sticks their face in my hair.

"But . . ." I take another deep breath, and all I can smell is Mateo's roses. It overwhelms me so much, I almost forget my train of thought. But I make myself focus. "I think we should also talk about . . . when you go back to California, what if I can't—"

"Penny." Mateo leans back and puts a finger against my lips. Their eyes are as dark and serious as I've ever seen them. "I've been thinking about this a lot too. I'll stop pressuring you about California schools, first of all, even though I *do* want to say that I think you could win a shit-ton of scholarships, but that's not the point. The point is"—they take a breath, speak carefully—"I'm tired of making myself miserable because I'm always stretching between my past and my future. It's what I've been doing ever since I moved here. But . . . I'm here. Now. With you. I just want to focus on that. No matter what happens later."

I think of my charts in my journal. Know that I've been thinking along the same lines. Still, my heart beats faster. I can't change my entire brain in a week. And not knowing the future—what's going to happen next, if or when Nikki's heart will give up, if my family will run out of money, what I'll do after graduation, when the next natural disaster will hit—has never been easy for me.

But when Mateo whispers, "Okay?" I know I can try.

"Okay," I whisper.

And then we're kissing again, harder this time, stumbling until Mateo's back hits the wall.

"Thank you for my flowers," they say against my lips between kisses, and I'm smiling when I kiss them next.

"You deserve them." Their fingers wrap around my hair. "I meant to bring you some at your gallery opening."

And when Mateo kisses me again, I sort of lose track of time. Until the door to the practice room opens.

Mateo and I jump apart when we hear an exasperated sigh.

"Really?" Mr. Phelps, the band teacher, throws up his hands. "On the first day?"

Rule-follower Penny jumps awake. "*OhmygodImsosorry.*"

We quickly grab our stuff. When I finally look back at Mr. Phelps, he's holding a hand over his forehead and muttering to himself, "Ten years to retirement. I still have ten years until retirement."

"It won't happen again," I promise as we rush past him.

"At least you weren't vaping in there while you were at it," Mr. Phelps says. He continues to mutter at our backs as we escape into the main band room: "These practice rooms are the worst things that have ever happened to me."

And then he disappears into his office, and Mateo and I are out the doors.

We pause when we hit the middle of the hallway, look at each other, and burst into laughter.

"He is never going to look at me the same way again."

Mateo lifts a shoulder, grinning. "At least he didn't write us up."

"True." I grin back.

A different kind of junior year.

"Hey." Mateo shoves the flowers under their arm and takes my hand. "I have something to show you."

And then we're running outside toward the parking lot. Where we are definitely not supposed to go during lunch.

But I suppose I did make Mateo risk arrest by breaking into a food-truck lot, so I let it go.

"Close your eyes," Mateo says.

"What?" I shout, laughing. "I can't run with my eyes closed!"

"Okay, okay." Mateo stops running, yanks on my hand so I slow down too. "Walk. And close your eyes."

I keep laughing but do as asked.

"Curb here," Mateo instructs, and I stumble my way along with them until we come to a stop. "Okay," they whisper. "Open your eyes."

I whip my eyes open, and—

"Oh my *God*," I shout. "Oh my God. Holy shit!" I twirl on Mateo, eyes wide. "It's a dusty-pink Bug!"

They laugh. "I *know*."

"Where did you even find it?"

"Saw it online one night last week. Drove up to Gresham first thing the next morning with Talanoa to get it. I don't really know anything about cars, and I think it's probably a piece of shit. Like, it could fall apart tomorrow, but—"

"But oh my God, Mateo. Still so worth it!"

"So worth it." They grin. "Honestly, it was worth it just to see the look on my dad's face."

My own grin drops.

"Don't look so upset, Penny. Like, sometimes *I* wonder if I do shit just to make my dad mad, but this . . . this one actually just felt good. And"—a satisfied smirk—"it's a stick shift, so he can't say shit."

I reach over and hold their hand.

"I saw he was at your gallery opening," I say, voice quietly questioning.

"I know you did," Mateo says, smirk still firmly in place. "Lía told me you were the first person to view all of her Stories." But then they look away, toward their new car, lips flattening. "My parents . . . I know it's complicated, but they love us. Love me. I know they do. And they were very proud of me that night. They think . . . I am very good at my hobby."

"Oh."

"Yeah." Mateo sighs. "But buying this car I've always wanted, with money I earned *myself* . . ." They shake their head. "I don't know. It felt different. I felt . . . in control." They look back at me. "I'm going to try to be braver with them. Correct them more. I think my mom will meet me there, eventually. My dad . . ." Mateo shrugs, squinting again. "It'll be up to him."

I squeeze their hand. "Yeah," I whisper.

"And I'm going to talk to Ms. Fuentes this year about applying for art schools."

I smile.

"Yeah, you are. And you'll talk to your parents about that too?" Mateo looks a little queasy at the question, but they nod. And then it hits me as I stare at them, standing next to the Bug. "Your hair! Did you dye it to match?"

They smile at me so big, face clearing. They do a little jerk of their head, letting the strands fly. "*Thank you* for noticing."

Feeling Their Queerness Smile.

"Although it turned out a lot lighter than I was expecting."

They laugh again. "Doesn't fully match. It's actually kind of incredible that you noticed. It looks kind of weird, right? I don't know how I feel about it yet."

I reach up and run my fingers through it. "No, Mateo. I mean, you can do whatever you want with your hair; you'll be hot no matter what, but believe me—this color. I am *very* into it."

"Yeah?" They grin.

"*Yes.*"

They lean down to kiss me.

And from the building behind us, the bell rings.

"Oh, shit." Mateo pulls back. Our feet are already moving. "Have you had lunch? Want a donut?"

They hold the pink box out to me. I take it, open the flap, and stop walking.

"Mateo!" I go to shove them, but they're two steps ahead of me. I chase after them. "You totally ate half the apple fritters!"

Mateo grins back at me. "Technically, Talanoa ate two. Whatever. They're good."

I glare at them. "You're damn right they're good."

And even though I've eaten approximately two hundred apple-fritter donuts over the past two months, the one I shove in my mouth now tastes the best.

Mateo's face looks a little funny as they watch me chew. "Do I have something in my teeth?"

"No, just . . . I've eaten, like, five donuts today and I feel—"

Ah. The feeling of too many donuts and too little anything else is a shape of nausea I now know well.

"Come on." I grab their hand and march us toward the cafeteria. "Let's try to grab you a cheese stick or something. I know we'll be late, but you need protein, stat. God, I can't believe you've been a fritter fan this whole time."

"All donuts are good, Penny."

"Except the jelly-filled."

"Dude, the jelly-filled are good too."

I come to another abrupt stop just outside the school doors.

"Mateo. That stuff can hardly even be called jelly. It's like . . . a weirdly gelatinous goo."

"Yeah, a weirdly gelatinous goo that tastes like candy." Mateo shrugs. "What's not to like?"

I shake my head and drag them down the hall.

"It's like I don't even know you," I say.

"Trust me." I hear the grin in Mateo's voice. "There's still, like, a world of annoying facts to learn about each other. We're on a whole journey now, Dexter. Hey, what classes do you have this afternoon?"

"Pre-calc, AP Chem, AP Lit."

I glance over to see Mateo's nose wrinkle. "Well, at least we'll have World History."

And I can't stop the smile that takes over my face, that radiates to my toes, as we wheedle some cheese sticks out of the cafeteria staff. Mateo presses a quick kiss to my temple before we separate; I turn right and they turn left for Ms. Fuentes's room.

"That'll be a tardy to start off the year, Miss Dexter," Mrs. Jones says over her glasses as I find an empty seat.

I nod. Try to look contrite.

And then I hide my reemergent smile behind my Chromebook.

A different kind of Penny—this year and maybe next, and the year after that.

A whole journey now.

ACKNOWLEDGMENTS

Thank you to Olivia Valcarce for seeing the promise in Penny and Mateo's story, and to Kimberly Lionetti for bringing it to her: this book wouldn't exist without you. Thank you to Alyssa Miele for picking up where Olivia left off, and truly bringing *Donut Summer* to its fullest, best life. It's been a long road, but I'm so grateful for what I'm holding at the finish line. Thank you thank you thank you.

Thank you to Max Reed for bringing Penny and Mateo (and especially Penny's freckles) so stunningly to life on the cover, and to Catherine Lee for designing the cutest book jacket of all time. Thanks to the rest of the Quill Tree team, including production editors Erin DeSalvatore and Alexandra Rakaczki; production manager Danielle McClelland; and proofreader Sarah Stowbridge. Thank you, too, to copyeditor, Tracy Roe, for deleting all five thousand of my extraneous commas.

Thank you to everyone who read early manuscripts or snippets of *Donut Summer*: Leigh Kramer and Hannah Y., your feedback was essential; thank you for encouraging me to take better care of Penny. Sandra Lopez and my other authenticity readers, thank you for making sure I took better care of Mateo. Thank you to Chandra Fisher, Elora Ditton, Jen St. Jude, Kaitlyn Hill, and Hugh Blackthorne for being the earliest readers and supporters of Penny's and Mateo's beginnings over three years ago. Thank you also to Taleen Voskuni for answering my Armenian pastry questions so kindly.

As always, thank you to Alicia Thompson and KT Hoffman for being Penny's and Mateo's biggest fans. I literally couldn't survive publishing without you. Thank you also to all of the authors who read and blurbed this book; entering the young adult realm has been a longtime but intimidating dream and your willingness to welcome me in felt like such a gift.

Thank you to my family and the small town that raised me; thank you in particular to my parents for always making sure my future felt wide open. Thank you to Oregon—in particular for this book, Silver Falls State Park—for all the ways you've made me feel so deeply at home.

Thank you to every educator and librarian who stands up for their students' right to be themselves and also their right to read, even in the face of cowardice and ignorance. Thank you to every young person who's braver and smarter than the adults around them: I can't wait for you to make the future better, brighter, gayer, and even more trans.

Thank you to Tyson for all of our donut dates, and to Manda for being with me from teenaged fan fiction to my young adult debut.

And to Kathy, for being the cooler-than-me dreamboat who somehow liked me back even when I barely knew myself. I love you.